THE 12TH GIRL

THE 12TH GIRL

Hunted. Escaped. Nameless.

A David Langwonaire Thriller

JOHN MYLROIE

The 12th Girl: Hunted. Escaped. Nameless (David Langwonaire Thriller Series)
Published by CIKM Publishing
Starkville, Mississippi

Library of Congress Control Number: 2022920327

MYLROIE, JOHN, Author
THE 12th GIRL
JOHN MYLROIE

Paperback ISBN: 978-1-959594-00-0
e-book ISBN: 978-1-959594-01-7

FICTION / Thriller / Crime

Book Design by Michelle M. White
Cover image derived from photo art by Haywiremedia | Dreamstime.com

Part One

IT STARTS

CHAPTER 1

RUNAWAY

SHE RAN, AS SHE ALWAYS COULD, fast and with endurance, but this time, it mattered, it really mattered. She could hear in the distance the baying of hounds, shouts of control. She understood she was not being hunted but driven; her fate was in front of her, not behind. Her small form and spare frame gave her the appearance of a child, but she was twenty-four and would not see another day if she did not think as well as run. The valley was broad to her left, the rushing stream to her right abutted high cliffs with a lower, narrow tree-studded slope right down to the water. She saw her chance and acted, stopping where a boulder jutted into the water. She reached down, unlaced her boots, and took them and her socks off. Stuffing the socks into the boots, rolling up her pants, and knotting the lacings so the boots would hang from her neck, she stepped out into the bracing cold water. She went upstream a few yards and out into the center of the stream, where tree branches, heavy with leaves, hung down. She reached up to the extent of her small height and was barely able to grasp a single leaf, the lowest of the lowest branch. She pulled gently, and the leaf and the twig that held it came down, and she grasped the twig, and in turn pulled it gently to her. Then she had a tiny limb, the width of her smallest finger, and she pulled some again and walked to bring more and more of the branch down, until it was as big as her thumb. She reached with her other hand, and began to pull, slowly so the branch creaked but did not crack. Then it was as big around as her slim wrist and she hung from it, walking her hands in and up towards the trunk. She was now free of the water and her feet dripped their goodbye to the stream below. She flung herself up, leg over and onto the branch, and reached for one higher still, larger and more robust. She climbed up to the new height, and the lower branch slowly rose back to its original position.

The hounds were closer, their masters' voices sharper. She climbed up the tree to a massive branch that went towards the cliff, and grasped a branch of the next tree, higher up the short slope. She climbed up that tree as well, and hung like a squirrel from a long branch, following it outward as it thinned and then bent under her weight. She stepped off onto a narrow ledge; she was twenty yards up the overhanging cliff, and she scuttled sideways along the ledge, grit grinding into her bare feet, fingers clinging to cracks and protrusions. She followed the cliff inward around a corner and the ledge narrowed to a few tiny footholds. She continued on, her fear of falling contesting with the sound of angry dogs approaching. The cliff straightened again, but at the turn, a narrow crack, a yard high and mere hand breadths wide, led into the cliff. The only way into that crevice was to slide her feet and then legs in, and hanging by one hand from a crumbly projection, wiggle her body into the tight confines. She had to snatch at her boots as they almost fell off, which would have given everything away. The crack was at least two yards long, enough to accept her entirely. She was invisible from below.

The hounds had arrived, their baying changing to confused barks and growls, as they searched unsuccessfully around the boulder for her scent. Voices floated up to her, gathered by the angling of the cliff that had been her savior.

"This one is a challenge. She ran hard to break contact and only then stepped into the water," a deep male voice stated.

"It's tough when they are fit both mentally and physically," a second voice said, also male, but younger. "Where did she go?"

"Not many choices," the older man replied. "She can't stay in the stream. It will slow her down and she has no cover."

"Did she cross over, try and hide in the bushes?" The younger man pursued.

"Fred's following on the west bank, if she's there he will flush her out," the older man answered. "Fred's a real tracker, nothing gets by him. We will go on downstream, if she pops up and out of the stream with wet feet, it will be obvious."

"Why didn't she cut east and try to lose us on the flood plain?" the younger man queried.

"She wouldn't lose my dogs, and she knows that; faster going here next to the stream, and she knows that, too," the older man responded.

"Do you think she would try the old breathe-through-a-reed trick?" The younger man seemed enthusiastic, almost rooting for their prey. Their last hunt had been slow and a bit agonizing, no challenge, no sport at all.

"That tiny lady?" the older man chuckled. "The water's cold, she would be cooled to a limp noodle in minutes. She isn't going to get behind us, she will keep going south, and then it's no longer our problem."

"What happens down there?" the younger man asked, nodding his head south, downstream.

"Nothing you need to know," the older man quickly replied. "You're not even supposed to think about it, let alone ask, you understand that. Let's keep driving, reach our marker, and go home."

■　■　■

Up in her crevice, Lauren ran the overheard conversation through her head. There was a follower, a sweeper to stop any escape north. She understood she wouldn't be going anywhere for a while. No food, no water, only the clothes on her back. How hard would they search when she didn't turn up at the marker they mentioned? How would she get out of this place? The tree branch she used to set down on the ledge had rebounded to its original position, out of reach. The ledge had petered out. Maybe she could use the upward continuation of this crack, only a finger width wide, to climb up and out. But not yet. Then she heard voices above her. That escape route was blocked.

"Hey Fred, watcha got?" the voice came down, from right above her.

"Shut up, you two!" Fred hissed back up at them. Lauren had not heard Fred approach at all. "How can I track the sucker if you two give me away? And you're dumping stuff off the top down here, messing up my track."

"Sorry Fred, too bad you can't seem to catch the little bitch," the voice above answered with sarcasm.

"Yeah, you scared she'll kick your ass?" a second voice above followed, with laughter.

"You do your patrol, and I'll do mine," was Fred's quiet reply. He had a job to do, a stupid job, a hateful job, the boys on the cliff top seemed to be oblivious to what was happening. But then, as Fred had heard stated down here earlier, they weren't even supposed to think about it. An advantage for them, thinking not being their strong suit.

Lauren realized her edging along the ledge, and her wiggling into the crevice could have dropped small debris down to the slope below. Fred appeared to be a tracker who knew what to look for and might have seen such stuff. The two men above her had contaminated the scene, as it were, and Fred moved on, unaware of who languished in the grip of hard rock above.

■ ■ ■

"How did I get here?" Lauren asked herself. She had been doing her morning run as a hike in her field clothes getting ready for the summer island expedition when classes were over. The dawn was coming, and the streets were gray. The van had come up alongside, quiet, maybe electric, she had never heard it. Her thoughts had been elsewhere, labs to teach, classes to attend. Suddenly two men were on her, wrapping her in a blanket or tarp and suddenly, she was in the van which accelerated away, her screams muffled and unheard, her arms and legs pinned in the wrapping fabric. Then the drive, a long drive, maybe hours. She could hear nothing, no voices, no radio, only the occasional bump, felt and not heard. Breathing was difficult. Her cell wasn't with her, she had only her keys. Maybe she should have been doing a run, but she wanted to get a feel for distance in her new hiking boots, discount store $25 specials. Hence the long-sleeved field shirt over her field pants. No hat, there being no sun. She had her student ID in her shirt zipper pocket, and a twenty-dollar bill for a latte at the end of the walk. Nothing she couldn't afford to lose if she was mugged. Now she could lose it all, including her life.

After a bouncy and rough last couple of miles, she had been dumped out of the van, still wrapped in the cloth prison. She had wormed her way out into the sun as the van turned and drove off to park. Facing her was a grizzled old man with a shotgun. Behind him, in a pickup truck perhaps as old as he, were dogs in cages. The man pointed as a younger man began to open the cages and leash the dogs. The sun was to the man's left, he was facing south, looking right at her.

"Run. Run now to save your life," the man had said, swinging the shotgun around to point at her. He had then aimed the pump-action shotgun at the sky and fired once, the booming sound rolling across a valley with cliffs on either side, with patches of trees and open grass with bushy areas interspersed. So she had begun to run, south, away from the men and their dogs, following the slightly more open area along the east side of the stream, running fast, her undergraduate days as a scholarship cross-country runner at a Division I school coming to the fore. She still had her keys, her ID, and twenty bucks, as if that made any difference.

As she ran, she thought. Running over rough country was second nature to her, her feet felt heavy and awkward in boots, but she was strong; she ran with a steady, distance-eating gait. She understood that this event was not new to the men behind her, they had acted with practiced ease and a sense of purpose. The young man had looked excited, but the old man, not bored, more doing a job that had to be done before he got back to his regular life. The shotgun blast had been a signal to others. So she ran, and she looked about, and she thought, and she went back to her childhood and tree-climbing days, and now she was here, in a crevice with at least five men and several dogs looking for her. Or they were driving her south, to some destination that could not be pleasant. Five men, a large group for a kidnapping. Lauren realized that kidnapping was the wrong term, she was never to be let free, never to go home, there would be no ransom demand. She was to die out here; what faces she saw, what names she heard, mattered not. Fred had called her a 'sucker,' she was to be eliminated, and she assumed it was for someone's pleasure or entertainment. Even if she got free, scooted away and home, would she still be hunted, a witness who must be eliminated? Which authorities could be trusted, which authorities would believe her? Would she even be missed?

Why her? They hadn't searched her; did they already know who she was? 'This one is a challenge' the old man had said, who were the other ones? How many? Was she just a random target, picked up off the street because she was there, available, vulnerable? There were too many questions without answers. She didn't have time for that now. Like the prey she had become, all she could do was hide.

CHAPTER 2

THE OLD NEW PROFESSOR

MAGGIE WAS ON THE OUTSIDE LOOKING IN. It was the story of her life, and it had become so routine that she not only accepted it, she adopted it as her superpower. She had become an intellectual spectator, watching from the sidelines, gazing around academic corners, and peeping through windows of thought. She had discovered that watching other people do great things, or hard things, or momentous things was more rewarding than doing such work herself. She fed off that second-hand success that she observed; not a scavenger, more of a tax collector, taking her cut of a positive outcome, her percentage. She correctly divined that her tasks and duties allowed the great people to do their thing, freed up their time and resources. In other words, as a clinical faculty person at a Research One university, she taught so that others could pursue the frontiers of their discipline. She worked the well-plowed ground behind those frontiers, nurturing the next crop of students to be fed into society's haphazard opportunities. Some few would move on to graduate school to become the next generation of curious, seeking minds, and a minor slice of them would become research professors, so the cycle would continue. Like fish spawning in the ocean, Maggie cast forth students by the thousands in the hope that a couple would persevere, and by skill or luck, more commonly both, become the next professorial generation.

At fifty-two, Maggie felt reborn. Her children were grown and gone, her husband had, to his mind, discarded her when he had in reality given Maggie her freedom. The alimony allowed her to become an MRS, a 'mature returning student' instead of a Mrs., the admissions office guidelines said, so she went to graduate school in geology, entering by dint of hard work into the master's program; then once she had proven her abilities, shifted directly to a PhD program after one semester. Her advisor had been old school in that he valued all aspects of an education and considered research to be the ultimate instructional activity. He was not old school when it came to his relationship with his students; he treated them all as individuals and did not put them into categories. They self-selected by ability and effort. Maggie never felt her gender, her appearance, or her age made any difference to Dr. Spencor. Dr. Spencor carried a large teaching load, and when he suddenly retired the same semester that Maggie walked the stage for her PhD sheepskin, the faculty decided to plug the gap with their newly minted Dr. Margaret Gerelli. It felt good to have status behind her maiden name, her being no maiden. It was a one-year adjunct appointment, but her performance with students was so obviously excellent, so non-threatening, that the Department accepted the administration's new program of 'clinical faculty' as a non-tenured type of teaching position. Maggie glided into this new faculty slot with its three-year rollover contract and no research obligation unless she wished to do so, but then only as ten percent of her work effort, maximum.

Maggie was of an age where the years showed, but the spirit was active. She had a rich social life full of friends who were always trying to pair her up. She avoided local entanglements and took her pleasures farther afield, with those who knew her and her limitations and rules but would still delight her with the unexpected. She was in no hurry; being a faculty member meant a high degree of control of one's own schedule, including plenty of time to travel, especially if it were part of her research mission, scanty as that was. She felt some of her colleagues no longer did research, they just managed it, the grad students and postdocs did the actual work, made the actual discoveries. For Maggie, the research was personal; simple projects that needed time more than money, topics that interested her and looked like they would be fun. She had done her PhD on fossil soils on limestone islands, work that allowed time in the field in wonderful tropical settings, and then lab work with expensive machinery she didn't need to maintain. Several good scientific papers had come out of that work, and she continued to dabble with it. All in all, Maggie was very satisfied with life. She avoided the angst younger female faculty had about raising children while building a career — that condition was all behind her. No trailing spouse issues, either. She loved teaching, both at the introductory level, and then with geology majors in higher level courses. She knew some faculty felt she was an old biddy who needed to know her place, but that approach did not sit well with younger faculty, both male and female. In meetings, she was always prepared, had the facts down, and would nail the unprepared, but so politely that colleagues would need to explain to the unsuspecting victim that they were done. Maggie felt she was playing with house money, and that she had paid her dues and was now entitled to be respected for her performance.

Maggie had her first graduate student, Lauren Tammers, who wanted to do field work on islands and observe and research how they were made. Not all types of islands, only those made of limestone, a rock created by living processes, a way to make a physical environment innately coupled to the life that lived and died close to an island's shores. Unlike children, who arrived and then one had to deal with them, graduate students were selected, one got to choose. Lauren was special, an athletic scholarship runner from a big-time program in which less than one percent of students were that good, male or female. Her Graduate Record exam scores had been in the top five percent. Smart, athletic, and diminutive, Lauren was a child scholar in Maggie's mind. Her very first grad student, fun to be around and they had shared how Lauren's career would advance. With her credentials, Lauren could have gone anywhere, but she came to Maggie as she had read her papers, and after the first meeting, they had hit it off. Lauren did not want to be a cog in a research machine, she wanted to do fun science on her own terms. Maggie loved her for it.

This morning, Maggie was concerned. Lauren had missed her first class, then her second. She had labs to teach in the afternoon. No text, e-mail, or phone call to explain. A call to Lauren's cell went to voice mail after eight rings. Lauren had no roommate. Maggie was slightly worried; Lauren was highly reliable and conscientious. It was a Wednesday, and it was unlikely that she would be sleeping off a hangover. Who partied on Tuesday nights? She went upstairs to the warren of graduate offices, no Lauren at her desk, no one had seen her, and no one knew why she might be absent. Maggie quickly set up students to cover Lauren's intro labs should she not show up in the afternoon. Then it was time to teach, and the routine swept her up. A call that night bounced to voice mail again; Maggie wondered whether to call Lauren's parents. They lived three states away, and there was nothing they could do in the immediate time frame, so she let it slide. If Lauren failed to appear Thursday morning, then it was twenty-four hours, and she could ask for an official police inquiry. Undergraduates might runaway, especially freshmen who got overwhelmed, but not grad students. Would the police take it seriously? Maggie worried — worried as she never had with her own children.

CHAPTER 3

HERE THERE BE DEMONS

TED KELLER LIKED HIS NAME, he always had. Switch a few letters, and he became 'Dead Killer', which as a kid had sounded awesome, and as an adult had become a reality. He knew he had a mental problem, and he was confounded by Joseph Heller's Catch-22 concept, that if he was crazy he wouldn't know it, and if he knew it he wasn't crazy. He was a nutcase and he knew it. He was wrapped fairly tight, and he kept hidden that inner disease. Acting on that sickness was what had taken time. Means, motive, and opportunity was what the crime aficionados talked about. Ted was brilliant and had used his brilliance to advance in the tech sector and become a billionaire. That gave him means and opportunity. The motive had always been there, a rot deep inside that had percolated through the years. He had resources to spare and could exploit and enjoy any perversion he wished. He had personal skills with all things computational and informational, which meant he could track his activities from the outside, a self-voyeur, watching what he did as others would. It was more than reading newspaper accounts, it was penetrating systems, following lines of investigation, smiling and laughing at the absurd types of inquiry developed by people con-fused by his purpose. He did the crime, then he took the time to see it ripple through law enforcement, families, and society. His actions were subtle, and somewhat open-ended. He was Malaysian Air flight 370, one person at a time — missing, gone, disappeared, but no body ever found. He enjoyed the cruelty of lack of closure, the agony of the still-hopeful, the despair that grew slowly and forever. He was a very sick creature.

So now he waited. He had heard the shotgun blast and knew his prey was being driven towards him. It was quite a logistical operation, seizing people off the street, having them transported hundreds of miles to his 4200-acre site, hiring rednecks and their hounds to drive the prey to him. He understood operational security, he knew how to keep information proprietary. Fred was his contact; Ted had not personally interacted with any of the people operating this show. He had files and dossiers on all of them of course, should it prove necessary to prune some people. They certainly knew nothing about him. Layers of shell companies hid the true owner of this land, docketed as a private hunting preserve. It was that certainly, but all that mattered was what was hunted. To Fred he was only 'the boss'; Fred had to know a little more, and he had to dispose of the evidence.

The prey came to him anonymously. Part of the game was to figure out who that prey was after the fact. It made the game so much more enriching, satisfying, rewarding. It also made it impossible to go back, to consider the value and worth of each victim. By the time he found out, the act was over; no regrets, no hindsight, just the focus on the events as they unfolded, as people tried to find the one who was lost, without a trace. Just gone. It thrilled Ted continually and, as his victims piled up, he could look at how things matured, and he could see at the same time old cases, fading as families and investigators gave up, contrasting with his latest efforts, where the frantic hope battling the walls of fear still reverberated. Ted understood probability, he knew that eventually something would go wrong with his scheme; it was like all things, entropic. He had experienced one blip already, a victim who had fought back. It had been close. After that unsettling event, he didn't use a spear, club, hatchet, or knife, only that which killed at a distance. Today it would be a crossbow. Only the twang and the thunk, then the scream. If necessary, if just to stop the noise, a second bolt. Otherwise, he would watch and stare, feeding on the scene the way a lion feeds on a wildebeest, committing to memory as with a favorite movie.

So he waited, but uncertainty grew. The hounds had stopped baying, he did not hear a victim crashing through the brush, the panting and gasping of a person driven to exhaustion by terror and effort to escape. He sat in his blind and waited some more. Nothing. Then, in his pocket, his walkie talkie vibrated. No cell phone use, no digital record; down in this valley, the walkie talkie worked just fine, no signal escaped. It was analogue anyway.

He pressed the transmit button. "Go ahead."

"We have a problem," Fred's voice came through as a static-laden statement.

"Go on," Ted replied. Ted and Fred, it sounded like a comedy duo, but no one was laughing.

"We lost her. The hounds can't find the track, I can't find any sign. She just … disappeared."

"She is supposed to disappear after I have finished with her, not before," Ted responded angrily, then took a moment to regain his calm. "What do you recommend?"

"We will continue the search, widen our perimeter, I thought you should know there would be a delay," Fred continued.

"Could she get free of our area?" Ted probed.

"I don't know, she might have gotten lucky and we missed her by chance, but I don't think so," Fred proposed. "She ran with energy and purpose. If she is out through the perimeter, then it becomes a radial search, and we don't have the manpower for that."

"Stick with the program for now, I can wait," Ted replied. "I will also be thinking of my options." He stated the latter to indicate that if nothing else, a new plan might be necessary and that could be fun. One of the options would be to close-up shop and move on. The Malaysian Air flight 370 again fascinated Ted; could that be done to a cruise ship? He might have to sacrifice Fred, but no others. What they knew was very different from what they suspected. Ted could just walk away. Or, he could let the show go to a new level, like an arcade game. Let one escape and then do the tracking. The look of surprise when the victim found out she wasn't really safe after all would be exemplary.

CHAPTER 4

DISAPPEAR

LAUREN SHIFTED HER BODY, sweeping away from under her some annoying pebbles and small chunks of rock, careful none went past her and out the entrance. The crevice was small, she lay on her side, unable to rotate flat or to her other side. She was in a downward spiral, knowing that she would slowly go hypothermic, lose energy and strength. It was late spring; the air outside was warmer than the mean annual temperature of the rock, but the night would be colder. She had no food and no water. She did not know the extent of her pursuit. Did she try and wait it out until the next morning, hoping the pursuers would give up? Or did she leave immediately, knowing she would never be stronger and faster than now? She could, she decided, wait a little longer.

Lauren waited, and Ted waited. Who would decide to change plans first?

She heard the dogs first, small barks and growls that were immediately quieted. Then voices again.

"Never heard you, but the dogs picked you up," came the older man's voice.

"Can't fool those dogs," the younger man bragged, but Lauren had fooled them.

"We will expand the search," Fred's voice displayed some frustration. "We know she got this far, did she double back and we missed the jump-off point?"

"Well, if she went in the water, the dogs and I can't figure out where she left the stream," the older man complained. "Nothing on the west side?"

"Nothing, no evidence she was ever there, dry or wet," was Fred's answer.

"She didn't get south, past the marker?" the old man persisted.

"If she had, we would all be heading home," Fred stated.

"Is she up in a tree?" the younger man asked.

"I can spot a raccoon in a tree, and she is bigger than that," the old man countered.

"I checked every tree on both sides, she didn't shinny up any of them," Fred replied. "I reckon she got out into the valley, to the east."

"Didn't go up the cliff?" the young man asked, imagining Lauren as more monkey than woman.

"Those sandstone ledges overhang the shale beds down at creek level, an impossible climb without hardware, which she doesn't have," Fred retorted. "Anyway, such work leaves obvious traces."

"If she was up and on that cliff, we would see her," the old man rejoined. "If she got on top, the van boys would have her."

"I am going to call those boys down here, we need to look east, out in the scrub," Fred decided. He had a distinct feeling they wouldn't find anything. He had watched the small girl run south, totally in control, setting a pace, looking around. The wind was from the east today, maybe the hounds would catch an air scent. He said as much to the old man.

"Might help, but I don't want to spend all day out here," the old man replied.

"You'll be compensated, you always are," Fred answered, pulling out his walkie talkie, changing the channel, and summoning the two men who had done the kidnapping and ferrying of the victim, telling them to come down off the west cliff.

■　■　■

Lauren had heard it all and re-evaluated her situation. Had the entire discussion been staged to make her come out of hiding? If that were true, then they had to assume she was within hearing distance, why not just search her out? Or were they going along the stream and repeating the show, time and again? No, they had met up here as this is where the dogs lost the scent. They would backtrack north to see if she had done a double back and then a long hop to go east. Then voices began above her yet again.

"So you lost her!" came a voice, as before.

"Now your sorry asses need our help to make it all good," came the second voice.

"Just shut up and go north and get down here, wait until we meet you at the dog truck," came Fred's angry reply. "Can't have you messing up what little trail we have."

"OK," was the haughty reply, and she could hear the men above jogging away.

They were vacating the field, Lauren thought then, to herself, I have a window of opportunity. She began to move, stiff and cramped, out of the crevice. She had a dilemma, how to get up and out? Could she reverse the maneuver she had used to get into her hiding spot? She squeezed out of the crevice and looked around. She was directly across from the rock she had used to step into the stream, her creeping along the ledge downstream had matched her distance upstream to catch a leaf. That had made the voices easy to hear. She moved out, and reached up for a handhold, which allowed her to rotate her hips and sit at the lip of the crevice, her face pressing against the cliff. She rearranged her boots so the laces didn't cut into her Adam's apple and considered her route up and away.

Slowly, and with care, she moved the boots and socks down to her lap, and she untied them, all with one hand. She switched hands as necessary, but she needed the handhold above her for balance and control. It took a while, but she got both socks on, and then both boots, which was awkward as they took up space on her feet, she had to keep one leg straight and the other bent at the knee. The crack that had widened to become a crevice where she sat continued up to the top of the cliff, maybe five yards up. It was wide enough to insert her fingers, with the far wall extending out a foot or so. She worked her way out of the crevice and stood up. She was now exposed for any at the stream to see, but the offset in the cliff she had gone around that morning kept her out of sight from the north. She inserted the fingers of one hand in the crack and did a layback, changing hands as she went up; she was soon at the lip of the outcrop. She peered over the top to see a cigarette butt right in front of her, still smoldering. She levered up and over and quickly stood up to move to some bushes and get out of sight.

Lauren had no idea where she was. The van ride had been for hours; she could be two hundred miles from Athens, Georgia. Then she applied her mind. The geology said she was in northeastern Alabama or southeastern Tennessee, the sandstone and shale layers of the cliff were lying essentially flat, and were old and hard, Paleozoic. She hadn't gone east or south into the coastal plain, and she wasn't to the north in the folded valley and ridge province of North America. They had made the dogs push her south in the valley to some ugly fate. Her searchers now went north to begin a recon to the east. Her choice was obvious, she would go west. Not only were they not looking that way at the moment, but it was away from home, away from Athens and the University. She was to have been killed out here today, she understood that much. She was to be killed and then made to disappear. She thought about going north and, as the dogs and men went east, disabling their vehicles, stealing stuff for her survival. She was no James Bond to pull such a stunt, no Bourne Supremacy here. She would follow their purpose; she would just disappear. She began to walk west, carefully, trying not to leave an obvious trail, knowing that if the dogs came up here, they would track her. She had only gone a few hundred yards when she came to a chain-link fence. No barbed wire on top. She repeated her tree climb stunt; pulling down a branch until she could work her way up and into the trunk, then pick a branch that went over the fence, work her way out hanging from it, and letting it bend gently to set her feet on the ground. Turning around, she saw a sign a few feet north. It said: "Private Hunting Property, Long Guns In Use, No Trespassing For Any Purpose." Small print underneath said only "Dead Rock Holdings." No address, no phone number, no URL. Lauren turned and continued west.

CHAPTER 5

OUT AND ABOUT

TED WAS IMPATIENT, he had waited and there had been no success. Fred had not been able to locate the woman who had simply disappeared. If she had broken their perimeter when she first went missing, she was miles away by now, even on foot. It was a new game. What was his risk? She had seen faces, knew that hunting hounds had been used. By now she might have an idea of where she was, where she had been taken in the van. But she hadn't seen Fred, and she had no idea the situation was set up by Ted for Ted's pleasure. He could just walk away. Send out a cash bonus and tell the participants it was all over, and to stay quiet. Walk away from the land as well, it would sit fallow for years, and then go up at auction for back taxes. Ted had billions, the land was a consumable. No regrets, time to move on. No, now it was a new game, a quarry that had escaped. She would go to the authorities, and they would have a hard time proving anything. They might think she made it all up to explain why she had missed her job; maybe that she had run from a boyfriend. Or girlfriend, there was no telling these days. He could track her down, that effort would be fun. Wait until she felt safe and secure, then explain to her in the most personal way how wrong she had been.

"We are done, wrap it up," Ted said into the walkie talkie.

"Done for today or done here forever?" was Fred's response.

"Done forever, I am afraid," Ted replied. "There will be a bonus for you and your colleagues at the usual spot. Explain that the program is moving to another country. You did good work. I may call on you again if you are willing."

"OK, Out," was Fred's last input. He was just as happy to be done for the day and to be done with 'the boss' for a while, maybe forever. He didn't worry about his personal safety, the way the boss conducted business meant Fred had no idea who he worked with. Bodies raise questions, that was why he had made all those dead young women disappear. It was no thrill for him, just business. Nasty business that he didn't think about. He had been paid very well, had enjoyed what the money had provided him, but he was glad to be done with it. Sometimes those silent and still faces came to him at night, always asking why, and he didn't know the reason.

Lauren crossed several dirt roads, but kept moving, she heard cars in front of her and assumed she would soon be at a major highway. Then find a convenience store, or a truck stop, and borrow a phone and call Dr. Gerelli. She moved more fluidly now, she was miles from the stream and cliff, no need to worry about leaving a trail. She could re-adjust her concentration inward, to think about her situation. She had escaped, she had escaped from a trap that had been sprung before, perhaps many times. The men searching for her had been practiced, experienced; they knew what they were doing. Was she the first to ever escape? What would be the reaction? Someone had waited for her to the south, she assumed it was more than a simple sex crime, too elaborate. She imagined she was to be hunted. Were the victims targets of convenience, were they always women? It was more than just a hunt, it had to be. Too involved to be human trafficking. Why hunt women? Or was the hunt just a side show, a warmup act? She was to disappear, to be gone without a trace. A mystery. Did the person who instigated all of this have a bigger result in mind, to make society react, to pay attention, so that he could sit in the shadows and say to himself 'they do all of this because of me?' It would explain taking women, the public always worries about women, right down to 'women and children first' when abandoning ship. Missing men? Men run all the time. No societal angst there.

Would she be tracked? Did they even know who she was? She hadn't been searched or photographed. They hadn't even checked for a cell phone, probably no reception down in that valley. She had been grabbed, transported, and dumped to run. She was not intended to ever come back. Now they would have to determine who she was. Her initial thought had been correct; she had to disappear, at least for now. Unless she had been specifically targeted, they wouldn't know who she was until a missing person case was filed from where she had been abducted. But what if it wasn't? Their plan had been elaborate, but also had holes in it. If her identity had been deemed unimportant at the beginning, did it matter at the end? It was as if the instigator knew her identity could always be determined later. That implied a skill operating on the web, tracking down people with more than a search engine. If she wanted to disappear, she had to leave no electronic signature.

Lauren was aware she was speculating on minimal evidence. There could be many reasons she had been taken, but she could not figure out a valid reason why she, Lauren Tammers, would be specifically targeted. She did not do drugs. Hell, for her undergraduate cross-country career she gave a pee sample every week to make sure. Her dad was an elementary school teacher, her mother a school librarian, not people of note or wealth. Not a kidnapping, not a hit, that was ridiculous. She felt she was a random abduction. In college, her psychology class had a visiting lecturer who talked about serial killers, Ted Bundy, John Wayne Gacy, and others. Serial killers looked for people who fit a type, usually not for a specific individual. For Bundy, women; for Gacy, younger men and boys. Was it her size? Did they mistake her for someone younger? Serial killers did not work with others; they were typically loners. The organized ones were smart, but not exceptionally so despite the common myth about their being geniuses. Smart enough to get victims, smart enough to not get caught for quite a while. Serial killers also liked to taunt the authorities, and they loved the publicity each killing got them. This had been a team effort, not a loner at work. It was different. How many ways was it different? Who had she been driven to? What was supposed to happen to her? What would happen now? Questions bounced in her head like an old-time pinball machine.

■　■　■

Ted was in no hurry, he knew his escapee had been picked up in Athens, Georgia. He would monitor there for a missing person report, or a police report, depending on when she got back home. He had no exposure, flying west at 35,000 feet in his private jet to LAX. His schedule was full, he would set up bots to troll the internet and see what came up in Athens. She might go to local authorities in Tennessee, it didn't matter, nothing could be connected to him. As regards the victim, he had very little to go on. He knew gender (unless the victim was transitioning); body size, small; hair color, brown. No eye color, no blood type, no DNA. Unless there was DNA in the van; the rug was by protocol already burned by now. Not much to go on. He was enthralled, he had a new game. Someone had escaped, had defeated Fred and his cronies; would she defeat him? He laughed at the thought. He had resources she couldn't imagine. Nonetheless, she had proven to be smart, decisive, capable. He would bring her down, at the time of his choosing, in the manner of his choosing. He was the decider, and the world listened and got out of the way.

▪ ▪ ▪

Lauren came out on the shoulder of US 41, so said a sign with another below it that stated "White City 5 miles." She ducked back into the tree line and walked there, parallel to the road, out of sight. No attempt at hitchhiking, as three things could happen, and two of them were bad. She could be picked up by friendly people and whisked to White City, she could be picked up by those who searched for her and be back where she started, or she could be picked up by a different bad guy and face a new challenge. So she stuck to the woods. It was slower going, but it was safer. It was dark by the time she reached a convenience store on the outskirts of town and ducked inside. A school bus was there with a girl's softball team crowding inside. Lauren fit right in. Two girls were sitting in a booth when Lauren skipped over.

"Can I borrow a phone? My mom grounded me and I can't use mine for a week," Lauren offered.

"Who are you?" one girl asked.

"Someone who needs to call her boyfriend, the one Mom doesn't like," Lauren replied, but got no response. "Look, I'll buy you a shake, then you let me make a call."

"Now that sounds better — chocolate," one of the girls said, and Lauren went and broke her twenty making the purchase; she got one for herself as well.

The shake and phone were traded, and Lauren stepped a few feet away and made a phone call, hauling the number up from memory; she learned this trick from doing field work in remote areas. "Hello?" came the voice on the receiving end.

CHAPTER 6

RECOVERY

MAGGIE SAT AT HER KITCHEN TABLE, trying to decide what to do. She looked at her phone as it lay next to the salt and pepper shakers and wondered who to call. Then the phone rang, and Maggie snatched it, feeling a psychic moment, an intervention. She didn't recognize the area code or the number, but it didn't matter. If someone was going to try and sell her a car repair warranty, they would get an earful.

"Hello?" Maggie asked, sliding red to green on the phone symbol.

"Dr. Gerelli, this is Lauren, I need your help," Lauren's voice said, fast and pinched. "Listen carefully, I am at Red's Safety Stop on the south side of White City on US 41, northwest of Chattanooga. I was kidnapped, but I escaped."

"Lauren, have you called the police?" Maggie responded with a question, uncertain why Lauren was calling her instead.

"I can't call the police, at least, not yet!" Lauren replied so forcefully that Maggie moved the phone away from her ear and stared at it. She realized Lauren needed special aid and needed it right now.

"I'll come and pick you up, stay there and wait, is that all right?" Maggie asked.

"OK, that would be great. Tell no one what you are doing; well, write it down and leave it in an envelope on your kitchen table," Lauren instructed. "I have borrowed a phone and I can't be reached again until you get here."

"I will do as you ask. Stay calm, stay safe, I'll be there in about three hours or so, I guess," Maggie offered.

"Thanks, I'll make this up to you, I promise, bye," and Lauren ended the call.

Maggie again stared at the phone in her hand, now silent. Her heart raced. Lauren was in some sort of trouble, and Maggie understood it wasn't Lauren's fault. Maggie had no one else she was as close to as her first grad student. She had to help.

■   ■   ■

Lauren walked back to the booth and gave the phone back to its owner. "Thanks, I really appreciate it, Bobby will come by and pick me up later, after he gets off work."

The girl nodded, and the bus driver stepped in the door and called to load the bus, and the convenience mart became a storm of confusion. Lauren went out in the middle of the crowd and slipped around the side of the store, and into the woods beyond. She wasn't dumb enough to hang out where she could be seen, be it by strangers, or any of the crew that had tried to take her life this day, and who might happen by. She sat on a downed log, and sipped her shake, which felt really good. Staring out at the cars whizzing by, and the gaudy lights of the store, she felt the first sense of relief since the moment she had been grabbed. To anyone in the store, she was on the county school bus headed back towards Chattanooga. To anyone on the bus, she lived in White City. She was with neither, and glad of it.

■   ■   ■

Maggie sat stone-still for a moment, running things through her mind. She suddenly jumped up and headed for her home office to type out a note, then she stopped. Lauren had said *write* it down. Lauren used a borrowed phone. She had escaped her kidnappers but wasn't yet free, or that was Lauren's thinking. Maggie wrote down where she was going and why. The note was a back-up measure; any reader should assume the worst. She wrote across the envelope 'Open If I Am Not Here' and leaned it upright against the saltshaker. She got out a small cooler and loaded in some drinks and snacks, grabbed some blankets, and picked up an extra flashlight to join the one always in the car. She also dug out some cash from the bedside table. From that same drawer she pulled out her Glock G43X and a ten-shot magazine of 9 mm rounds. She took the second loaded magazine as well. Had Lauren been forced to lead her into a trap? It seemed completely unreasonable, but Maggie thought it best to be prepared. She hopped into her Hyundai Sentra. She was going to use a GPS app, but she turned off her phone and dragged out an old road atlas instead, looking over her route. It was night, traffic would be low, it was run and gun.

The drive was long and boring, but Maggie had plenty to think about as she flew through the dark. Lauren, kidnapped? It certainly explained her failing to show up for class and her lab teaching. Why all the secret agent stuff, what was that all about? Lauren had sounded scared, but in control. She was out there now, all alone; maybe people were looking for her. Finally, Maggie was north on US 41, driving through a very empty area, few lights, houses, or towns. She saw a sign, 'White City 5 miles' and she became hyper-alert. Would Lauren be in the store, or hiding where she could watch the place? Maggie would drive up to the pump, walk in the store and give the clerk a twenty-dollar bill and put gas in the tank. Lauren should make an appearance somewhere during that activity. Maggie pulled into Red's Safety Stop, went inside with the money, came out and then pumped the fuel. Lauren hadn't been in the store, and she wasn't coming to the car. Maggie scanned around, and realized the pumps were in field of view of at least two surveillance cameras. Maggie got in the car and pulled it ahead, out of the light and to the far edge of a parking area where she stopped. Before she could react, Lauren was at the passenger door and Maggie pushed the unlock button. Lauren hopped in.

"Drive north and west, slowly, then go to I-24 and head back to Atlanta," Lauren said, as if ordering a burger and fries. Then she burst into tears. "Thank you, thank you, I really needed you here, I am really scared."

"Drinks and snacks in the cooler between the seats," Maggie offered, to help calm the girl down. "When you are ready, tell me what happened."

Lauren had opened a bag of Cheetos and a grape soda, holding and eating each Cheeto as if it were the first she had ever seen, sipping her soda as if each sip might be her last. Maggie drove; she was fatigued but not sleepy, eager to know what the Hell was going on, but patient, too. After a few minutes, Lauren seemed to settle.

"OK, I am going to tell you what happened, and then I am going to tell you what I think it means," Lauren began.

"Observation, then interpretation; good approach, just like in field work," Maggie soothed.

Lauren then gave a narrative of everything from when she went out on the sidewalk to break in her boots, to the abduction, to the release and flight, to the hiding in the crevice, to the overheard conversations, to her climb out and escape west, to the convenience mart and the phone call, and the long wait. There was some backtracking as she remembered a detail, added a fact, or clarified something. Finally, she stated, "That's what happened."

"I see," Maggie replied, not seeing at all, but intrigued by what had been done to Lauren, and how she had extricated herself from a very bad situation. "What do you think it all meant, what was going to happen?"

"I was prey; I was being driven to the south, where I would have been hunted and killed," Lauren said simply. "The men I saw did not care that I saw them, they knew I was not coming back. I saw five men, well, saw four and heard a fifth, there could have been more, and whoever was waiting for me to the south, one or more additional people. They had done this before, every move was practiced, prepared, well learned. They had come two hundred miles to take me. It is a big operation, hard to keep secret. It requires a lot of resources. The person or persons behind all of this have money, big money, but also power and the knowledge of how to use it. They made no effort to identify me and collected nothing from me. I was meant… to disappear."

"You were not targeted for who you are but what you are," Maggie interpreted, trying to enter the one-sided discussion.

"I was to be entertainment," Lauren said loudly, trying not to believe it. "Someone wanted to make me disappear and then watch what happened. I was a game piece. They want a missing persons report, they want my parents to plead on television. Whoever is behind this will watch, will make it a game to find out who I was and then track all the events around my disappearance, knowing the whole time that I am in a grave in southeastern Tennessee." Lauren started to cry, loud whooping sobs.

"But you escaped! We can get the authorities on this and run these guys to ground," Maggie explained, trying to calm Lauren down.

"I don't think it is over," Lauren stated, snot running from her nose, her eyes puffy, her lips tight. "I think the game just went up a notch, I think he now wants to watch the police deal with me, a survivor. The investigation will be a dead end; he has cut all those Tennessee people loose. Then he will stalk and kill me, when he assumes I think it is all over. I cannot go to the police, they won't believe me, but they will talk about it. He will know. That is what 'Me Too' is all about: rejection, disbelief, inaction. Rape kits stacked up in police departments across the country, by the thousands, never run. They won't believe me, and worse, they won't care."

"That is quite a speculation, Lauren," Maggie interjected. How had Lauren worked her thoughts into this wild reasoning?

"I am working from a worst-case scenario," Lauren answered. "I might be killed right away, to keep any investigation from happening, before the cops start looking at who owns hunting dogs in White City."

"You sound like you have a plan," Maggie volunteered.

"Oh, I do, I certainly do," Lauren brightened. "I am going to disappear as if I never was, and I am going to hunt this bastard down." Maggie listened, realizing Lauren was fixed on her role in a game she fully believed herself to be playing. She was a survivor, scorned.

CHAPTER 7

HOME IS WHERE THE SECRET IS

LAUREN FELL ASLEEP, and Maggie drove as dawn began to break to her left. She was dead tired, but her mind raced with what Lauren had told her, both about what had happened and about what it meant. Maggie had no doubts about the veracity and accuracy of Lauren's tale. The girl had been kidnapped and dumped out to run for her life. The number of people involved, and the organizational effort, were astounding. Then the interpretations had begun to creep in. Lauren's opinion that the men were used to it, that they had done this action before, that they knew what they were doing. Nothing to counter that argument, right down to how the men had spoken when overheard. A big operation, run many times, how had it gone unnoticed? Snatching people for no apparent reason from widely separated locations could explain why no one had determined a pattern. If it had been younger women, then the runaway syndrome, how women sometimes just ran away, would be considered by initial investigators, confusing the issue. Lauren thought it was all theater, that a man or men — she had never speculated that it was a woman in charge — enjoyed the hunting, the kill, and were then thrilled at the response. A demon who fed on the sorrow and despair of others. So very scary, so vile, it numbed Maggie to just consider it. The business of how the perpetrator watched it from afar, using modern technology, seemed a bit of a stretch. Then she remembered the Zodiac Killer in California and his codes and ciphers. Lauren's serial killer may have moved to a new style of play.

Maggie pulled into her carport, Lauren never stirred; so, she unlocked the house and put on coffee for herself. It had been years since she had pulled an all-nighter; she went and woke Lauren, walking her into the guest bedroom and urging her to sleep. She showered and prepared to get back into her normal Thursday morning schedule — class at 9:30 and again at 11:00. When she was ready to go, she got Lauren up and sent her to the bathroom while she moved the cooler out of the car. Then she sat on the bed as Lauren struggled back under the covers.

"I am off to teach class. I'll get your labs covered again," she said to Lauren. She held up her pistol and the spare clip. "I'll leave this with you, here on the bedside table. You know how to use it?"

"I'm used to hunting rifles, but I have fired pistols," Lauren answered. "That toy is not a man-stopper, but it will do."

"OK, stay here today, stay off the computer, just rest, plenty of food in the fridge," Maggie advised. "Might be good to write this all down, too. My home office is next door, the desk has writing pads. I agree we stay off electronics for now. Maybe we order in pizza tonight?"

"Sounds good," Lauren mumbled, then she straightened up. "Thank you, Dr. Gerelli. You are the only one in this town I trust." She lay back down and shut her eyes to escape both the present and the past.

◼   ◼   ◼

"Lauren had a minor medical problem, a woman thing, so she had a treatment yesterday and all is fine. She is convalescing and I will get this last week of her labs covered, and she will finish her coursework with me remotely," Maggie explained to the Department Head, Joe Connerly. Maggie had wondered what the difference was between a 'Head' and a 'Chair,' and Joe had explained that the Head served at the pleasure of the administration, a Chair at the pleasure of the department. Joe gave her a look, and Maggie said simply "It wasn't an abortion." And that was that.

Maggie hadn't said where Lauren was and had fudged the bit about the remote instruction. Lauren wasn't getting online again for some time; she and Maggie would handle the course material face-to-face. Maggie got through the day without taking a nap, but as soon as her last class was over, she went home. She entered from the carport cautiously, calling out "I'm home," thinking of Jack Nicholson and 'redrum,' 'redrum.'

Lauren was in Maggie's office, writing at the desk, and for some time apparently, as Lauren looked at the stack of papers filled with hand-writing. Her Glock was sitting on top of the stack as a paperweight.

"Everything is set at school. You have a minor medical problem and will finish the semester online, your last lab is covered, so you are part way disappeared," Maggie stated to open a conversation on what was next.

"I can't go back to my apartment. I am supposed to disappear. My lease runs out at the end of the month, anyway," Lauren replied. "I can't stay here, though. I am putting you in danger."

"For now, you are staying here," Maggie wanted no doubt in Lauren's mind. "It is a matter of simple security. Right now, I am the only one besides your abductors who knows what is going on. We keep that circle small. I am in hip-deep anyway."

"Do you think I am paranoid?" Lauren rejoined.

"You are here, now, with me, only because you ran fast and thought fast, and defeated a better-equipped foe," Maggie rebutted. "If you didn't display a little paranoia, I'd be worried." What Maggie was worried about was PTSD.

"So, what's next?" Lauren queried.

"We have to decide on a strategy, then we think about tactics," Maggie replied. "Right now, you are unidentified. If this perpetrator is the web genius you think he is, he is expecting a missing person's report to turn up, or a police report. You got away; if he thinks you went into hiding without telling anybody, he will expect a missing person's report. If he thinks you went to the cops, he expects a police report. He doesn't expect either action to not occur. So, I imagine several girls go missing a week in this part of Georgia. He will see those reports and weigh the descriptions with what he knows about you, which is gender, size, race, and hair color, what his people saw when they took you and when they sent you running. He will see no report about an attempted abduction that ended hundreds of miles away in Tennessee."

"So, if I don't disappear, and there is no missing person's report or police report, then what?" Lauren asked.

"OK, let me put myself in his shoes," Maggie responded. "You got away, so he has probably shut down his Tennessee operation. You offer a new hunting opportunity, a difficult one if you plan to stay hidden, as he has no initial trigger on your identity, which would be those reports that aren't going to happen. The lack of a police report says you are trying to hide."

"How does he get the reports?" Lauren asked. "Aren't they supposed to be confidential?"

"A police report, yes, to a certain extent, but then out goes a bulletin to alert other jurisdictions, not hard to hack into that file," Maggie offered. "Missing persons reports are public, 'have you seen this individual?' type of announcements. Easy to check."

"He comes up with nothing, so what does he do?" Lauren asked.

"He then knows you are hiding," Maggie answered. "Or died during your escape and your body is lost in the woods somewhere in Tennessee. He will doubt that, based on your effective initial escape. So, he will start at your abduction point, and look for routine surveillance video. He needs an image or an address."

"He can get that?" Lauren was wide-eyed.

"We assume he can," Maggie replied. "You made it harder for him, as those videos would have been checked for either a missing person's report or a police report and be in a file. That didn't happen. He has to now hack into the actual device or its storage component. Much harder to do, as there are all sorts of security checks on that stuff. Not so much after the police do a download, then it's in their system and there are dozens of ways in."

"So, we assume he is going to get my name, eventually, get my ID," Lauren looked disconsolate.

"If he can track you backwards from the abduction site, yes, he will be able to narrow it down to your apartment building, I assume," Maggie detailed.

"He will hack my university records, he will know I am a student, he will know I am your student."

"Who finished the semester and disappeared," Maggie noted. "That is when he will get frustrated, and start fishing, or to use a digital term, spell it with a ph."

"That's a good thing?" Lauren inquired. "It means he is getting closer."

"It means he has switched from passive looking at records to actively asking questions, he will have gone from reactive to proactive, he will expose himself if anyone is watching," Maggie said with a smile of triumph.

"So, what do we do?" Lauren was lost, disappearing was looking to be much harder than she had imagined. "He will go from me to you eventually."

"Why come to me?" Maggie asked. "He doesn't know I picked you up in Tennessee, he doesn't know you made a phone call, he doesn't know if anyone helped you. I am going to move you out of your apartment this weekend, notify the manager you are gone for the summer. I will close out your bank account after your last TA check direct deposits next week. Your phone will be flat, your computer unbooted, you have no digital presence at all. You wear a wig and glasses to fool facial recognition software."

"What good will these actions do?" Lauren was observing Maggie go through this conspiratorial process like she was watching a movie. She had to remind herself this was about her, her life, and her future.

"He will get frustrated, and frustrated men make mistakes," Maggie replied. "I know. I was married to one for twenty-seven years."

Maggie stepped back and thought. How had she let herself get so deep into Lauren's problem? It was a human thing to do, help another in distress, but she was now doing special agent stuff. Was she role playing, in it for the thrill? For Lauren? Maggie had felt the insults of trying to re-make her life as a professional woman in a man's world. This was a chance to strike back. Someone had come for Lauren, *her* Lauren.

CHAPTER 8

BATTLELINES

MAGGIE WAS CORRECT, Ted Keller was getting frustrated. His bots had zero, zilch, nada. No police report on a human hunting ranch in Tennessee. Lots of missing persons reports in the general Atlanta and Athens areas, but the profiles had been close in only a few cases; it didn't look like his 'Little Miss,' as he thought of her, was among them. So he either gave it up and moved on, or he got to digging. He, of course, did the latter. He liked the challenge, he liked the new, tougher game, but most of all, he was pissed. The little bitch had gotten away. He had to shut down one of his favorite toys. He had billions, actual cash in addition to stocks, options, and all the rest of the 'funny money' in business and finance. His cash reserves alone would dwarf the total economies of many small third-world countries. He couldn't spend his way to victory here, he would have to put in the legwork himself. A bought victory would be hollow, and he didn't want to risk letting anyone else know of his search, because the why of that search would always be present, and unanswered. He employed smart people; he didn't need to arouse their curiosity.

Ted wasn't surprised his Little Miss had gone silent. She had been smart enough to beat his bush drivers, his support team. She would have counted that they were four people plus more unseen, such as himself. Ted didn't realize his Little Miss knew about Fred. She would have observed that the four men knew what they were doing. She saw a big, polished operation, which meant money. The Tennessee site was clean, the people back to their daily routine, nothing in the valley but eleven well-hidden graves. Fred was the weak point, but he knew he needed to keep quiet; Tennessee still had the death penalty. Fred was also smart and, more to the point, cunning. He probably had a complete account of his actions squirreled away somewhere, maybe even with images. It would stay hidden as long as Fred was OK, but surface if Fred met trouble or disappeared. Still no connection to Ted, a brush fire six states away. Ted had written it all off.

Ted did all his clandestine computer work from an office down the hall, his secure room, as he called it. Separate fiber optic line to a building three blocks away, owned by a shell company who, on the official record, was a competitor. It was set up to appear as if the company was trying to spy on him, should it be discovered. From the servers there, Ted could get on-line to anywhere, and make it look as if it came from Russia, or Iran, or Luxembourg. His abductors had told Fred exactly where they had collected the girl, and Fred had passed that on to Ted as the last item of business as Ted severed the relationship. The corner of Lakewood and Magnolia on the University side of Athens. Ted put his bots to work, to build a list of where in that area there were cameras. They came in all sorts of conditions and situations. Home residence security, really hard to access unless the password was 1234. All sorts of traffic cams and license plate readers. Business security cameras. And, in light of recent Black Lives Matter protests, city-owned cameras for direct observation of the public. To get those images would require skill. Many image files were deleted after certain time limits, so Ted needed to secure imagery quickly. Once secured, he could review it at his leisure. Ted was eager but knew when to be in a hurry, and when not.

Ted was certain he would locate his woman, this Little Miss, so he began to think about how he would end her. Quickly, like hitting a light switch, or slowly, so she fully understood? Ted liked efficiency, but there was something about human despair that reached deep into him. He would keep her until she despaired. He was confident he could make that happen. He had never felt despair himself as an adult, he had always succeeded, at least eventually. He had hunted; what was it like to be hunted, to be cornered, to know the game was up? He passed on those thoughts as silly; his ego was strong. Continuous victory did that to a person. He hadn't met his match yet.

*   *   *

"We are still stuck on tactics," Maggie complained to Lauren. "We attend to the tasks as described, and we get you disappeared. Then what?"

"Disappearing is a strategy, Dr. Gerelli," Lauren countered. "If we can make that work, then we can move ahead with other strategies. If this guy finds me and eliminates me, then the rest of the strategies won't matter. So we are doing the necessary initial first step."

"Fair enough, what do you think is the next step?" Maggie queried.

"We expose the Tennessee operation," Lauren responded.

"He won't have any connection that will be found," Maggie rebutted.

"That is what he thinks," Lauren countered. "He is ninety-five percent sure, but he isn't one-hundred percent sure; if we expose this part of his game, he will be concerned, he will pay attention."

"He will be distracted," Maggie nodded. "He will also suspect that it is you who has blown that operation. It will increase his motivation to find you and get rid of you."

"It will increase the likelihood that he will make a mistake," Lauren proposed. "Anyway, there is a bigger issue here, which is to let the families know what happened to their girls."

"That will really piss off the perp," Maggie stated.

"Take away his joy, what better answer to what he has done?" Lauren queried.

"How are we going to do this?" Maggie inquired.

"We go to White City, we find Fred, and we induce him to make a video confession, with details," Lauren answered with a grim smirk. "Then we send that video to a number of law enforcement agencies and news outlets."

"Isn't that against the law?" Maggie felt a coldness in her gut. "Will we kill him in the end?"

"I believe the term is 'extrajudicial removal'," Lauren answered, "and it is fine by me. He makes the tape, the police find the bodies, the FBI comes in, and the pressure mounts," Lauren continued.

"And we just sidle away?" Maggie asked.

"This Fred guy was a central figure in the murder of maybe five women, maybe ten," Lauren argued. "He has earned his death, and he will reveal nothing about us."

"Fred is not the leader, the originator. He was a pawn," Maggie countered.

"There is a monster out there, with huge resources. We won't bring him down with polite words and well-written legal briefs," Lauren proposed. "We get him by using his own game. Let him have a taste of fear, let him start running, in his head. He will see the video, he will see what happens, he will worry."

"You really will do this?" Maggie asked.

"By myself if I have to, but you would make it easier," Lauren admitted.

"Let me think about it," Maggie said. Thinking about it would only make it more likely. "How would you make Fred talk, waterboard him?"

"This monster likes electronics. I have a soldering iron. Fred will literally smell his pain," Lauren said with determination, "and the monster will know it."

Maggie looked at Lauren, a whirlpool who was drawing her in. They were talking about murdering a human being. A very guilty human being, but a living person, nonetheless. Then she thought of the other girls, the ones who didn't get away. Who had families that didn't know. Something in her heart hardened as she thought about it.

CHAPTER 9

LOOSE ENDS

"THE FLAW IN OUR ARGUMENT is that the perpetrator will quickly connect you, Dr. Gerelli, to me," Lauren noted. "We have to demonstrate that you are as far into the dark as everyone else about me and what happened to me."

"I already told the Department Head you had contacted me about a medical problem," Maggie rebutted.

Lauren paused for a moment. "You found a note from me in the front seat of your car Thursday morning, along with my Special Hours project and the two take-home finals for my courses. I have them almost completed anyway. The note said I had a medical problem, and I was taking a leave to address it with the proper medical treatment. I had a bout with Hodgkin's Lymphoma when I was younger, pre-pubescent, and I beat it, but let everyone assume I had a re-occurrence. I expect our opponent will access my medical records and find out. That will send him down a rabbit hole that will lead nowhere, trying to determine where I am getting treatment." Maggie now accepted that the opponent was theirs, not just Lauren's.

"So I enter your final grades and as far as anyone knows, you and I are done for now," Maggie answered.

"The note could also ask you to collect my things from my apartment and put them into storage, that I left money in an envelope in my apartment," Lauren proposed.

"That is when I can pick up your reports and exams and have them in my files," Maggie replied, warming to the subject. "What about your car?"

"I don't have a car here," Lauren answered. "I walk to school, ride my bike, or take the shuttle. Put the bike in storage, it's inside the apartment right now."

"The perp will wonder how you got from Tennessee to Athens, and then how you left," Maggie said.

"I stole a car, of course," Lauren smiled. "That will occur to our opponent, and he will go down another non-existent rabbit hole."

"Either you stole a car or made good friends in Tennessee really quickly," Maggie observed.

"Will he back-trace the phone call I made to you from the convenience mart?" Lauren queried.

"The call I got trying to sell me a car warranty?" Maggie feigned. "Your call was short, the number was ghosted."

"More believable than you dropping everything and coming 200 miles to rescue me," Lauren agreed. "You will post my grades, a sophisticated hacker will see that, and perhaps wonder why you did that instead of entering incompletes," Lauren speculated.

"So would Joe," Maggie answered, considering the Department Head. "I'll just tell him you turned everything in so I scored it all and calculated your final average and entered the grades."

"What about me finishing up online? Isn't that what you told him this morning?" Lauren inquired.

"I'll tell him, if he asks, that you finished up remotely, which isn't necessarily online, and I'll have the documentation to prove it," Maggie replied. "I'll act a little pissed off, that your departure messes up my summer field plans."

"I am very sorry about that," Lauren apologized.

"Oh please!" Maggie exclaimed. "We are now involved in a much bigger thesis project than we had initially contemplated. We do have a field trip to Tennessee to do, remember?"

▪ ▪ ▪

Maggie recruited a couple of graduate students to help her out on Saturday mid-day. She had called the apartment manager and explained that Lauren left school and wouldn't renew her lease. The manager was helpful, and when Maggie showed up with the key, the lady went in with Maggie and determined that the apartment was in good shape and the damage deposit would be returned. It was a furnished apartment, right down to the utensils, almost a vacation rental setup. Lauren did not have much stuff. Maggie had two wardrobe boxes from her divorce and property separation, and all of Lauren's hanging clothes fit in just fine. It took about a dozen other boxes to wrap up, not much, but then Lauren lived simply. Maggie found the reports and exams on the small desk, and carefully boxed all the academic stuff; it would go home with her, as would the laptop. Maggie also made certain a box held toiletries and other things that Lauren would need right now, including some clothes, were included. The manager agreed to return the $300 deposit in cash which solved another problem: no bank transaction, no un-deposited check. Maggie had rented a small storage container on Friday, and when she and the grad students had loaded all of Lauren's stuff inside, it still seemed mostly empty. The rental was for three months, to give the appearance that Lauren would return for the fall semester. Another rabbit hole, it was becoming a warren of rabbit holes for Lauren's enemy. Maggie had worked from a list that Lauren had given her, and Lauren was happy to have some of her things back in her possession when Maggie returned to the house.

◼ ◼ ◼

The house was dark when Maggie strolled in, carrying a box of Lauren's papers and books. "As a single woman, I always have my curtains and shades drawn," Maggie noted. "You can have some lights on."

"One of the easiest things to get a hold of online would be your utility records," Lauren announced. "We can't have a sudden increase in water and electricity usage that coincides with my disappearance."

"Wow, now that sounds paranoid, but you are correct," Maggie replied. "Same with food purchases, looks like spending cash at the farmer's market is in play. It is good that I don't eat out much, no change in pattern there."

"I fully understand that I am basically under house arrest, and off the web as well," Lauren stated. "All the more reason to move quickly, both to keep our opponent off-balance, and to keep me from going stir crazy."

"Finals start Monday, Commencement is Saturday, then I am essentially free of duties at the Department," Maggie responded. "My nine-month contract runs through to the 15th, but no one is counting."

"I have been working up some plans," Lauren said with enthusiasm.

"OK, what is step one?" Maggie asked, knowing that the beginning always has a beginning.

"We drive to Tennessee, and we steal a car," Lauren said with relish. Maggie caught that tone and wondered if they were both drifting into a role-playing game, one that reversed roles.

CHAPTER 10

TACTICS

TED WAS BECOMING MORE FRUSTRATED. It was taking time, too much time, to review video from Athens. He had electronically posed as law enforcement from Florida and gotten traffic video and had identified the van used by his abductors. From that he got the license tag, which he hadn't known. That allowed him to use the tag ID feature on patrol cars and street videos, and he was able to map the van's travel into and out of Athens. He already knew where the abduction had occurred, so that effort was a dead end, really to no purpose. Ted had gotten caught up in the game of tracking a van he didn't need to track. He was angry at himself for falling into that trap. Finally, some street video catalogued at 5:50 am local time showed a short person walking briskly towards the abduction site. It was grainy and indistinct as such video always was, especially in the dark. Useless for facial recognition programs, but now he had two points, which determines a line, and he could work backwards on that travel path. One small discovery that greatly reduced the search area. A second small discovery was how the person was dressed. Not shoes or sneakers, but boots. Not sweatshirt and pants, or running clothes, but field clothes. Ted hadn't known that detail; Fred did but had not relayed it on. Baggy clothes that didn't reveal gender, and the ponytail was a hint but not determinative these days. Still, he hadn't found anything else of value, so he went with it.

Ted now had a geographic information system (GIS) map of a portion of Athens, and on it he had plotted the abduction site, and the camera location with the supposed victim's images. There weren't a lot of city cameras in the area, but city records showed him where the apartment buildings were. One of Ted's problems was he didn't know if the victim was leaving or returning to her apartment when abducted; a line goes two ways.

It was now several days since the abduction and subsequent escape, and still no police report. No missing persons report either that seemed to fit what he knew of his victim. Plenty of likely candidates in terms of age and stature, but no one who should have been abroad in that portion of Athens at 5:50 am. Ted was forced to consider that his Little Miss had gone to ground, without telling anyone. He wondered at that choice by his target. Was she just totally scared? Had she run to her parents and said that she was afraid, that they shouldn't do anything? That would explain no police report, no missing person's report. How had she done that? Had the van guys, by chance, taken someone from Athens who lived in eastern Tennessee? That would have simplified things for the girl. She could have borrowed a phone and called home. Loving parents would have driven 500 miles to pick up their child from an attempted kidnapping. Still, why no police report? It implied that his Little Miss had an idea of what she was up against. She had gotten away, she was smart, she knew what the setup had been. Ted's frustration battled with his excitement. This was worthy prey.

■　■　■

"We have a strategy, to pressure our opponent, and succor his victim's families, by blowing up his Tennessee hunting ranch," Lauren stated. "It is a tactics question now. We can't use the web, and we can't travel openly, and we have to be careful how we use funds, cash only."

"Margaret Davenport can help," Maggie replied.

Lauren, who had been face down at the kitchen table looking at her handwritten notes, jerked her head up. "Who is that, can we trust her?"

"Davenport was my married name, and when the divorce was being negotiated, Paul, my beloved husband, demanded that my alimony funds be in an account under my married name," Maggie explained. "A last bit of control for a man for who control was everything. It was an easy thing to do. It allowed my lawyer to agree after negotiating a further gouge of the man's bank account."

"So we can do things under the Davenport name that won't ring alarms?" Lauren queried.

"I think so. If our guy determines who you are and is watching the actions of faculty in your department, especially your advisor, then it is some protection," Maggie agreed.

"It means we can go to Tennessee as mother and daughter. Do we need to spend cash?" Lauren asked.

"I access the account by a credit card, and I have all my old ID," Maggie replied with a grin.

"Good! We drive to Chattanooga, park your car at the airport's long-term parking, rent a car, and do our business in White City," Lauren exclaimed.

"And what business is that?" Maggie inquired.

"How you want to surprise your husband with a hunting trip run by people who know how to do such things," Lauren replied. "Your husband has had some trouble with the law and has to be careful where he goes to shoot guns. He must be careful about flying, so it has to be somewhere he can easily drive to."

"I like it, but is it too soon? And what will you be doing?" Maggie followed up.

"Looking for a remote rental where we can do our interrogation," Lauren said. "You will need to wear a wig, not obvious but observable, and explain it's because of chemo."

"Another rabbit hole?" Maggie asked.

"It seems they breed just as rabbits do," Lauren laughed.

"What's next?" Maggie asked.

"We go to Atlanta, buy a cheap laptop, and set up a free email account at a coffee shop," Lauren explained. "We need to be able to get anonymously on the web."

"What do we look for first?" Maggie queried.

"Hunting club and camp operators in eastern Tennessee. The old man with the hounds, he may use his dogs on contract with such people. We start there," Lauren advised. "He leads us to Fred."

"We blow up Fred and our perp gets nervous," Maggie proposed.

"Especially when Fred looks into the camera and says, 'They know boss, they know everything. And they are coming for you,'" Lauren mused. Maggie, upon listening to Lauren, again worried about the possibility of PTSD.

CHAPTER 11

SETTING UP A SETUP

THERE WERE DOZENS OF HUNTING CLUBS in eastern Tennessee, all the way up and down I-81, east of McMinnville. Most boldly advertised how they followed all state and federal regulations for hunting. A few were notable for not having such a disclaimer; some of those instead talked about the unique and wild experience they offered. The type of people who would use hounds to drive deer to their city-slicker clientele, sitting comfortable in a blind with both a heater and a cooler.

"I think we have several candidates, all close to White City, all with promotional material which suggests activities that might shade the law a bit," Maggie pronounced as they sat sipping lattes in downtown Atlanta. "I am prepared to approach a few."

Lauren was reading the instructions for the two burner phones they had just purchased; she looked up. "You think you can find out if they use hounds or not?"

"Paul, the dear boy, liked to hunt," Maggie explained. "He did it in the west; he loved the open air and the sharp peaks, but he would brag about how to evade limits, where to bait a site, when to pay for people to drive his four-legged victims to him."

"Aren't these operators suspicious of people who come on to them asking for illegal activities?" Lauren asked. "I can see them smelling a setup."

"Of course, which is why I explain my situation and let them make the offer," Maggie replied.

"And your situation is?" Lauren queried.

"My husband is an ex-felon who cannot own a gun. He must be able to drive to the location as he is on the no-fly list," Maggie began. "And he has a limp from an incident, and still carries fragments in his left leg."

"You make him sound like a Mafia Don," Lauren exclaimed.

"Not the Don, too public, too traceable," Maggie cautioned. "More like a made man high up in the ranks, semi-retired. Helps with the books, but the street work is long over."

"Your husband Paul did this?" Lauren's eyes were wide.

"No, not Paul. He didn't have the balls for that sort of stuff. He, as they say, knew people who knew people," Maggie responded. "What he admired was that the Don would give an order, and it would be obeyed. As I said, Paul liked control."

■　■　■

"I have two likely sites, the Highland Hunting Club and Dudley's Dude Ranch, they are both within ten miles of White City," Maggie offered. "Based on how the website for each is laid out, I suspect a common owner/operator."

"Why do you suspect that?" Lauren asked.

"They each have a photo album, and a couple of pictures are the same," Maggie answered. "The key is the same phone number for deliveries. In any event, I think Dudley's Dude Ranch is the filter, and Highland Hunting Club is where the real action occurs."

"Because…" Lauren probed.

"The Dudley name is a joke, and implies easy going; it's a dude ranch," Maggie replied. "Highland Hunting Club sounds professional, serious. It's also much more remote than the dude ranch, which is not far off US Route 41 just north of White City. Highland is to the south."

"Closer to where I was hunted," Lauren whispered. "So, what's next?"

"I make an online inquiry. I expect after some back and forth, I'll be asked to make a call. Those phones all set up?"

■　■　■

"Well Mrs. Smith, thank you for calling," the man's voice said politely. The e-mails had said he was Sam Fairbanks, but Maggie made no assumptions.

"Good to talk with a live human being, Mr. Fairbanks. I hope this phone call moves things along, I dislike hunching over keyboards," Maggie answered.

"Well, let's see if we can address your needs, and call me Sam," the voice replied. It went on, "I see your husband has some movement restrictions, travel limitations, and has to be careful regarding his use of firearms. Is that correct?"

"Mr. Fairbanks, I am in no mood to play footsy," Maggie growled back. "My husband is a convicted felon, which is why he cannot own a gun. His reputation has gotten his ass on the Homeland Security no-fly list, and he has bullet fragments from a police revolver in his left leg. That is his condition in plain English. Is that clear enough for your southern ears?"

"Yes, yes, of course, Mrs. Smith," Sam was quick to reply, seeming to take no offense. A person with special needs gets special prices. "We are very experienced with a wide variety of clientele from numerous backgrounds, I am sure we can accommodate your husband."

"Good, because I want to surprise him with this hunting club trip; he thinks we are going to visit relatives," Maggie was making it up as she went along, reading the man on the phone. "He doesn't want to see them, and they don't want to see him, so this place of yours has to be good enough to meet his needs."

"I see," Sam replied, and he did see, not only the situation but the reward that could be there for him. A deep-pockets man who needed to be unseen and yet have a good time. "We are very discreet, and we can cater to almost any hunting specialty."

"What about law enforcement. You have a good relationship with them? I'm not sending my husband into a set-up," Maggie barked.

"Law enforcement has no interest in my operations, Mrs. Smith," Sam answered in his best 'trust me' voice. "We have never been cited; hell, we have never even been inspected."

"Good, because I have some specific questions," Maggie responded. "First, are you recording this call? Tennessee is a one-party state, so I need to know." Georgia was also a one-party state and Maggie *was* recording the call.

"No ma'am, we do not record phone calls, not for quality control or anything else," Sam replied, beginning to sense this was a serious approach, while Maggie began to sense that she had a fish on the line, so to speak.

"OK, that's good, but you could be lying," Maggie answered. "Second question, can you make it happen so the deer or bears or whatever are made to show up where my husband can see to shoot them?"

Sam could see the woman knew what she wanted but was not literate in hunting terminology. "Yes ma'am. We do it a variety of ways. We can have people make a disturbance that forces the animals where we want them to go."

"That sounds gimmicky, like a Disney World show," Maggie retorted.

"Well, we can make it like the movies, and have hounds baying and driving the prey to your husband," Sam offered.

"You can do that? He is always saying 'loose the hounds,' he would love it," Maggie chortled. "You have a man who knows what he is doing? I don't want my husband attacked by dogs."

"Josh Ketchum is the best hound master in eastern Tennessee. He has been written up in *Field and Stream* a few times. It was a while ago, but he still has the touch, and his dogs are the most active, but fully controlled."

"I see, good," Maggie replied. "Next question, Tennessee has some funny laws regarding alcohol; what goes on at your place?"

"We are private property, we can do anything we want," Sam, replied, liking where the conversation was going. Specifics, like alcohol, indicated the sale was half made.

"Do I need to drop him off? Do you do pickups at the front gate, or does he drive in, or what?" Maggie was into detailed specifics now.

"Whatever works best for you, ma'am," Sam answered. "You could look the place over if you like or drop him and forget about it until pick-up later. How long are you thinking about?"

"That is open-ended. If he gets there and doesn't like what he sees, we will leave. Or he may love it and want to spend ten days there," Maggie proposed.

"Fine with us. We can do on-the-spot arrangements," Sam replied, recognizing that this Mrs. Smith, he didn't believe for a second that was her real name, was sharp and careful. "I can pencil you in for whenever."

"It would be next month, I think. I'll get back to you," Maggie responded. "I can call at this number and ask for you?"

"That would be fine. Thank you very much for your interest," Sam answered, keeping the disappointment out of his voice. A callback might never happen. He was right.

"Excellent. Goodbye," and Maggie ended the call. She had made the call from a quiet spot in a park. Lauren looked at her expectantly.

"Now what?" Lauren asked.

"Now we go to the library," Maggie smiled.

■　■　■

"How do we find an article or two about some guy who runs hounds in eastern Tennessee?" Lauren asked as they walked into the Fulton County Public Library, One Margaret Mitchell Square, a name that pleased Maggie no end.

"You are a child of your generation. Let an ancient biddy show you how it was done in olden times," Maggie answered, channeling Forrest Gump. "We will look at an index. I suspect it is now searchable. We will do so carefully by looking into a topic such as 'which hunting dogs make good pets'. That way if someone is watching to see if we were looking for Josh Ketchum, they won't know."

"They will when we download the article," Lauren protested.

"My dear Lauren, we will go into the stacks and look at a hard copy," Maggie laughed. "An advantage for us — I suspect our perpetrator is between us in age. He may never have looked in the stacks either. He is blind to old school ways."

■　■　■

They found Josh Ketchum. He lived a few miles east of White City, at least he had when the most recent article had been written, about fifteen years earlier. Lauren looked at the images, it was the second one that caught her eye.

"That is the truck, in better shape than when I saw it, but that is the truck; see how the cages are tied into the railing in the back?" Lauren almost shouted, Maggie had to shush her.

"What about the pictures of Josh himself? Is that the man with the shotgun?" Maggie kept Lauren on task.

"I have to age him in my mind, but there is nothing I see that would say he is not the old man I saw," Lauren replied. A good, objective answer.

"Look at this! He says he hunts with a lot of friends, and sometimes they hunt each other for kicks," Maggie read. "The only one who ever got away was Fred Dossett, he calls him 'a whisp in the woods.' That sounds like your Fred."

CHAPTER 12

HUNTING

IT WAS TO PHONE BOOKS NEXT. It had been years since anyone had published a phone book, but they still sat in microfilm, the youngest one for White City and the general area of Grundy County, Tennessee, was eleven years old. That led to an address for a Fred Dossett in the tiny burg of Oak Grove, just south of where Lauren had stumbled on to US 41. The biggest town in the area was Tracey City, west of White City on US 41. Fred was a proud graduate, it would seem, of Grundy County High School, a school that was 95% white with fewer than 700 students. Now they could go online to look at a yearbook. They found Fred in the 1979 volume of the *Mountain Laurel* with a notation beneath his picture — 'Mr. Mountain Man' — which hinted at his skill as a tracker. The seventeen-year-old face looked back, now a man pushing 60, but still active it would seem, were he Lauren's Fred, which appeared likely.

Nothing more they could do at this end. Any attempt to search voter roles or tax roles would be too bold. The yearbook said he had been a three-sports letter winner. Maybe it was time to go to Grundy County and see what they could find. They could be tourists who liked nature. There was a state park, Savage Gulf, and there were cemeteries where they could come up with the name of an old friend for Maggie. Then hit a diner or two and see if there was anyone talkative. Make Lauren a teenage boy, Maggie a grandmother. Time to roll the dice.

*　　*　　*

Lauren's small, slim stature made a convincing sixteen-year-old boy. She had enough vocal range to sound like a guy making the physiological move through puberty towards adulthood. With a wig and judicious use of make-up, Maggie had aged herself and she now looked mid-60s as compared to early 50s. They were Nancy Davenport and Jack, her grandson, off on an adventure of sorts. They had driven to Chattanooga, put Maggie's car in long-term parking, and rented a Toyota. They drove up I-24 to Monteagle and came into Tracey City from the south. They tooled around the main roads and got a feel for the area. They went south down US 41 and past the 'White City 5 miles sign' each of them had seen last on that fateful day. Back up into Tracey City to a local motel, very old fashioned, individual cottages, weathered but not rundown. It could have been 1955. Maggie strolled in the motel office, Lauren trailing, looking bored but polite. A bell sat on the counter, Maggie gave it a tap of her hand, and a voice rang out from the back, "Coming!" Lauren sat in a metal chair and began looking through an old issue of *Guns and Ammo*. An older woman, grey-haired and worn, came up to the counter; while not Nancy Davenport's twin, they could have been sisters.

"Yes ma'am, you need a room?" the lady inquired.

"If you have one for me and my grandson — twin beds?" Maggie asked with a hopeful smile.

"Of course, how many nights?"

"I don't know, we like to wander around and see the land," Maggie replied. "We're from eastern Arkansas and Jack wanted to see some mountains."

"Long drive gettin' here," the owner responded.

"Oh no, Jack's father does sales and travels a lot. We flew on his miles. He has them stacked up," Maggie countered.

"So your car's a rental? I wondered about the Florida plates," the manager stated, alerting Maggie that sleepy-looking people may not be asleep.

"Yup, flew into Chattanooga this morning after the short drive to Memphis," Maggie revealed. She had checked out that such a flight did occur.

"What do you plan to do here, besides look at cliffs and mountains?" the manager was between being friendly and being a snoop.

"I had a roommate in college who had a friend from here, graduated from the county high school, who talked about all the history and family culture, how it was simple but rich."

"Who was that?" the manager was suddenly beyond simple curiosity.

"Ann Fastnot, I don't know where she is now." Actually, Maggie knew she was in the Laurel Mountain cemetery down near Monteagle. Lauren had spotted the grave and checked it against the list of names from the 1979 high school yearbook; the gravestone had said 'Ann Fastnot Wilson,' so she had been married and now dead a decade. Ann had been listed as 'Going to be a teacher' and she was going to Murray State in Kentucky, a long way from Tracey City. She clearly had wanted to get away from eastern Tennessee, but she had come back.

"Oh yes, she married the Wilson boy and taught in the private academy in Monteagle," the manager replied. "Died of breast cancer, she had the barking gene or whatever."

Maggie as a post-menopausal woman knew the lady meant the BRCA gene and wondered how such personal medical information was common knowledge. "That is too bad. I'd hoped for a cup of coffee and to share old times," Maggie sighed. "I know what she went through." She tapped her wig. "Chemo."

"You a teacher too?" the manager inquired.

"Retired now," Maggie nodded. "Taught in Arkansas, that's where my daughter met Jack's father. By the way, I'm Nancy Davenport." Maggie stuck her hand over the counter.

"Lucy Banks," the lady answered, and gave a quick handshake. She looked over at Lauren. "You like guns, boy?' she asked.

"I like hunting, at least, I think I do. Don't get to do much on the Arkansas floodplain," Lauren, aka Jack, answered.

"He's at that age, wants to do manly things but not sure how to go about it," Maggie interjected.

"That's a father's job, not a grandma's" Lucy responded.

"Like I said, his father is on the road all the time," Maggie replied, more with accusation than as an excuse. "There a good place to eat? Not a tourist joint, but where the locals go? If I can't talk to Ann, maybe I can soak in what she grew up with."

"You want to pay with a credit card or with cash?" Lucy said, wanting to close the deal and move on. "It's five percent more for a credit card. Fees, you know."

"Cash is fine. How much for a night?" Maggie asked.

"$55. Towels in the room," Lucy said, and they concluded the transaction. "I'd recommend Dockey's, right downtown on 41. An old timer's place. Won't get a quiet meal there, you being a stranger. They'll talk your ears off."

■　■　■

They loaded their luggage into the room, kept the laptop in the car, under the front seat, as there would be no wifi in this place. Working from Maggie's road atlas, they found the high school and looked around, as if Lauren might be a student there in the fall. They stopped at a road-side plaque commemorating a small civil war battle, a skirmish actually, and then it seemed the right time to hit Dockey's. Maggie parked the car several blocks away and they strolled along Main Street, with every third business boarded up, it was typical small-town America.

Dockey's offered booths and tables, all had nice checkered red-and-white tablecloths. They took a table — more likely to get conversation there then stuck away in a booth. Lauren had dyed her hair dark and trimmed it back. She had on sneakers, no hiking boots, worn jeans that had an honestly distressed look to them, and a flannel shirt. Maggie wore baggy pants and a blue blouse; functional clothes that said she was old, that she knew it, and that fashion did not matter. They seated themselves, picked up the laminated menu, and looked it over. They were completely into their roles now.

A waitress came by and gave them the visual once-over. "What'll it be for you folks? You look new here. Need any explanation?"

"What is the house special?" Maggie, aka Nancy, asked.

"Tonight it's the pork barbecue plate, cole slaw, and fries or onion rings, your choice," the waitress spoke a well-repeated line.

"Sounds good. Jack, what about you?" Maggie queried her grandson.

"Yup, make mine with onion rings, and a sweet tea," Jack answered.

The waitress looked over at Nancy. "I'll have the fries and just water, thanks."

Knowing that strangers could tip low or high, the waitress followed up. "Doing the tourist thing?" she asked.

"Sort of. Jack, my grandson, wanted to see mountains, not many in eastern Arkansas. He thinks he might want to be a professional hunter. That's today, anyway. Tomorrow, he might want to join the circus," Nancy said with a chuckle. Jack gave her a stare and rolled his eyes. The waitress, an older lady maybe in her forties, gave a knowing nod and drifted off to turn in their order.

Their order came, and they continued their faux conversation about hunting. Did Jack want to hunt big game or fowl? Use regular guns or go with muzzle loaders, or bow and arrow? They weren't arguing, but they didn't talk subtly. The whole point was to be noticed. They were wrapping up the meal. Jack had a refill of his sweet tea, and then a gentleman came by.

"My apologies. Billy Concendus," he said, introducing himself. "I heard your grandson here likes hunting," the man said.

"Nancy Davenport and my grandson, Jack," Nancy replied. "I guess being new in town is pretty obvious."

"I don't mean no offense, ma'am, it's just that we are off the beaten track here, so a new face means a new conversation," Billy said apologetically.

"No offense at all. We are here and not at the Denny's down on the interstate because we want to get a feel for the neighborhood," Nancy soothed. Talking up strangers was a big deal on the remote islands she visited. Grundy County was an island of sorts. "Jack knows of hunting, but he doesn't know about doing hunting, if you know what I mean." Jack looked uncomfortable, but eagerness to get the real deal about hunting shown in his eyes. Lauren was playing the role very well.

"Well, Jack, I hunt a lot, and I work with some of the best hunters in all of Tennessee, right here in Grundy County," Billy began.

Maggie had a sudden insight as to how Lauren's serial killer had selected this spot for his game. He had done something similar to what they were doing now, but he had done it remotely, online. He probably also had dug deep into some of these people, found out what they owed, who needed money, or who needed a way to wipe a record clean. He had the power to bargain, right down to what was the foundation of a few men's souls. The conversation went on, right through peach cobbler and coffee for Nancy and Billy. Billy waved a man over.

"This here is Sam Fairbanks. If it's about hunting in Grundy County, he knows it all," Billy bragged.

CHAPTER 13

PREY ID

"WHAT'S HUNTING LIKE?" Jack asked, looking to Billy on his left and Sam on his right.

"Well, a lot of people think hunting is all about the shot, the taking down of the quarry," Sam began. "But it is really all that goes on before that moment, the preparation. The aligning of gun sights, the check on the weather, the proper meals so you are fit and ready to go. Knowing your prey. And you haven't even left the house yet."

Maggie, as Nancy, had kept her mouth shut. She didn't know how good an ear Sam had for voices, and she had spoken quite a bit on the phone with him. She was using a faint southern accent here in Grundy County, and she had tried to be imperious on the phone with a flatter accent. She sure as hell couldn't change up now, not after talking with Billy for a quarter of an hour. Sam wasn't paying any attention to her anyway. Jack was an acolyte, a boy who wanted to hunt like a man, and Sam had a missionary zeal about him.

Sam was holding court, talking process, he hadn't gotten to war stories yet; it was the war stories that might yield names. Jack knew he had to push the conversation forward.

"So how do you find the deer, do you use drones, or are there special satellite images you can download?" Jack's voice was eager. His statement broke Billy up, Sam was more careful to not make Jack look stupid.

"You do it just the way our ancestors did, be it Native Americans on this continent or clans in Europe," Sam explained. "You track them, you look for all the signs an animal leaves as it lives in the wild. You look for scat, you look for where they bed down, you find their trails, you look for where they forage." He went on at some length, appearing and sounding really into his own explanation. Billy took his leave; it was hard to compete with Sam.

"You can do all of this?" Jack asked, eyes wide. Sam was sold on the kid.

"Oh yes, I can do all that," Sam said. "There are shortcuts, like baiting the deer by putting corn out in a pasture, efficient but not really sport, more like notching your gun. Or you can use dogs to help, following the scent. Again, efficient but not really your own work, you understand."

"Like with bloodhounds. I saw that in a movie, but they were hunting people, slaves fleeing to the north," Jack said. He was really pushing now. Maggie and Lauren had agreed the persona Jack would drive the conversation, and Maggie as Nancy would watch and evaluate. They even had little signals. Rub an eye to back off, scratch an ear to follow up, stuff like that. Maggie scratched an ear.

"We have them here. We have some people really good with the hounds. They will demonstrate for tourists at some of the city-slicker hunting camps hereabouts," Sam continued. "Josh Ketchum has made a name for himself, had articles in *Field and Stream* published. It takes a lot of training to get a dog setup that'll hunt reliably. Josh is the best I ever knew."

"But the real mountain men, they track just by themselves? Any good ones around here" Jack pursued.

"Old Fred Dossett, he was the best I ever saw, or didn't see; he could go into a one-acre woodlot, and you would never find him," Sam laughed. "He still does the work, hires out now and then, but he has slowed down, rarely leaves his place in Oak Grove. Has his beer every Saturday night down at the Iron Anvil as you come into town on 41."

"You aren't going to any bar, Jack," Maggie said, laying on her southern accent a bit more with Billy no longer present.

"Just as well, Fred can be hard to talk with. He don't like strangers, unless they're women," Sam said apologetically.

"What about choice of guns, I mean, I know it is birdshot for quail, and a rifle for deer, but does make and model matter that much?" Jack pressed. Lauren and Maggie didn't want the last piece of conversation to be about Fred Dossett.

That question sent Sam off on a long discussion before Maggie interrupted. "Sam, that is great stuff. I'm sure Jack now has an idea what hunting is all about. You have shown him how a true believer looks at it, not some urban journalist, I like that. We have had a long day, up early to get to Memphis, the flight, the drive out here, I think we need to call it a day." Jack looked disappointed, but he yawned just then, which sold the ploy.

"Of course, you are right, hunting is my life; I run a dude ranch and a hunting club, but that is to put food on the table so I can do all the hunting I want," Sam extolled. He stood up and went over and shook Jack's hand, which earned him a big smile. He nodded to Maggie and left.

Maggie put down a decent tip, paid the bill, and they walked back to their car. Only after they had pulled away from the curb did they speak.

"Was that productive, or did we just confirm what we already knew?" Lauren asked.

"I think it is without a doubt that Fred Dossett is our man, our link, tenuous as it is, to the perpetrator," Maggie replied.

"So, what next?" Lauren continued.

"I use a lot of different make up, no wig, drop twenty years, and go hit on Fred Dossett in the Iron Anvil," Maggie replied.

"This is where it gets dangerous, doesn't it," Lauren made it a statement.

"It has always been dangerous, right from when they took you off the street, Lauren. This is a long-distance race, not a sprint," Maggie chided.

"I know, I meant dangerous for you," Lauren chided back.

"I hear their voices sometimes when I'm alone working on this project," Maggie replied softly. "I have children; it is personal for me now."

"Whose voices?" Lauren queried. "Fred or Josh?"

"The victims, the dead ones, buried in unknown graves, families left to wonder and mourn," Maggie almost sobbed. "And he watches, he loves it, he lives for it." Maggie had bought in, totally.

"Then he will die for it," Lauren said with a firm voice, a convincing voice.

They pulled up to their cabin and walked into the tiny structure with its two twin beds, small bathroom, but a sink, tiny fridge, and microwave with a small counter on one wall. No phone, no cable so no TV. Comfortable but primitive; sheets and towels were clean. They would check out in the morning. They had gear in the trunk, they had to locate a place to use it. They had lined up some options, backcountry rentals. They would look in the morning, make a decision, and then go hunting.

CHAPTER 14

INTO THE DEPTHS

UP EARLY IN THE MORNING, they had doughnuts and orange juice in the room as they went over their list of rental places set back in the woods. Maggie went up to the office to check out.

"Leaving so soon?" Lucy asked, clearly wanting more business.

"Jack wants to go deep into the woods. We had a great meal last night and met a hunter guy who gave Jack a real introduction to the ins and outs of hunting," Maggie replied.

"Who was that?" Lucy, ever nosey, inquired.

"First it was a guy named Billy, but he waved over a second man, uh, Stan or Sid, something like that," Maggie fumbled.

"Sam Fairbanks?" Lucy suggested.

"Yeah, that's it, says he owns some hunting operations around here," Maggie stated. "He gave Jack a real good idea of what hunting is all about. He talked so much that Billy gave up and wandered away."

"That's Sam all right," Lucy said as Maggie handed over the cash.

* * *

The second place they looked at seemed that it would do just fine. It was an A-frame construction, which gave a high central room with a balcony in front of the second-floor accommodations. Plenty of space for the rigging they had planned. They were still in their Nancy and Jack identities, looking at a place that her family could rent that summer for a vacation.

"So you were at Lucy's place last night?" Susie asked with a grin. She was young and personable and if she could close the deal here and now, she would get the rest of her Saturday back.

"Lucy was pleasant and interested in us," Maggie said diplomatically.

"Nice turn of phrase. Lucy is a nosey gossip and she probably called Billy to let him know you were in town," Susie laughed. "He's her nephew."

"Small southern towns are all alike; it's the same in Arkansas," Maggie chuckled. "This house looks good; plenty of room, way off the main road, nice conveniences, even satellite TV."

"So you will reserve for this summer?" Susie was hopeful.

"No, we will spend the night, just the two of us, and give it a good check out," Maggie replied. "Then I have to sell it to my family, a harder sell than you have had with us." Maggie gave her cash for the one night, and Susie left in her own car, which Maggie had previously followed up the long dirt road to the house.

■ ■ ■

The balcony had been the key, and the high roof. Maggie and Lauren set up the tarp and the cables where Fred would rest. They had bought a strong wooden chair in Atlanta at a thrift store, with cash, naturally, and that would be the foundation for the interrogation. They plotted out camera angles. Nothing was to be seen in the video but a blue tarp and Fred, that and what was to be done to him. No one would see, no one would hear, except Lauren and Maggie and the microphone. The questions would be asked by a computer program from a typed list. All the preparation wasn't just to protect their identity, it was to add to the mystery. They wanted the man behind all of this to be totally blown away.

"Not too late to back away, to say let's just call it in and let it go at that," Maggie proposed. Was she up for torture and murder?

"No, this is something that has to be done," Lauren countered. "Josh has to see this and know he could be next. The same for his assistant and for the two guys in the van. They may say, or think, that they really weren't complicit. But they were. Those girls are dead because they helped. They took their pay and were satisfied."

"OK, I see, but let's be blunt," Maggie rebutted. "We are going to do our own kidnapping, we are going to torture a man to give us all he knows, and then we are going to kill him. You down with that?"

"We will kill him cleanly, and leave his body to be found," Lauren said calmly. "That is better than what he did for all those girls before me, who ran in fear down that valley. What about you? And where did you get a roofie, and the fentanyl?"

"A state university with dozens of fraternities? It was easy."

"I always worried about that, getting drugged and then being taken over. Then, the drug residue showing up in my weekly drug test."

"My goal is forward looking," Maggie answered, getting away from drugging people. "I will be pleased to see these Grundy County Deliverance creeps get their due. I will be satisfied to know a bunch of families will get closure. But what I really want is the man who put this all together, not only stopped, but prevented from doing some more nasty stuff in the future. The dead are gone, we need to keep the living alive." An inversion of the Stockholm Syndrome, on steroids.

■　■　■

Maggie completed her next transformation. Gone was the grandmother of 65, also gone was the college professor of 52. In their place was Deidre, a 45-year-old recently divorced woman looking for a good time. Smart enough to get out of Chattanooga to play, warped enough to want a country boy with experience. She drove to the Iron Anvil as Lauren lay on the floor of the back seat with a blanket over her. Maggie, now Deidre, parked in the gravel lot and went into a roadhouse that could have been in any of a dozen or so Hollywood movies. The rental car now had a license plate stolen from a parked car in Tracey City.

Maggie walked into a loud, warm room with waves of cigarette and cigar smoke. Music rang from a jukebox. It was timeless; Maggie could think of quite a few places like this one she had been in when younger, before Paul had put the clamps on her. She knew the routine and knew it would work in a joint like this. She pulled up to the bar, ordered a Bud. Young men ignored her for now. If it got near to closing time, and they had struck out, she might get a nibble. She was at the end of the bar and could sit relaxed on her stool and scan the entire room. Based on what Sam had said, Fred Dossett was tall and dark, but not particularly handsome. He was gruff, and sat alone, and watched. She saw a likely suspect, back against the far wall, alone at a table that would hold only two. He had a mug in his hand, he drank draft. His eyes wandered around the crowd, from the pool table where men argued and shouted, to where couples danced in a ritual as old as time. He looked at other people, guys telling jokes at a big round table, other guys leaning in to hear a story that must not be overheard, this in its tenth retelling. She let her eyes do the same, knowing that their gazes would cross and then meet. He had looked at her several times when she caught him with her stare. She stood up and walked over, his spot was strangely quiet, as if the hubbub around them was shielded somehow. Probably why he sat in this specific place.

"You dance, or do you just sit and stare?" Maggie asked.

"Who's asking?" the man said.

"Deidre," Maggie answered. "And who are you?"

"Deidre has no last name?" the man asked.

"She does, but Deidre will do for now," Maggie parried.

"You aren't from around here," the man continued.

"Well, points to you for noticing," Maggie observed. "Does a lady get to sit?"

"You're no lady, but you can sit if you like," the man said.

Maggie sat, put her Bud on the table, and looked at the man with an appraising stare. "So you must be from around here, Mr. Man with no name. At least I got one."

That last barb got home. "Aren't you the smart ass? You come up from Chattanooga or down from Nashville to play with the ignorant?" The man feigned indignation, but Maggie could see he was interested.

"I came up from Chattanooga so I could get free of all those posers and fakers. I am interested in a real man who does real stuff," Maggie responded.

"Well, I am a real man. Name's Fred Dossett, and I am a tracker," Dossett stated with pride.

"Do you make tracks or follow them?" Maggie queried. That got a chuckle from Dossett.

"You could leave now, and I could track you all the way to Chattanooga," Dossett bragged.

"The point in coming here was to be not tracked back home," Maggie chided, smiling.

"I'm not buying you a beer," Dossett scolded.

"I'm not here for beer," Maggie replied, leaning her cleavage forward.

Dossett took a last pull on his mug and waved two fingers at the bar. "Have what I'm having?"

"Sure, it hasn't killed you yet," Maggie chuckled. A young girl, not looking old enough to work there, came over with two mugs and set them down. Maggie pushed one over to Dossett, casually dropping in a roofie on the way. The talk continued, Maggie let Dossett carry the conversation and played the eager divorcee role to perfection while she waited for the roofie biochemistry to do its thing.

■　■　■

As Maggie and Dossett staggered out of the bar, Lauren was up and out of the vehicle, holding the rear door open while Maggie laid him in. No one was paying attention. It wasn't a place to have surveillance cameras. They drove off quietly and made their way back to the house, where all was ready.

CHAPTER 15

INSPECTED AND INJECTED

DOSSETT WAS STILL OUT when they got him naked into the chair and handcuffed him, wrists and ankles, in a spread-eagled pattern, the cuffs connected to eye loops in cables that stretched to the wall beams at the floor for the ankles, and to the balcony beam for the wrists. Behind him was a featureless blue tarp, of the type seen on roofs after tornadoes and hurricanes. It flowed down under the chair and across the floor. The tarp edge on the floor was up on boards to keep any fluids from escaping. The house lights were off, flood lamps on stands illuminated the scene. His eyes had been duct-taped shut. There was nothing present to provide any hint of where Dossett had been for this interview. His body would be dumped in Grundy County. The soldering iron was mounted on a pole, so none of Lauren's limbs would ever appear onscreen as she reached the soldering iron out to touch him anywhere she chose. The computer with its list of questions to drive the electronic voice was set up next to the camera. Maggie had her Glock in its holster. She would operate the camera. The computer clock had been set to zeros for time and date, as had the video camera. Everything was ready.

"We are still able to call this all off," Maggie advised Lauren.

"I appreciate the motivational check, but this is a go," Lauren answered. She had as determined a look as Maggie had ever seen on a human being. Would she purge old demons tonight, or create new ones? Trade one PTSD experience for another? They were outfitted in personal protection equipment right out of a pandemic newscast and had wiped any surface in the building they may have touched. Gloves had been on when using the duct tape. Neither lady had ever been fingerprinted or had any ancestry DNA work done. Dossett stirred; he pissed himself immediately, a continuous dribble, not a stream.

"It is time," Lauren whispered. Maggie started the camera. The microphone was to the left so it wouldn't hear any key tapping on the computer, or any breathing by Lauren or Maggie. The women both had only a pad of paper and a marker to communicate; they would not speak while the camera ran. To say Dossett looked uncomfortable would be an understatement; there was no slack in any of the four cables. His waist had been duct-taped to the chair. He was fully immobilized. He began to mumble, then, as his head cleared, he tried to speak.

"Uh, Deidre, is this some sort of joke? Are we playing a game?" Fred slurred his words.

Maggie tapped a key on the computer board. "State your full name, address, and age," commanded the speaker plugged into a USB port on the computer. Each key had been set up to ask a specific question. The voice was a default setting on the common text-to-voice program, off-the-shelf stuff.

"Come on, what is this all about?" Fred asked.

Maggie tapped the same key mercilessly, "State your full name, address, and age," followed by "If you do not answer, you will receive this motivation." Lauren reached out with the pole, the soldering iron and cord was wrapped in duct tape, only the heated tip stuck out. She stuck him in the left bicep.

"Ow, shit, don't do that!" came out as a yelp. Maggie repeated the initial question for the third time.

"OK, OK, I am Frederick Richard Dossett, age 58, I live at 23 Travis Road in Oak Grove, Tennessee."

"Explain your relationship with Dead Rock Holdings," the computer said.

Fred was quiet for a moment. Lauren poked him in the bicep again, drawing the tip along the arm for a few inches. He screamed, then "OK, I see what this is all about. I am here because of the girl who escaped, I know some things, but I don't know who was in charge, I don't know why he did what he did."

"How many girls were killed?" the electronic voice intoned.

Dossett tried to squirm. He pulled, he wiggled, but he could only move a fraction of an inch. Lauren reached with the pole and drew a smoking line across his stomach. Dossett screamed. "It was eleven, it was supposed to be twelve but the last one got away, escaped somehow."

"Where are the bodies?" Came the dry electronic voice with no emotion.

Again a pause, again a smoking line, this time on a thigh. "I buried them, deep. It took a lot of effort. They are in black plastic garbage bags. I didn't kill any of them. He did."

The questions continued: how the girls were killed, the names of the two van men, the name of Josh Ketchum's assistant. Was there anyone else who participated or knew what was going on? How was contact made by 'the boss'? How were payments done?

Then, "Did you take evidence, or trophies?" To this there was quite a long pause. Lauren reached in and stuck Dossett's left testicle. He screamed mightily at this act and started crying. "I took photographs and put a lock of hair and a drop of blood in an envelope, but it wasn't trophies, it was protection in case the boss turned on me or did to me what you are doing. I thought he would just knock me off. I didn't think he would torture me."

Maggie realized that Dossett thought they had been sent by the boss, that it wasn't Lauren as the escapee.

They had thought he might have collected and hidden some information, so there was a question for it. "Where is the evidence?"

"If I tell you, you will just kill me," Dossett shouted. Lauren stabbed him in the side of the neck. "OK, OK, I get it, I will die tonight in any event, and you will torture me until I tell you what you want to know. If I give it all up, will you just kill me, make it easy?"

Torture isn't all about the pain, it is about the fear and the uncertainty. Drunk, drugged, blinded, Fred was full of fear. He could smell his burnt flesh, feel the tight shackles, hear an impersonal machine voice. He was terrified. He gave up.

A key tap from Maggie, "Yes."

"I made notes of each event, detailed. I know where each girl was taken, its all there, in one spot," Dossett sobbed.

"Where is the evidence?" was repeated. It had to be somewhere easy to get to, as he updated it every time he was part of a kill. He had probably updated Lauren's case. It also would need to surface if he didn't show up.

"It is in a safe deposit box at Citizens Bank in Monteagle," Dossett gasped. "Box number 438, the key is in my truck, under the horn button. I pay every quarter. If I don't, the box is opened, and the contents examined."

"What do you know about the man in charge?" came the electronic question.

"It was just one person, it was a male, I never saw him, I would get a text telling me where to go, and he would call me on a walkie talkie, channel 13," Dossett's voice was raspy, he had done some screaming when Lauren had worked on his motivation. "He sounded middle age, his accent wasn't southern, in fact he had no accent."

Maggie ran a few more questions through the computer, but it was clear Dossett had been bled dry. She wrote 'Done?' on her pad, and Lauren nodded back. She faded to black on the camera, shut it off, ejected the chip and loaded the video onto the computer, then put it on a couple of thumb drives.

She got out a used insulin syringe she had scavenged from a friend's trash. She loaded in a very big hit of fentanyl. Lauren came over and made certain the camera was off, unplugged, and she put it back in its case. She and Maggie had discussed who should do the lethal injection. Maggie had agreed to let Lauren do it, to kill this demon. Lauren took the syringe over to Dossett.

"Fred Dossett, I was up in that cliff while you and your dogs searched in vain for me. My name is Lauren, and you have been cooperative, so the torture is over, now you will be sent to Hell." She inserted the needle into a bulging vein as Dossett whimpered, and she gave him the full syringe load. It was 2 a.m. Then, the cleanup started.

CHAPTER 16

THE PUZZLE BEGINS

FRED DOSSETT'S BODY WAS WRAPPED IN TWO WHITE GARBAGE BAGS, one over his head, one pulled up over his legs. The bags were duct-taped together, and they hauled his lanky frame out to the backseat of the car. The various components of the interrogation were loaded in as well, some in the trunk. They straightened up the house, packed their luggage, locked the door with the key left under a rock near the picture window as Susie had instructed, and drove off. At 4 a.m., they left the body on the road underneath I-24 at the Pelham exit overpass, knowing that the white bag would attract immediate attention. On to I-24 and southeast to Chattanooga. The stolen plate, wooden chair and blue tarp went over the US 41 bridge into the Tennessee River as the traffic was less than on I-24 at 5 a.m. The handcuffs and other small items like the PPE went into parking-lot trash receptacles at a McDonald's, a Wendy's, and a Denny's. The cables were left in a ditch next to a construction site near Kimball. The floodlights were left with other equipment behind a Methodist church in South Pittsburgh, to look like a donation. By the time they pulled into the Chattanooga airport and turned in the rental car, only the laptop computer remained from the interrogation scene. They took the shuttle out to long-term parking, got in Maggie's Hyundai, and drove back to Athens by way of Atlanta. They pulled into Maggie's carport after twelve noon, entered the house, and crashed as they were completely beat.

They had talked little, mostly about the items they were disposing of and were they doing it properly, safely. The mood had been gloomy until they left Fred Dossett's plastic sarcophagus in the middle of a highway. Then it became more of a game, dropping off bits and pieces of their crime here and there. Still, there were long periods of quiet as they struggled with mental and physical exhaustion, and with the big step they had just taken in Lauren's kidnapping. They had killed a man, they had tortured him and taken from him all he knew about Lauren's abduction, and the entire scheme behind it. There was not a sense of triumph, more like satisfaction that a necessary unpleasant task had been done. They were cleaning up some filth left by others. Lauren remembered the lecture on serial killers, how they partitioned and pigeonholed their crimes from the rest of themselves. Could she do the same? Maggie felt some release; poor Fred had been the recipient of pent-up trauma that Maggie had carried within her for decades. Fred was a worthy victim, but did that make it all OK?

All that remained was to send off letters to the FBI, Tennessee State Police, and a few media outlets, letters that contained a jump drive with the interrogation video. The two law enforcement letters would be printed out at the Birmingham, Alabama, public library but mailed from Tuscaloosa. The three media letters, CNN, *Washington Post*, and *NY Times* would be printed in the Montgomery, Alabama Public Library and mailed from Georgia. A long road trip. The law enforcement letters would go out first, with a warning that the media would receive the same letter in three days. Time enough to get Fred Dossett's safety deposit box open and perhaps notify the families before the media storm erupted. Then Maggie and Lauren would become passive observers, just like their adversary.

*   *   *

Trooper Chad Bensen got the dispatcher call about a body on the road at the I-24 Pelham exit, and he took off, blue and whites and siren active. It was near the end of his shift, and he thought of the bad luck of catching something like this just when he wanted to go home and crawl into bed. He beat the county sheriff to the site, which meant he could control the scene. There was only one car present when he drove up: Mr. and Mrs. Cotterly, retirees on their way to open the Revival Baptist Church for an early morning service when they saw the bag. Mr. Cotterly had stopped the car to move the bag so no one would hit it and send household garbage all over the place when he realized there was a body inside. He placed a 911 call while Mrs. Cotterly's love of 'Law and Order' had her out and about, securing the scene, lighting up a road flare and directing traffic around the body. She was quite enjoying herself and didn't think about what was in the bag.

A body in white plastic bags wasn't a suicide, or a hit and run. Bensen knew he had a murder, and unless the body had rolled off a truck by accident, a body placed so as to be found. A message was being sent. He called in the situation and recommended that a state coroner in Chattanooga handle the autopsy. The Grundy County Sheriff objected; it was his turf and he wanted full control, but Bensen merely said it could be terrorism, so the state had dominance of the crime scene. It wasn't the crime scene, Bensen knew that, just the body location, but he had a sense that this was big. He stayed on-scene after sending the Cotterlys on their way with thanks for their quick thinking. They became a minor center of attention as the facts spilled out, having discovered what would become a famous body, a body that anyone could have found. The state crime scene investigator appeared eventually from Nashville, but there wasn't much to see. No evidence a vehicle had stopped abruptly to leave skid marks, no recent cigarette butts, no shell casings. It was a body dump, not much evidence to be expected outside the white plastic sheath. By that time, the body was in an ambulance approaching Chattanooga, so the investigator went on to catch up to it. Chad Bensen went home, wondering if the body was local or some gangbanger from Atlanta or Nashville.

■ ■ ■

Tom Stass watched as the plastic bag was cut open. The coroner was Linda Usteuss, a pro. Tom had worked with her a number of times and knew to let her do her thing, at her speed. She began with a brief description of what she saw as an assistant took fluid samples for drug analysis.

"White male, late middle age, tall and fit. Numerous burn marks on the left side limbs, neck, abdomen, and chest. One also on the left testicle. Done with a pointed but blunt object that was quite hot. Done while the victim was alive. If conscious at the time, quite painful." Linda looked over at Tom as she said those words. "Duct tape over the eyes, and across the hips. Bruising on each wrist and ankle, consistent with being bound. The burn marks on the left arm indicate the arm was outstretched when the burning was done. Same for the left leg." Again, a look over to Tom, indicating the obvious — this wasn't routine. "I am going to expedite this case. It looks like we had a serious perpetrator. No hesitancy on the burn marks. Each was made with purpose and intent. I would speculate the man was tortured, but not for fun. Possibly to gain information."

"If they planned to kill him at the end, why cover his eyes?" Tom inquired.

"To increase the fear, to remove the option of pleading by facial expression," Linda replied. "The mouth shows no signs of being gagged, they wanted him to be free to talk, and wherever this was done, they knew no one else could hear. That, too, added to the fear. I expect this man told them everything they wanted to know. He could have probably withstood more pain, but he knew it wasn't going to end, that it would only escalate. He may have bargained to give it all up if they made it end quickly."

"How would they know if he had given it all up?" Tom pursued.

"If he had specific data, like a phone number, a password, an account number, something they could check in real time, they would know," Linda responded.

"Cause of death?" Tom asked, knowing it was early.

Linda went back to the left arm. "A needle mark here. No other needle marks. This guy didn't inject himself with drugs. I expect they gave him a drug overdose and put him away peacefully. These were practiced pros. They knew what they wanted and how to get it." It was Linda's only error of the autopsy, a result of careful thought and planning by Maggie and Lauren, and their very determined attitude.

"Can we get an ID?" Tom continued.

"I'll roll his prints, we will do DNA, I'll check dental records. The man was killed sometime after midnight, so the interrogation took place nearby where he was found. It is unlikely he was brought in from far away to a specific location for the questioning."

"Why do you think that?" Tom queried.

"Why go to all that trouble and then dump the body nearby?" Linda explained. "I think this guy is local. This was a capture, question, and kill all at one time in one general place. It may be a while before a missing person's report is filed. He has no wedding ring, no wedding ring scar. He could live alone; his hands are calloused. Maybe does part-time jobs, like construction or ag work."

"Thanks Linda, you have given me stuff to start with," Tom stated. "I have a feeling this isn't some disagreement or minor feud, but something much bigger."

"I agree," Linda volunteered. "I'll get you more when the tox screen comes back, and I look at the stomach contents."

Tom left. He had to call Nashville and let them know something big might be on the radar screen. He had a friend at the FBI, Sal Munoz. He'd give Sal a call and see if they had run across anything like this before.

CHAPTER 17

PIECES COME TOGETHER

THE LOCAL PRESS WAS ENTHUSIASTIC; something like this rarely happened in Grundy County. They had no specifics except Mrs. Cotterly's lavish description of the scene. No identity for the body, no idea where it came from. So certainly no idea of who had done it. The collective wisdom was that it was a dump by gangs out of Nashville, Atlanta, or maybe Chattanooga. People would soon move on.

Someone who didn't move on was Paul Essinger, who owned and operated the Iron Anvil. Fred Dossett's truck was still in the parking lot Sunday afternoon. Fred doted on that truck, bragged about all it could do. It was new and shiny, Paul wondered if Fred ever took it off-road or only talked of what it could do if he did. He also wondered where Fred got the $45,000 it took to buy such a behemoth. Fred had left with a woman, one Paul had not seen before, a stranger. He must have gone off in her car. Why had Fred not tried to show off his power wagon? He decided to call the Sheriff. The Sheriff was still miffed about being taken off the I-24 body case, to have come up with a potential lead would restore some of his mojo. He called Chad Bensen, who had just gotten out of bed. Chad called Tom and went to take a shower. It was a game of telephone but the facts were simple.

Tom ran the name of Fred Dossett into his usual search programs. Fred's name came up several times. He had been busted on some hunting violations, mostly off-season taking of deer, but it meant his prints were in the system. He notified Linda. She called back a confirmation of identity, John Doe became Fred Dossett. He was local, and he had known something that other people desperately wanted to have. A true case was developing.

■ ■ ■

Ted's bots finally came up with something, but not what he expected. Fred Dossett was being looked at by the Tennessee State Police — a search had been run on his name. Ted wondered what Fred had done now, maybe a DUI and an accident that killed someone? Or another hunting violation, but on state land, like Savage Canyon State Park? No details yet, and he expected none until a report was filed. Maybe someone thought Fred had witnessed a stick up or something and it all would fade. Fred was always getting into minor scrapes, a barroom fight, speeding, stuff like that. Ted was happy his bots had been alert and found something, but he dismissed it for now. He couldn't be distracted from his Little Miss search, which was still unproductive. He liked games when he was winning, he wasn't winning this one yet. He forced his frustration to become patience and went back to his daily chores. Being a billionaire still meant you had to work if you wanted to keep it all. Little Miss could wait, but Little Miss wasn't waiting, as Ted would soon find out.

■ ■ ■

"Sal, how are you doing?" Tom asked with true cheerfulness, now back in his Nashville office. Sal was a guy who was a pro but still knew how to have fun, a pleasure to work with. No pretense.

"Good to hear from you, Tom, what's up?" Sal responded.

"I have a strange case down near Chattanooga, and I wanted to check to see if you have any indication that it matches a pattern," Tom related.

"Hit me with it, I need a break from tax cheats and lawyers," Sal replied jovially. Tom then went with what he had on one Fred Dossett, tortured and then executed.

"Sounds more like interrogated with harsh methods and then eliminated; executions commonly are public, to make a statement," Sal proposed. "Let me adjust that, yes, an interrogation, but the body was placed to be found, so that makes it an execution. Someone sending a message?"

"What message gets sent by killing a part-time worker who hunts a lot?" asked Tom.

"You said he owned a new, big-time truck. How did he get the funds for that?" Sal inquired. "He is a backwoodsman. He knows the territory. Maybe he ferried drugs or acted as a local drug commissary. Whatever it was, he was paid well."

"He's been paid off for certain," Tom rebutted. "So, no pattern you are familiar with?"

"Well, it's a common pattern from a strategic viewpoint, someone is muscling in on another gang's territory, grabbing info," Sal speculated. "The tactics are new, very precise. Most of what I see is clumsy, lots of blood. I'll keep an eye out. If DEA starts to take a look, I'll let you know."

"Thanks, Sal. As I get more information, I'll let you know. Somewhere along the line I may have to go official," Tom said.

"Fine by me. I work as well with gossip as with real paper. Bye," Sal replied as they both ended the call; no one hung up anymore.

"Linda, calling me already, that was fast work," Tom said into his cell as he walked to his car at the end of the day, a long day with the early morning drive down I-24 to the crime scene and on to Chattanooga, then the drive back.

"I'll be sending a report later, but I wanted to update you on what we got," Linda replied. "It has been slow here, so I am caught up, and this case disturbs me, even more now. I pushed a lot of stuff through."

"OK, hit me with it," Tom said, repeating Sal's line.

"First of all, the burn wounds were likely done with a soldering iron. The early marks especially have lead and tin in them," Linda began. "That allows a lot of precision and control. The body had both traces of a roofie, you know, Rohypnol, as well as a lethal dose of fentanyl, with alcohol. He had cheap pizza for dinner, probably in the same bar where he got the beer."

"So, he gets drugged in the bar, goes outside with his killer, gets put in a car, probably a woman's, which is why his truck was still at the bar. He gets taken somewhere close by, is interrogated, and then pumped with a kill dose," Tom laid out the events as he saw them.

"That was my scenario as well," Linda agreed. "The 'close by' part is accurate, the roofie was still in his system, the pizza was barely digested, he wasn't taken far before he was worked on."

"Any hint of where that was?" Tom was hoping but not expecting.

"He was strung up while seated. There is a chair out there with duct tape on it and probably his DNA. He both pissed and pooped in a sitting position," Linda advised.

"Really, you can tell that?" Tom was surprised.

"I've got three kids. I know what a diaper looks like when it is filled in the sitting position," Linda rejoined. "The point is, he was probably cuffed, the bruises are sharp and there are no fibers. His limbs were outstretched. Another point is he wasn't interrogated in the back of a van, or even a motel room. There had to be a high ceiling is my guess."

"So I am looking for a place that was used only one night, a rental of some sort," Tom stated as much to himself as to Linda. "Maybe an abandoned barn, I doubt these people would leave a trace by renting a place."

"It had to be remote, this guy was probably screaming for a while," Linda added. "The nature of the burns bothers me. It was like there was no malice, that it was necessary, like pruning a bush."

"Not a revenge killing then?" Tom pursued.

"No, unless the revenge is about someone this guy worked for," Linda supposed. "Eventually this all becomes part of the public record. Dossett's boss will know what happened. The precise coldness of the work should be a message in and of itself." Linda used a name for the body for the first time. It humanized the man at the very last.

CHAPTER 18

THE EXPLOSION BEGINS

SUNDAY WAS INDEED A DAY OF REST for Lauren and Maggie. They slept right through to Monday dawn. Up with the sun, they made their thumb drive copies and headed off to Birmingham, where they went to the public library at 2100 Park Place and typed in their letters and ran them off for a cash fee on the library printer. Then they folded the pages, placed them in the envelopes with the thumb drives, and laid on the typed addresses, 312 Rosa L. Parks Avenue in Nashville for the state police, and 1501 Dowell Springs in Knoxville for the FBI. All was done with PPE gloves on, and the envelopes were fresh from the box, purchased with cash at Walmart. They then mailed the letters at post boxes in different zip codes in Tuscaloosa, then drove I-20 back to Atlanta. They would go to Montgomery on Wednesday and print the media letters at the public library. They had decided on CNN, because of its Atlanta base, the *Washington Post* because of its reach, and *The New Yorker* magazine because of its reputation. They decided to mail from Columbus, Georgia, to keep things mixed up.

They focused on their tasks and did not discuss the implications of torturing and killing a man. It was done, they had done it, good would come out of it. Feeling guilty could wait.

Then they entered the waiting game. They did not try and track events in Grundy County; it would all become very public very soon. Maggie went onto campus now and then to check in, do some paperwork, and to be seen. Joe Connerly did come to her office and ask about Lauren, to which Maggie gave her pre-prepared answer. His main concern was what to do with her teaching assistantship for the fall. Maggie advised a wait-and-see approach. Joe had nodded and gone off. Lauren remained disappeared and was adjusting with a stoic earnestness to her home arrest in Maggie's guest room, plotting and planning but really waiting for the news to break.

■ ■ ■

Tom came into work for a normal Wednesday morning, managing both old cases and new. The Fred Dossett murder still intrigued him, but he hadn't gotten approval to go back down to Grundy County to sniff around. Then he got a call to go to the Director's office.

Roger Basten was a very traditional state policeman, with the emphasis on "man." While not openly misogynistic, he felt that law enforcement was a man's job and women did lesser things. He and Tom got along just fine, with Tom ignoring Roger's attitude and admiring the man's instincts in an investigation.

"What's up, Roger? You called me directly and were very mysterious," Tom said as he strolled into the Director's office.

"Close the door," Roger barked, and Tom quickly did that, realizing something serious was on the table. "This letter came in to our office this morning; read it and tell me what you think." He had gloves on as he set the letter down on a table.

"No forensics yet?" Tom inquired as he leaned over to read the text.

"If you think it is for real, then we go full bore," Roger replied.

Tom started reading.

> To The Tennessee State Police: By now you have found and identified the body of Fred Dossett. Mr. Dossett was involved in a serial killer's scheme to hunt young women like animals and then make their bodies disappear. The enclosed thumb drive contains a detailed confession given by Mr. Dossett before his death. He has claimed to have physical evidence in a safety deposit box. It is

recommended that you secure this evidence at the earliest time, as a similar letter, with the thumb drive, will be sent to numerous media outlets later this week. The perpetrator of this horrific killing rampage remains on the loose, and unidentified. It is hypothesized that the killer is male, with significant resources to field such a large operation and keep it secret. It is also believed this man watches as each missing case unfolds, and delights in the anguish he has created and watches with pleasure. Please remove this monster. The activities in Grundy County, Tennessee, have been ended forever, but he is still out there.

Tom stared at the letter, read it again, and stared some more. He brought up his head and looked over at Roger. "Have you opened the thumb drive and looked at its contents?" Tom already knew. It would be a video of Fred Dossetts's torture and confession. A chill went up Tom's spine.

"No, I wanted your evaluation before I moved on anything," Roger replied. "You think it's for real?"

"This is real, this is very real," Tom sputtered. "We have to get out in front of this. The letter is correct — we have a day or two to secure things. If it is real, and I think it is, the media will go on a feeding frenzy over this that will be unreal."

"OK, I had Madison look at the drive. She said it is clean of any virus or malware, so here goes," Roger said, plugging the drive into his computer as the wall screen activated. He went to Explorer to see the MP3 file, the only thing on the drive, and he clicked on it.

■ ■ ■

Fred Dossett sat bound naked to a wooden chair, his arms and legs taut and outstretched. Then the questions began, emanating as a computer-generated voice. The answers came, one after the other, sometimes initiated by a soldering iron on a pole. It went on for quite some time. Then it abruptly ended.

Roger was ashen faced. "That was for real?"

"There is a body in Chattanooga identified as Fred Dossett that has actual burn marks on it," Tom answered. "I have seen the body. This is for real."

"I will need to have the dialogue transcribed. We don't want people looking at this," Roger suggested.

"Good idea, but warn whoever does the transcribing that it will be grim," Tom advised. "And remember, the media will have this in a few days, so no need to play nice with our own people. Better to hear it from ourselves, then see it on TV."

"This won't get broadcasted," Roger exclaimed.

"Maybe not, but it will be on the web," Tom rebutted. "Have Sally Quinn do the transcription. She did two tours as a combat medic in Iraq." Tom still saw women as women first, but he judged them by their professional actions and outcomes.

"You are in charge of this investigation. Assign resources as you see fit," Roger said with finality.

"I assume the FBI will be part of this. Should I set up a liaison?" Tom queried.

"You know some people over there. Approach them as you think it necessary," Roger said with a wave of his hand. "Now I need to prepare for the political fall out. Keep me posted."

Tom got up and walked out.

■　■　■

He had just gotten into his office and shut the door when his cell rang, it was Sal Munoz. "Hello Sal, what do you have?"

"You got the Dossett letter?" Sal was tight, clipped in his speech.

"Yes," Tom replied.

"You watched the video?" Sal was still tight.

"Yes, and I have approval to work with the FBI through you," Tom responded. "I have been given the charge of working this case. Will we be able to team up?"

"My boss asked if anyone was interested in following up, that we would give initial priority to Tennessee. I said I know people in

Nashville and had already been given a preliminary briefing," Sal stated. "So, I am now your FBI contact and teammate. My partner, Peter Comstock, will be with me."

"We need to set up a field office in Grundy County and work with the Sheriff's Department," Tom recommended.

"What works best, if you approach him or I approach him?" Sal inquired.

"The Sheriff there has a reputation of meddling and aggrandizing himself, so if you brought the weight of the feds down on him, then I can be the good cop," Tom proposed.

"Works for me. When will you go down?" Sal answered.

"I need to set things up here, and I need to get a warrant for the safety deposit box, as well as Dossett's truck. Better to have the key," Tom stated.

"OK, I am coming down from Knoxville tonight. I want to secure the truck," Sal said. "I'll let you know where Peter and I hunker down."

- - -

Tom worked to get the paper flow set up to run the Dossett operation. He still hadn't processed what he had seen, hadn't gotten past the visuals to the substance of the question and answers. It was late afternoon when Sally Quinn knocked on his door, and he called, "Come in."

She gave him a manila folder full of paper. "The transcript from the video of Fred Dossett's interrogation," she said.

"You watched it. What did you think?" Tom asked.

"You watched it, Tom. I transcribed it. I weighed every word. You haven't thought it through yet, have you?" Sally was accusatory, and correctly so.

"We have a serial killer on our hands, but those killings will stop," Tom suggested.

"Tom," Sally said with frustration, "we have eleven dead women and the man responsible is still out there. The thugs are all going to be removed, but the mastermind is loose. What will be his next game? Maybe men, that might get your attention."

"You're right, Sally, I'm stuck in amongst the trees and I didn't see the forest," Tom responded. "Look, you just demonstrated that we will need perspective to go after this guy. Will you be part of the field team? We also have Dossett's killer to go after."

"That interrogation wasn't a one-man job. There are a minimum of two people involved," Sally observed. "Going after those people is not our priority, nor our second focus. Those heroes are a third-tier problem."

"If so, and the mastermind is top tier, what is second tier?" Tom asked, truly confused.

"Finding those dead girls and getting them back to their families!" Sally shouted. "Then the mastermind doesn't have his grieving families to torment as much."

"You buy into the letter's supposition that this mastermind is watching the pain and grief caused by those girls going missing?" Tom was skeptical.

"Of course I do; why else would the bodies be hidden, the girls snatched from so far away?" Sally was calm now, reasoned. "There was no sexual attack, Dossett said, just the killing and the walking away."

"The letter is correct in that the perpetrator has resources; this was a big operation," Tom stated. "Now we start digging."

"For the girls, we will know where to dig; for the killer, it will take a big effort, but I am set. I really want this guy," Sally retorted.

"You seem to take this personally," Tom noted.

"I'm buying a soldering iron," Sally said with a serious tone as she walked out of the office.

CHAPTER 19

THE TEAM

THEY DROVE DOWN I-24 in a department minivan, with some forensic gear in the back with their luggage. It was early, the sun was barely up, almost directly in their eyes as they went southeast.

"Look, I realize that whoever interrogated Fred Dossett is a tertiary target, but still, how did they find out about what is going on, how did they know to ask such specific questions?" Tom was earnest; this case had problems going in all directions.

"Someone who stumbled onto the plot would have just reported it, and have let the authorities handle it," Sally replied. "This sounded personal."

"I agree, but that means the family or friends of one of the dead girls figured it all out. How could that happen?" Tom was caught up in the puzzle.

Sally rode silently for a few miles, then spoke up. "The twelfth girl."

"There is no twelfth girl, not that Fred Dossett knew about," Tom rebutted. Sally didn't answer, but she had a small smile on her lips. She waited.

It didn't take long. "The twelfth girl escaped; Dossett said he thought his interrogation was about the escapee. She set this all in motion," Tom exclaimed. "But there was no police report, no missing person's report."

"She figured out what the perp was up to, the voyeur aspect; she denied him that display," Sally answered. "Dossett said they never took any ID from the victims, didn't know their names."

"So, the twelfth girl is loose, creating havoc, and the perp doesn't know who it is," Tom said with enthusiasm.

"I want to meet this girl. She is smart, fierce," Sally stated.

"And a murderer," Tom advised.

"Justifiable homicide, and the torture was just an interrogation technique. I saw the inside of Abu Ghraib prison. Don't talk to me about interrogation techniques," Sally said with force.

"The letters were postmarked from Tuscaloosa, so it appears she, and her teammate, if there is one, are still in the south," Tom said, building an investigation in his head.

"Stop it, Tom. We aren't going after the twelfth girl, at least not yet. We have a much bigger fish to fry," Sally warned. "She didn't go after any of the other named suspects. She left them for us."

"She hasn't gotten to them yet, you mean," Tom was playing a very poor bad cop.

"If that had been her intention, we wouldn't have gotten the letter until she was done with those guys," Sally rebutted. "No, she wants us to do it."

"So why send out a video to the media, just to enrage the perp?" Tom asked.

"To scare him, to let him know he is hunted," Sally surmised. "Up to now, it has been smooth sailing for him. Now the twelfth girl has ended his Tennessee game and sent him a message that she is looking for him. It won't be just a few burn marks when she finds him."

"Think he will make a mistake or two?" Tom asked.

"He already has. She is loose and on the hunt," Sally laughed. "Godspeed to her."

■　■　■

Tom had called ahead. Sal and Pete would meet them at Citizen's Bank in Monteagle. Sal already had the safe-deposit box key.

"You could have waited for the warrant," Tom chided.

"Exigent circumstances, this is a murder case," Sal chuckled back. "Anyway, Dossett is dead, his truck is part of a crime scene."

Tom pulled into the bank parking lot, Sal and Peter's unmarked car wasn't obvious as Tom's was, so those two would be able to skulk around better. The two men were in the lobby, and introductions were made all around. Then they approached the bank manager, who had been alerted, showed him the warrant, and they went down to the vault. Peter took the manager out of the vault after he had inserted his key and played nice with him while the other three used Dossett's key and opened the box and took out the contents with gloves on, which went into an evidence container that was sealed with tape. They thanked the manager, avoided all his questions, and went back outside where the box went into Tom's vehicle. Chain of custody issues are always paramount.

"Next?" Tom asked.

"Time to see the sheriff up in Tracey City," Sal said. "We will go in your official car to impress the old SOB."

As they drove along, Sally turned back to Sal, who was seated behind Tom. "Anything useful from Dossett's truck?"

"He kept it clean. I was surprised," Sal began. "The bar owner came out when we were stringing police tape around the vehicle, said Dossett loved the vehicle, bragged about it all the time. He also wanted to know when we would tow it."

"I have a call in. Forensics is on their way. They will load up the truck and take the safe deposit box contents back to their lab in Nashville, but I want to peek at it first," Tom replied. "Where do we do lunch?"

"In Monteagle, where we will look like tourists. Don't want to mix with the locals up in the county when we plan to arrest a few," Peter spoke for the first time. "Got you two rooms where we are, at the Comfort Inn."

* * *

Sheriff Phil Koslowsky was gruff, imperious, but also a bit off his feed. He hadn't had to deal with such high-powered law enforcement personnel before. He wanted to stake out his own turf, but on the other hand, he didn't want to be staked out on his own turf. The best way to go about it was to give him some tasks to do. Right now, the business forensics people in Nashville were pouring over the finances of the five named men from the video.

"We will be making arrests very soon, maybe tomorrow, so we would like your office to do that. Since you know the people of this county, we would like to avoid any bad takedowns," Tom explained.

"We are still developing the case, but we have been tipped off that some items will go public by the end of the week, so we need to get a bunch done before then," Peter said, with his very professional demeanor.

"For now, you can explain we are nosing around as the dead body might be a big drug kingpin, and we want to make sure what he was about has nothing to do with the people of Grundy County," Sally interjected. "Just a place to dump a body."

"Typical police work. Eliminate potential suspects so everyone can get on with their lives," Sal suggested.

"But they won't. You are going to have me arrest a bunch of people right here," Koslowsky complained.

"When the full story comes out, and it will be out by the end of the week, you will be glad we played it this way," Tom soothed. "I will be back with warrants tomorrow and you can get to work."

That approach seemed to mollify the Sheriff, and they departed on good terms.

Back in the car, Tom was more relaxed. "Let's do lunch, and look in the box, see if Dossett told everything truly."

"If not, let me know. I am willing to go down to Chattanooga and give his body a few more burns," Sally said. She didn't appear to be kidding.

CHAPTER 20

THE BIG WAIT

TED'S BOTS ALERTED HIM TO MORE INTEREST in Fred Dossett, and Ted got to work and wormed his way into a police report on a dead body in Grundy County. That got him the coroner's report, and he saw that the body was Fred Dossett's. It looked like Fred had gotten scalped by a working girl, a stranger in the Iron Anvil who left with Fred, and there he was, dead the next morning. Ted had paid Dossett a lot of cash over the two years the hunting gig had been operating, so Ted assumed he'd flashed a roll one too many times and had been set up. Tortured to give up the rest of his stash. Given the description of the body, Fred had surrendered rather soon, and then he was overdosed and left in a bag on the road. In a way, that was good. Fred hadn't known much, but he had known more than anyone else in Tennessee, so someone had done Ted a favor and wrapped up that loose end nice and tight.

Still nothing on his Little Miss. Unlike New York and California, landlords didn't need to keep and report many records about their operations in Georgia. Ted couldn't figure out which apartment block his Little Miss had come from, or been going to, when she was grabbed by his boys. It was all quiet in the ether, not a peep about the girl being missing, nor a police report on his human hunting plot. Maybe she had some misfortune and was dead out in the forest. Good luck had gotten her away from his team, and bad luck had killed her anyway. That seemed a nice symmetrical balance, so he decided to coast for a few days and see what happened. The 'what happened' part would prove a big deal at the end of the week.

*   *   *

The team looked over the safe deposit box material with great care. It was all there as Dossett had stated under duress: photos, envelopes with hair and blood samples in them, and a sketch map that showed the Dead Rock Holdings property and where the bodies were buried, all numbered, probably in the order of the killings. Pen colors were commonly different; he had added each grave after burial, when he came to the bank to drop off his non-trophy trophies. The write-up was the same, and different pen colors were there, too, with details on where the abductions had occurred. This was hard evidence, more than enough to get a warrant for the two van guys, and the two hound guys. Koslowsky would have a busy day rounding them all up. Roger would get a judge to sign warrants tonight. They'd be here in the morning, and those four would be off the board before the public got any wind of what was happening. There was cash in the box as well, thousands of dollars. Those bills would be recorded and tracked, but Tom doubted that avenue would yield anything at all about who was behind the human hunting plot. In the old days, they would have carefully scanned the documents; now, they just took photos with their cell phones and uploaded the images onto their laptops. The map especially needed to be printed out. The digital age was wonderful, but once you made an electronic copy of anything, it had a habit of getting where it shouldn't go.

"Sal, give Koslowsky a call, see who he uses to dig up buried bodies. Tell him we think we have a drug stash in a cemetery," Tom requested. "We have to get those bodies to Chattanooga and get them identified."

"Why not Nashville?" Peter asked.

"Linda Usteuss did the Dossett autopsy, so she is already invested," Tom explained. "She works fast, and she is very, very good. All the victims are female, so the families will have the comfort that their naked, dead little girls were viewed by a mother of three."

Sally looked up from where she had been reading Dossett's notes. "Christ, this operation had reach. Two from North Carolina, two from Alabama, three from Georgia, two from central Tennessee, and two from eastern Kentucky."

"That's why no one saw a pattern," Peter noted. "A very disparate geography of abductions and missing persons reports. It doesn't look as if the women were selected randomly when they actually were."

"But they were, a geographic destination was selected, and the abductors went there and took the low-hanging fruit," Sally contended. "No notes on a potential twelfth victim."

"He always reported after the fact," Tom decided. "He didn't bury the twelfth abduction. She escaped."

Sal came back into the room. "Koslowsky uses a company down here in Monteagle. They do contract work for the state on maintaining this section of I-24, which is a difficult stretch with the lanes separated and all, down that big hill. We can get backhoes, dump trucks, whatever we need. As long as we pay for it, he reminded me."

"OK good, let's get up on Google Earth and see how we get into those sites marked on Dossett's map. Tomorrow will be ugly," Tom concluded.

"Body recovery always is," Sal agreed.

"I'll begin to catalogue missing persons reports for young women from the area of the eleven abductions for the dates in question," Sally proposed. "It will help Dr. Usteuss with the body identifications."

▪   ▪   ▪

Lauren was strangely calm. Before the big expedition to Grundy County, she had been fidgety, prone to pacing. Now she was contemplative and wrote up outlines of possible plans to locate the man behind it all. Maggie tried to function normally, as if she had not impersonated a lot of people, lied to dozens, and helped torture and execute a man. It was useful that it all needed doing, but it was a weight nonetheless. They now expected that the FBI and State of Tennessee had viewed the video, and that things were happening behind the scenes. That would end by Friday when the media received their copies. If not Friday night, Saturday's news would be loaded with it. Boredom warred with expectation. People already hurting; even those who had given up hope would be devastated by the news. Their girls were truly dead, and in an awful, horrific manner, dying full of fear and pain. That was Lauren and Maggie's gift — the price of closure, of knowing. There was possible guilt at the killing of Fred Dossett, a man who deserved to die, without a doubt. There was possible guilt at bringing this reckoning onto eleven families. The alternative had been to walk away, to let five guilty men go free, to let eleven families never know the truth. Lauren and Maggie wrestled with it, each in their own way. For Maggie, she was an on-looker, the entire affair was somewhat theoretical, as if watched from afar. For Lauren, who had run in fear, who had heard the men lightly talk about little bitches and what was coming to them, it was deeply personal, visceral. Maggie wondered if she had done too much; Lauren if she had done too little. So, they waited.

CHAPTER 21

CONSOLIDATION

ROGER BASTEN TOOK ONE LOOK at the photos, map and sample envelopes, and realized he had a bigger problem than he had thought. He called Memphis and Knoxville and mobilized their entire forensic teams. The Memphis team boarded a flight to Chattanooga on a state plane in the evening; the Knoxville team would drive down I-81 early Thursday morning. They would gather in Monteagle and go to the burial site and begin the body recoveries. Those eleven bodies needed to be found and in autopsy before the news broke on Friday afternoon.

It had taken a senior judge no time at all, after viewing the video and seeing the safety-deposit box material, to approve four warrants for the two van men and the two hound men. A State Trooper ferried the paperwork to Tom at the Comfort Inn that night. Tom called the Sheriff.

"Sheriff Koslowsky, Tom Stass here. I have the warrants to arrest four citizens of Grundy County, do you want me to bring them over tonight?"

"What's the rush?" Koslowsky growled.

Tom decided it was no longer necessary to play charades. "The warrants are for eleven counts of first-degree murder for each man. That's forty-four counts — enough to make it worth rushing for?" Tom growled back.

"Oh my God," Koslowsky murmured, then louder, "Who got killed, eleven gangbangers?"

"Eleven young women, Sheriff," Tom used the man's title to keep the focus on the law, not personalities.

"That is what you are digging up tomorrow?" Koslowsky queried.

"That is *who* we are digging up tomorrow, Sheriff," Tom corrected. "I need these four men locked up before we make our move. There can be no way you allow these men to slip away."

"You telling me how to do my job?" Koslowsky bristled.

"Sheriff, I don't care how you do your job, just do it. Get those men locked up," Tom challenged. "This affair is going public on Friday, and the media will be all over Grundy County. You will have to show how quickly and firmly you acted before people ask how you let these grotesque crimes happen."

"I didn't let anything happen! I didn't know," Koslowsky protested.

"People will ask if you should have known. That is why you need to get out in front of all of this," Tom cajoled. "Look, I agree, there was no way you could have known. None of the women are from anywhere around here. It was a stealthy operation. Nonetheless, you can't afford to have any hint of dragging your heels or being sloppy."

"Should I go out and get them now?" Koslowsky asked, still waiting to be nudged to do what he should already be doing.

"Yes, that's obvious. I'll bring the warrants to your office now. Call me back when you have them locked up in a cell," Tom affirmed. He ended the call.

"That went well," Sal mused, looking up from his laptop where he was registering the sketch map done by Fred Dossett onto a lidar image overlay of the Dead Rock Holdings property plat document. "The graves are all at the south end of the property. Two gates, one in the north, one in the south. It looks like the women were dropped at the north end and driven south, to where the leader of the operation waited. Then he killed them and left by the south gate. Dossett came by later and buried the bodies, one at a time."

Sally and Peter looked up from their laptops, where Sally had been reading missing persons reports from five states and Peter had been looking up the four men named on the warrants. Sally responded first.

"These four men, the abductors and the drivers, what were they thinking?" She asked. "They captured the women, brought them here, and sent them to a certain death. Drove them like a game animal. It had to be more than money."

"All of them have a record of petty violations, most involving hunting, moonshine, marijuana cultivation, fights in bars, reckless driving, DUI, but nothing major," Peter reported.

"Did they ache for something bigger, but never had the balls to do it?" Sally questioned. "Did our boss man sell it to them: the thrill, the excitement of real danger, real death?"

"Sickos one and all," Sal volunteered. "Death penalty cases for certain."

"Oh no, Sal. I want these guys to get life without parole," Sally countered. "To be locked up and hunted by the other inmates, never knowing when the shiv is going in."

"They'd be like child molesters, despised by all around them. I like it," Tom agreed. They were all steeling themselves for the grim task they faced the next day. Tom left to deliver the warrants.

■　■　■

Maggie and Lauren faced each other across the kitchen table, where they ate toasted cheese sandwiches with tomato soup. Comfort food.

"They have it all now: Dossett's body, the video, and probably the safe-deposit box," Lauren stated, as if reporting a sports score.

"They have his map. They will probably dig tomorrow, start the autopsies and forensics to identify the bodies," Maggie agreed.

"Did we do the right thing, sending that material to the media?" Lauren queried.

"Initially, it motivated the Tennessee State Police and the FBI," Maggie replied. "Knowing that a media storm was coming, I bet they have moved fast and efficiently, knowing any tiny delay or error will hit them hard."

"So a better, more thorough investigation this way?" Lauren now showed some uncertainty.

"If we had sent a detailed letter of what you experienced, including Dossett and Ketchum's names, and the landowner, Dead Rock Holdings, what would have happened?" Maggie asked. "Little to nothing. We wouldn't have been taken seriously. Even if they sent someone down to Grundy County to interview people, Dossett and Ketchum would have merely denied it. Dead Rock Holdings wouldn't be approachable. That entity probably went up in smoke the day you escaped. Dossett said the perp had ended it all. Not even probable cause."

"So we had to do it?" Lauren questioned.

"Of course we did. And we did it well," Maggie argued. "This man had to be stopped. You saw that from the beginning, you convinced me, and after listening to Dossett, I have no regrets. None." Maggie hoped it was true.

"So we watch CNN Friday night?" Lauren inquired.

"It will be hard, Lauren. It will bring back things to you. It will open up the identities of all those young women who were in that valley before you were," Maggie counseled.

"It will be a public record that the arc of justice is falling towards the land, and the man behind this horror will know it, feel it, sweat it," Lauren whispered. "Does this end it for us? There will be state and federal agencies all over this problem. We can't even go online. We can't hunt him down."

"We can draw him out," Maggie advised. "You will become Q."

"Q? What do you mean?" Lauren asked.

"The Q of QAnon; we will make you a meme, we will enlist thousands of other people to search out our perpetrator," Maggie responded. "You will become your very own conspiracy theory."

"Human parallel processing, people each looking and searching, hunting down private jet flight records, car rentals, who had the money to do this, all sorts of things," Lauren smiled as her tension eased. "He won't be searching for me because I am probing. He will have thousands of probing people to watch out for, from grandmas to tech wizards. And I will be online, calling him out, dropping details of how I escaped. I will goad him."

"And also law enforcement, who may want to get their hands on the murderer of Fred Dossett," Maggie warned.

"Knowing what we did and proving it are two very different things," Lauren rejoined. "Proving it and getting a jury to agree may be a bridge too far."

CHAPTER 22

FROM THE DEPTHS

THE ONLY GOOD THING ABOUT THE DAY was that it was clear, the soil dry from a week of fair weather. Rain and mud would have slowed everything down, made people who were psychologically miserable physically miserable as well. Sal had done a good job with his map overlay. Copies were handed out; people were looking for disturbed earth. Cadaver dogs were employed, as was GPR, ground penetrating radar. These were determined people. Tom had decided to shock them by having everyone in the conference room see the Dossett video. Not standard practice, but it would be on the web the next day anyway, so he used it as a motivator. Backhoes began to work as sites were confirmed. Black plastic bags were found. Now, it was for real: bodies of young women cruelly murdered made the teams working the scene harder in expression, more terse with words. A careful, British-style cops in a shoulder-to-shoulder line search found what were interpreted to be blinds where the murderer had hidden. Two yellow metal discs had been found on two trees north of the blinds, the markers Dossett had described, beyond which the hounds and their master were never to go. By and large, this search in the valley was a failure. No cigarette butts, no candy wrappers, no soda cans. Evidence of travel, but no clear footprints. The killer, and Dossett after him, had been careful and skilled. One cigarette butt from on top of the west cliff was found late in the day. Rain was forecast overnight, so hard effort engaged to look for evidence from the escapee. The eleven previous graves had seen many rainfalls. Nothing. The bodies, still in their plastic bag wrappings, had been loaded into traditional body bags, zipped up, and carried with care to ambulances which loaded two by two took those lost souls to Chattanooga. The last one alone, where Linda Usteuss waited to begin her necessary but emotionally difficult work, with additional helpers from across the state agency.

— — —

It was mid-afternoon as Tom, Sally, Peter, and Sal sat eating a simple lunch in Monteagle. All the bodies had been found; the initial forensics sweep had been done. Some investigators remained behind to continue to look around and evaluate. Sheriff Koslowsky had come around to see how things were going. Tom asked him for deputies to secure the site; the curious and the weird might be coming by after Friday's news hit the public. The four men under warrant had been apprehended at their homes at three in the morning without incident. They were totally unaware that they had been identified.

"What's next?" Sally asked. She was hungry but at the same time her appetite was subdued — being around eleven tragic bodies did that to her. She ate because she knew she needed fuel, but it was without relish.

"You and I should go to the county jail and see if one of our arrested accomplices has anything to say," Tom replied. "Then we need to go to Chattanooga and see how the work there is going. Our priority now is identifying the bodies."

"Peter and I are done here, actually," Sal stated. "We will go back to the Knoxville office and begin to work on who the man behind all of this is."

"You aren't interested in the murder of Fred Dossett?" Tom inquired.

"Dossett did his crime in Grundy County, he was murdered in Grundy County, and his body was found in Grundy County," Peter observed. "It is a Grundy County problem, unless they want help, but I suspect they have their hands full right now and don't need that distraction."

"You don't think this is a problem that needs action now before the trail goes cold?" Tom interjected.

"Tom, I saw the video, these guys are pros. There is no trail to get cold," Peter cautioned. "This isn't a forensics problem. It is a thought problem." He looked at Sally. "You think the escapee did this, the girl who got away?"

Sally gave a nod but said nothing. That action said more than words.

"You will have a hard time proving the escapee did this. You don't even know who she is," Peter displayed a bit of exasperation. He saw where the real problem was, the man behind the scene. "If she did this murder on her own, she is scarily capable. Leave it be for now. There is a monster to catch. No jury will ever convict her anyway."

■　■　■

Only Josh Ketchum was willing to talk. The others had seen too much crime television and only wanted a lawyer. Ketchum said he didn't care. He walked into the holding room and sat down. Two deputies were behind him. Sally and Tom sat across the table. It was very much like what was seen on television.

"What have you got?" Ketchum spoke first.

"Fred Dossett's full confession and eleven bodies in black garbage bags for starters," Tom replied. "We are, of course, sweating your assistant and the two guys who did the abductions."

"So why are you here? What do you want? You've got me dead to rights," Ketchum volunteered.

"The specifics of how you were approached, the reward package, for starters," Sally stated.

"And then what?" Ketchum looked hard at Sally, who didn't flinch.

"Why you agreed to do it. Why you sent girls you didn't know to their deaths," Sally answered.

"That's what you really want to know," Ketchum sighed. "The amount of money, the purging of my felony record, none of that would be enough if I hadn't wanted to do it."

"Exactly what did you want?" Sally pursued. Tom could see Sally had forged a link with Ketchum, and he let her run with it. No good cop, bad cop now.

"To hunt a human being," Ketchum said with some passion. "With my dogs, I could catch anything. Deer, elk, panther, bears, fox, bobcats, whatever. A person, could I track a person, could I keep my dogs from being fooled? It was intoxicating. I never saw any of them die. I never truly knew they were dead. Maybe the boss man gave them a big check and sent them home, I didn't know. Dossett didn't talk."

"You chose not to know, you lied to yourself," Sally charged. "The boss man was killing them for sport, and you got off on the tiny thrill of driving those poor girls to him."

"You see it as a tiny thrill, but for me, it was big," Ketchum seized the moment. "All my life, knocking around these woods, doing the fetch and call for city people with lots of money and few brains. This was real. This meant something to those girls. They were focused, focused on me."

"You knew it was wrong," Sally said.

"Of course I did. That was part of the excitement, to walk down Tracey City Main Street and look at people and think 'you don't know what I did, you don't know what I am capable of' and know myself to be more than they would ever be." He paused, looked over at Tom. He had connected with Sally, but he saw Tom as the leader. "Now what happens to me?"

"You go to trial, get convicted and then go to jail," Tom replied calmly.

"Jail or death by lethal injection?" Ketchum queried.

"That may be up to you. If you have any information that might be useful, a plea bargain might save your life," Tom surmised.

"I don't know, you seem to have it all," Ketchum responded, but he was looking at Sally. His head gave a slight nod. "You want to know about the last one, the one who escaped." Sally didn't move. "Don't play poker, lady. You can't hide what you are thinking." He stared hard at Sally. "You want the girl who got away. That is what busted this all open. You got tipped off, but you don't know by who. I bet it was her."

"What have you got to say about her?" Sally inquired.

"Nothing now, I just got a bargaining chip," Ketchum chuckled. "I know I'm going to jail, but maybe I can stay off the drug gurney."

Tom stood up. "Make your decision soon. We just started this investigation, and we may get what we want elsewhere, so don't sit on it. I don't mind if you bargain, but my advice to the prosecutor will be to set a time limit. You will still need to provide us with something useful."

"I may stay quiet, I may take the needle," Ketchum said with determination. "She beat me. She beat my dogs. No one ever did that, not human, not animal. I have to admire that skill, respect that courage. Maybe it is better I die to atone for what I did. Maybe it was right for her to turn me in. Payback — I have to accept that. If you don't know who she is, maybe she doesn't want to be found. I helped kill eleven women, but maybe I can help this one stay free." Ketchum stood up and walked back to the deputies.

Tom and Sally buzzed the door and left the room. They didn't talk until they were back in the department vehicle and headed to Chattanooga.

"I believed him," Sally said.

"Believed the reason he did it, or believe he saw something in the twelfth girl that will help us identify her?" Tom asked.

"Both," Sally replied. "And I believe he admires the one who outwitted him."

CHAPTER 23

ELEVEN LADIES WEEPING

LINDA STARED AT THE SCENE. Eleven gurneys, eleven black plastic bags, eleven dead women. She would open each bag herself, do the initial description and inspection, then pass the body off for the sampling and the cutting. She had plenty of help — Tom had seen to that. He had called ahead; said he was coming just as the first ambulance pulled up. She also knew that Sally had worked up a list of possible IDs with weight, height, hair color, eye color, race, clothing — characteristics which would allow Linda to quickly eliminate possible choices. Because Dossett had numbered the sites on his map, Sally knew the geographic origin of each abducted girl and the date each had been taken. The next steps would be dental records and DNA. Dental records could be done in real time; DNA would take some effort, never as fast as on TV. She had been alerted that some bodies might have ID on them, that the girls were taken off the street, wrapped up in a tarp, and never searched. There could be cell phones. Masked, Linda took a scalpel and cut open bag number one.

In the end, there was little drama. Seven of the bodies had identification on them — if not an actual ID, a piece of jewelry or other diagnostic listed in the missing person's report. The bodies were essentially mummified. The graves had been too deep for any scavengers; the temperature in the graves had been close to mean annual temperature, for this plateau area of eastern Tennessee, that was about 56° F. Not exactly refrigeration, but decay had been slowed. Clothing was mostly intact. By the time dental records had been examined, as well as blood type, the identification was essentially done. DNA was being processed as a confirmation. This stage was near midnight. Beginning Friday morning, the notification process would begin.

The women had been killed in a variety of ways, all violent. Some were shot, others were stabbed. One was clubbed. The guns used were of a variety of calibers, including a shotgun; the stab wounds were made by blades large and small, suggesting swords or spears in two cases. A bow and arrow at least once. All gruesome deaths, only two gunshot victims appeared to have died immediately. Linda had not seen the Dossett video as to help maintain her objectivity when doing her analyses. She subsequently would never watch it.

Tom had crafted, with Sally's help, a letter that would accompany each notification, to be read over the phone if necessary. The letter explained that an anonymous tip had revealed where the body would be found. It explained that the victim was part of a serial killer's actions, one of eleven bodies. The hard part, in what was always a hard thing, this notification process, was that the tipster had also said that specific information regarding the killings would be released to the media Friday or soon after, and that the authorities had no way to halt that release. Several participants in the killings had been apprehended, but the actual killer remained unknown and was not in custody.

Roger Basten approved the letter and began to prepare for a press conference that would be given noon on Friday if all next of kin notifications had been made. He would get Tennessee out in front of this issue; it was his only option. He was thankful that the tipster had notified law enforcement first, but the later release of the video would create a sensationalism that would strain the ability of law enforcement to control the situation. Tom, Sally, and Roger had talked on a Zoom call over what to do about the video. Sally had said simply to just show it after a short announcement; it explained what had happened by the words of one participant, now dead. No fifth amendment issues. To not show a video that would soon be public anyway might create cries of cover up, and sow suspicion with the public. Tom suggested asking the reporters present to form a pool of maybe ten people, who would watch the video in a closed room, and then have the press conference proceed. Everyone agreed there would be no passing out of thumb drives with the video on it or posting it as a download on the Department website. The call ended with no decision. Sally and Tom were to drive back to Nashville, catch a few hours sleep, and help set up the press conference. Back in Chattanooga, Linda would write up a preliminary report in the morning. She had made a discovery that needed to remain secret. That aspect would not yet be reported.

Sally drove west from the headquarters building after Tom dropped her off; she was only a couple of minutes from her apartment and a few hours sleep before the press conference was vital. False dawn creased the horizon behind her as she went down empty and silent streets. She had her radio tuned to her favorite oldies channel, one of several in a music town like Nashville. She liked this one because it played a lot of folk songs, songs her grandpa had played from honest-to-God vinyl records when she would visit, a fairy-tale time now long gone. In the early morning hours, the station would play a full album with minimal commentary. Today it was *Album 1700* by Peter, Paul and Mary that wafted up from the speaker. 'No Other Name' was playing, sung hauntingly by Mary Travers. When her voice said the words 'the stone at my head will say I am dead, it knows me by no other name,' Sally pulled suddenly to the curb and cried, great bursts of sobs exploding from her chest as she rocked in her seat, her swings of motion only limited by the steering wheel. Eleven young women, lying in the earth, and no one had known but their killers. They had run in fear alone, been killed alone, and buried alone. Eternity had engulfed them as it would us all, she thought, but so alone, so torn from the fabric of their lives, and then that life was torn away as well.

She calmed down, turned off the radio, and steadied herself. Roger Basten would have nodded disapprovingly had he witnessed this moment of angst from Sally. Typical of a woman, he would say, not recognizing how his attitude separated him from what truly made us human: our sense of community, our dependence on each other. Maybe that was why men were so violent — they kept it all inside, not realizing the pressure they held until it exploded. The twelfth girl, the one who had killed Frederick Dossett, Sally loved her, loved her with all her heart. She had saved those eleven women in the end, had brought them back to the light. The families would cry their pain, as they had for a long time, but it would end now; they knew now, their girls were safe now, back in the family bosom that had loved and nurtured them and could now lay them to rest. A final peace. Sally cried again, but soft tears, honoring lives lost so falsely, but now with a completion. She got home, flipped off her shoes and lay on the bed, her mind strangely quiet, and she was soon asleep. No dark dreams troubled her exhaustion, the waking reality was bad enough.

■　■　■

Tom did not fall asleep easily; his mind raced on all the implications that had stung him this week, from a dead body in a white bag on a white concrete road, to eleven dead bodies in black bags in equally black earth. A man murdered in the coldest of blood, and he understood why. To get their attention and force an investigation. To taunt the killer of young women and force him to the light. To repair hopeless families and give them peace. So much to do. He was central to it all, Basten would pass it all off to him. 'Our representative in this investigation is Tom Stass, he will answer your questions.' How could Tom do that task when he had so many questions himself? He finally dropped off, but his body remained tense. He would wake up with aches and pains as if he had been beaten. And he had been beaten, beaten by what he had seen, eleven black bags and the awarding of names, as if it had been a contest. The prize of being found, being discovered, being returned to the world of air and sunlight, if only for a brief time. Death is the ultimate anonymity. It had been unfair to let them lie anonymous in that deep dirt darkness.

CHAPTER 24

THE FUSE IS LIT

ROGER DECIDED HE LIKED TOM'S IDEA; there would be a preview showing of the tape to a small group of journalists selected by Tom. Tom learned this as he called in during his morning groggy drive back to headquarters. He decided on a first come, first served basis, the first six reporters who showed up would be ushered into a conference room and shown the video, cold turkey with no introduction or preparation. Let them see it as Tom had first seen it. He called Kyle Lastiwitz, reporter for *The Tennessean*, who had always struck Tom as highly professional and levelheaded, with an overriding respect for the truth.

"Kyle, Tom Stass here," Tom said as he rang up Kyle's personal cell number.

"You are calling me?" Kyle acted flabbergasted. "Something big must be going on."

"You think you know what it is?" Tom replied in confirmation.

"Things have been hopping down in Grundy County, I know that," Kyle stated. "I'll be at the noon press conference to hear all about it."

"Well, you are right, and here is my tip, be there early, at least an hour early," Tom confided.

"Why, so I can be first against the wall for the firing squad?" Kyle laughed. He had recently done a piece about South Carolina using the firing squad again for executions since the lethal injection drugs were so hard for states to get.

"Just be there, main conference room," Tom answered in a dry tone. The main conference room was really an auditorium, but such terminology did not look good at state budget hearings.

Tom parked and scooted up to his office for a quick e-mail check. Linda's report was there; he downloaded it and printed it off, the printer humming behind him as he completed a quick scan of the contents on the screen. The eleven women were all young, of all types, however none were overweight. Tom realized that the latter factor was likely due to the element of the hunt. It had to be at least slightly competitive. Some were married, some of those with children. They had been jogging, shopping, walking — none were carjacked. The variety of deaths came as no surprise. Tom had begun to peer into the perpetrator's psyche and understood the killer would experiment, that he was playing, and he had so many toys. Time to check in with Roger.

■　■　■

"Are you ready for this, Tom?" Roger asked, with true concern, as Tom walked in. He knew it would be tough. Roger would do the overview; Tom would have to deal with the painful specifics.

"We are going ahead. All next of kin notifications have been completed?" Tom queried.

"Yes, all done," Roger answered. "Rushed, I know, but I put our best people on it and it went, well, not smoothly, nothing like this ever does, but efficiently and with compassion. It was very emotional, no one would call more than two families."

"Are we releasing names at this time?" Tom asked.

"No, the video will have no names, at least not of any of the victims," Roger responded, knowing that the named suspects were in custody, or in Dossett's case, dead. "You can tell the press that we know that information but are not releasing it out of respect for the families."

"You know some publicity-seeking official in one of the girl's jurisdictions will blab," Tom complained.

"We can't do anything about it except suggest these identities be treated as with a sexual assault case," Roger advised. Good advice it was; Tom would use it if Roger didn't at the podium.

"I will have Sally with me to assist, be a tag team as I think questions will go on for some time," Tom proposed.

"Tough case for a woman to face in the spotlight," Roger scolded.

"It's eleven dead women, Roger. You need her at the podium to check subsequent bad commentary," Tom rebutted, to which Roger nodded. He was a jerk in some respects, but he wasn't stupid, and he had a male-oriented compassion that made some women pull towards him.

"I have briefed the governor. I'll let him decide who else to talk with so the very important people in government don't get caught unawares," Roger reported, always covering the political end, which the entire department appreciated. He had their backs.

"Good, we don't need any internal flack. What we get from the outside will be bad enough," Tom explained. "I need to get going to make sure I have my press pool lined up."

■ ■ ■

Tom knocked on the open door to Sally Quinn's office. "You all set?" he asked.

"Depends where I'll be," Sally replied. She looked a lot fresher than Tom felt.

"You'll be at Roger's right, I'll be at his left, up on the podium," Tom replied.

"That's OK with Roger?" Sally queried.

"I told him you needed to be at the podium," Tom answered. "He understands we are talking about eleven dead women."

"He did after you explained it to him," Sally said, with a smile.

"You will be on his right, and will speak first after he does his introduction," Tom stated, knowing that Roger did not realize that specific part. "You will have plenty of time to figure out what you want to say while I have the press pool watching the video. Just play off what he says, and when you have had enough, I'll pick it up from there. We're good at this Sally, that's why we are at headquarters and not in the boonies."

"Until afterwards," Sally grimaced. "Then I may want to be in the boonies, as long as it isn't Grundy County."

"You see Linda's report?" Tom inquired.

"Just did a scan," Sally said.

"What stood out to you?" Tom asked.

"The circumstances of the bodies, what they had been wearing, what they had on their person, their stomach contents, the indicators of who they were and what they were about at the moment of their abduction," Sally revealed.

Tom paused; he had looked most deeply at their deaths, but Sally had focused on their lives. "Did you see any clues as to who we are up against?"

"He was playing, with them, and with his imagination," Sally offered. "He didn't give them any grace strike to end it. He let them die, some slowly, and I bet he watched."

"We aren't saying that at the press conference," Tom challenged.

"We aren't saying anything beyond what they will learn from the letter and the video," Sally replied.

"We will be asked about manner of death," Tom observed.

"The investigation is ongoing. We release no details that will reveal how much we have," Sally said as if by rote.

"Excellent, see you at the podium," Tom responded, and went downstairs to gather his press pool, happy to be teamed with Sally.

CHAPTER 25

FEEDING TO AVOID A FRENZY

TOM STEPPED OUT INTO THE HALLWAY from the staircase, and saw that reporters had gathered already, and it was just 10:45 a.m. He spotted Kyle, who came up as fast as he could without looking to be so doing.

"Well, I'm here, looks like you called everyone," Kyle accused.

"No, it was only you, Kyle. I promise," Tom responded. He saw a lot of faces he didn't recognize.

"Out of town reporters with nothing else to do. Some from Memphis, some from Knoxville, one from Chattanooga. Atlanta is here, as is Louisville and Birmingham," Kyle informed Tom. "That is the reason we have an early crowd. I knew you didn't call them."

"Good, since you know these guys, you are the Nashville rep. Go select one for each of the other six cities. The boss is limiting me to a seven-reporter pool," Tom said, relieving himself of one onerous duty. "The rest can cool their heels."

Kyle gave Tom a questioning look, not sure if he was being set up for a sucker punch or receiving a rare privilege. "Got it, give me a moment." He was off, and soon Tom was leading his seven people away to a small conference room down the hall from the auditorium. The four men and three women came in, wondering what was up.

"Please take a seat where you can see the screen on the far wall," Tom said politely, like he was selling kitchenware. He moved to a small podium adjacent to the screen, which now was up and showing the Tennessee State Police logo.

"Wednesday morning we received a letter from an unknown source," Tom began. "With the letter was a thumb drive. We subsequently learned that the FBI office in Knoxville had received the same letter." Tom then read the letter, verbatim.

Kyle's hand was up with the rest of the seven, but he didn't wait. As was common in the press these days, he shouted out his question, "What is on the thumb drive?"

"Folks, no shouting, let's be civil and polite. I'm not walking to Marine One in here," Tom scolded. That statement earned an embarrassed silence. "I have read you the letter exactly as I read it on Wednesday. The thumb drive has a single file, a video, which I will now play for you. This letter and video are, of course, the topic of the press conference today."

The lady from Birmingham shouted, "You are only showing this to us because it will be out later today," she accused.

"Of course that is the case. We need to get out in front of this story," Tom answered mildly. "Normally, a piece of evidence like this would be kept confidential as we conducted our investigation. This viewing is a courtesy to you all, so I expect some courtesy in return." He did not glance at the Birmingham reporter as he said this; it wasn't necessary. He began the video and stepped to the side and sat down.

As the video ran, Tom could hear whispers: "You can't see anyone but him." "That voice is computer-generated." "The burning fits the definition of torture," and others. The video ended, and hands went up.

"Some more information," Tom said, ignoring the upraised hands. "Frederick Dossett's body was found under an I-24 exit in Grundy County Sunday morning by passersby. It was wrapped in two white plastic garbage bags and taped shut. An autopsy revealed death by fentanyl injection. Time of death was after midnight Saturday. I was the state investigator on that murder, so when the letter and video arrived Wednesday morning, we had no doubt as to the reality of what we read and saw. Now, no questions in this format. After the Director Basten has given his introduction, and Sally Quinn has followed with her briefing, then we will accept questions. You seven have been pre-tuned, so to speak, and will be given question priority. It would be a great help if, as you ask your question, you preface it with 'having seen the video, I would like to know…' so as to cut off a lot of unnecessary questions about the video from the other reporters."

The reporters filed out. Roger Basten was approaching the podium; Sally was already there. Tom nodded to Roger, and the Director readied himself.

"Thank you all for coming on short notice," Basten began. "I regret to inform you and the people of the southeastern United States that a horrific crime has been discovered, and the investigation is ongoing. I can report the murder of eleven young women over a period of two years. The victims were from Tennessee and four surrounding states, ages sixteen to thirty-one. The bodies were all recovered from a single site in Grundy County. Each body has been identified, and next of kin have been notified. This discovery has closed eleven missing persons cases in five states. We learned of this crime from a letter sent to us, and to the FBI office in Knoxville, by an anonymous source. I repeat, an anonymous source, not a confidential one. We do not know who the informant is. With the letter was a computer thumb drive that contained a video of the harsh interrogation of a man, Frederick Dossett, who confessed under extreme duress to the crimes, and gave the location and number of a safe-deposit box that contained detailed information about the crimes. That information allowed us to do a body recovery Thursday. We are doing this early press conference as the anonymous source said in the letter that they had sent a similar letter with a thumb drive to a number of media outlets, and that they expect the situation would go public later Friday, which is today. Frederick Dossett's body had been found Sunday morning under an overpass at an I-24 exit in Grundy County. Autopsy indicated he had been killed by a drug overdose. When the letter and thumb drive arrived on Wednesday, the Dossett case told us we had reason to accept the contents as real and not staged. The subsequent body recoveries gave proof of that reality. I must state that Mr. Dossett is not the killer. He was an accomplice and claimed he did not know the man who did the actual killings. That man is still unidentified, his whereabouts unknown. This is an active case. Four other accomplices were arrested Thursday morning in Grundy County and are in jail. I now turn the press conference over to the investigators who will provide some more specifics, and then take questions. Thank you." Basten stepped down from the podium, He would watch the rest of it on the flat screen in his office, while he fielded phone calls that were sure to come from the political end of things.

Sally stepped up to the microphone; Tom stood off behind her left shoulder. There were conversations going on, whispers drifted up, some cell phones were out and active.

"Good morning, folks," Sally began, sliding past any gender identity issues that the term 'ladies and gentlemen' might create. "I am Detective Sally Quinn. Director Basten gave you a summary of what this case is all about. We are in an active investigation situation, and our hand has been forced, as the media will soon have actual copies of both the letter and the video. To avoid confusion and speculation, let me review some facts. Most importantly, we have recovered eleven female bodies, and the families of those women have been notified. We will treat those identities as we would a sexual assault victim, and we ask that you do the same if you learn the identities. Please keep them confidential to spare the families any further pain. We do know the identity of the actual kidnappers. We have in custody four people who assisted in the abduction of the women, and in their delivery to the actual killer. The man who did the after-act burials of the victims, Mr. Dossett, is dead. His coerced confession provided factual evidence that allowed the bodies to be recovered and the four accomplices to be arrested. Finally, we do not know who sent the letter and video. We assume that person or persons to be the same as who conducted the interrogation of Mr. Dossett. Mr. Dossett's interrogation and death are both crimes, so the footprint of this case has expanded. Detective Tom Stass will now offer additional material."

Tom stepped to the podium with a nod to Sally. "Cases like this, especially one that is in the very early stages of investigation, as this one is, invite a lot of speculation and theorizing," Tom stated. "As you might expect, we have been doing that ourselves, trying to figure out who the actual killer is, the motive, and if anyone else beyond him is involved. Mr. Dossett stated that he believed the assailant to be male, and we have no reason to think otherwise, but that is an unproven assumption. This is a very strange case, and it will require imagination as well as good police work to solve. In anticipation of some of your questions, let me offer some speculations. The placement of Fred Dossett's body in a public place was deliberate, to make us take the subsequent letter and video seriously. The choice of Grundy County was planned by the assailant to allow a remote place for his crimes. The involvement of five other people in those crimes suggests an assailant with resources. We have two unknowns here, the mastermind assailant, and then whoever did the interrogation and murder of Mr. Dossett. We will prioritize the mastermind as we do not know if these eleven killings are all he has committed, or all he has planned. Detective Quinn and I will now take questions."

Within an hour of the end of the press conference, CNN broke into its regular news broadcasting to announce it had received a letter and a video. The video was not shown, but the face of Fred Dossett was. It did not take long for the identities of the four men in the Grundy County jail to be exposed, as their arrests were part of the public record as well as being given in the video. Their background, and interviews with neighbors, led to a lot of speculation, but the term hunting came up a lot, especially because of the Dead Rock Holdings land being identified as the site of the body recoveries.

■ ■ ■

In Athens, Maggie and Lauren watched the press conference, and then CNN began its coverage. "Now he sweats," was all Lauren said. Maggie wondered now about being a fugitive. It was strange to listen to others talk about the torture and killing she had assisted. She kept waiting for a wave of guilt. It still didn't come.

- - -

Ted Keller was indeed sweating. His bots had quickly alerted him that Fred Dossett's name was all over the news. He clicked on CNN in his L.A. office and went ashen; he hadn't known that Fred had *actually* kept records, evidence, details. What else had he kept, or discovered? What else did the authorities have? Now he knew why his Little Miss had disappeared. She had done this; she had set it all up. He not only had lost his Tennessee playground, she had made it clear that she was coming for him. The mouse attacking the tiger, he thought, momentarily amused. Then, he reconsidered; what if that mouse was rabid?

CHAPTER 26

FALL OUT

THE NEWS SPREAD LIKE WILDFIRE, as to be expected, and a headline titled 'Grundy County Massacre' rose to the top, which was unfortunate for the inhabitants of Grundy County, since it also gave the incorrect impression that the eleven murders had happened all at once. The video became a sensation, although it took some time for a copy to be leaked, first to the dark web and then more commonly across the public and private spectrum of media. The public reaction was typical, first horror at the crimes as the names of the dead slowly began to filter to the press. With one murder participant dead, and four in jail, the public seemed to lose sight of the fact that the main perpetrator, the actual killer, remained on the loose. Later court filings in Josh Ketchum's case revealed how the affair had been conducted, the hunting of women with dogs, driven to a bloody end. That set fire again to the public, as all five accomplices were from Grundy County. The people there took big hits on social media. The county commissioner took down all the 'Now Entering Grundy County' signs on the roads coming in, and the 'Now Leaving Grundy County' signs as well. Sam Fairbanks lost a lot of business as people canceled, not wanting to be hunted by dogs and then shot.

Sam had thoughts about the grandmother and teenage boy he had talked with in Dockey's, the night before Fred Dossett was killed. Lucy wondered about that same pair, who came, stayed a night, and then were gone the day Fred was murdered. Susie thought the A-Frame was remarkably clean after having held a teenage boy for a night, and also wondered why she never again heard from the grandmother about the family reunion. Then, realizing no one would come to Grundy County for such a gathering after the massacre news, let it slide. If those three had ever sat down for a cup of coffee together, then maybe some interesting lines of conversation might have appeared. Sheriff Koslowsky never followed up with those three as none of them approached him about strangers in town. He did follow up on the mysterious woman who had escorted Fred Dossett out of the Iron Anvil, but Maggie's skilled transformation from a 65-year-old grandmother to a 45-year-old divorcee on the prowl made that inquiry a very dead end.

Only Sam thought to see a pattern; a phone call from a mafia wife that had brought up hunting with hounds but that led to nothing, a boy who was strangely ignorant about hunting but who asked a lot of questions and was also excited about hunting with hounds. How Sam had given the grandmother Fred Dossett's name, and where he could be found. Sam was appalled at what Fred had done, more appalled than by what was subsequently done to Fred. Wages of sin, fully paid up was how Sam saw it. He had two teenage daughters. If it had been one of his girls buried on the Dead Rock Holdings property, the torture video would have run for several more hours until the soldering iron melted down. Sam was the best positioned to get a start on figuring out Fred Dossett's murder, and he wasn't telling anyone.

■ ■ ■

America loves murder mysteries, and the Grundy County Massacre case had a lot of mystery. Online forums soon appeared, focused on the case. Some of it was conspiracy crap, that the bodies weren't real, it was a Deep State plot to damage Tennessee and get the Republicans there out of power. Another opined that the bodies were extraterrestrial, killed by courageous Tennessee vigilantes before they could supplant humans. Several were serious, free of speculative garbage, trying to do a competent analysis of what was known and what was unknown. The mystery of the mastermind played out in these posts and discussions, but it was thin gruel as so little was known other than he was male and had serious mental problems. The scale of the resources applied to the murders was noted, and deemed to eliminate drifters, the homeless, and small-time wannabes. To some people, a mentally sick person with resources equaled a politician. One item that did create waves was the timeline. Fred Dossett's evidence allowed people to reconstruct the where and when of each kidnapping and realize that the murders likely occurred within 24 hours of the abductions. Anyone who had an ironclad alibi for that time window eliminated them from the suspect list, such as Hillary Clinton or George Bush. Much time by these amateur Sherlock Holmes was spent looking at the very rich and what they were doing on the dates of the abductions. That approach was also not very productive. Such persons could not have an alibi for any one of the eleven abductions, as one person was believed to have done all the murders. A few people solved that problem by making it a conspiracy of many people, with each one getting their shot at a shot, as it were.

There was more fascination with who had made the videotape, who had killed Fred Dossett. There was general agreement with Tom Stass' early private assessment that the video, as shown, had required two people. It also made Dossett's seizure easier to explain, even though Maggie had essentially done that part herself. Dossett's killer or killers were considered heroes by almost all the online crowd. The deliberate, controlled method of inducing Dossett to talk was greatly admired and, in some quarters, feared. It could happen to you. The planning and successful operation of the big reveal was also celebrated. Women especially appreciated the steps taken to make law enforcement see the problem as real and serious. The homecoming for the victims was hailed as a wonderful humanitarian gesture. The public clamored to know who these heroes were. Some felt the authorities knew who it was and kept them secret for a variety of reasons: to cover their asses, to protect the heroes from pre-arrest publicity, to avoid trial as no jury would convict, to offer them additional black-ops assignments, and so on.

Dossett's comment about the one that got away, the twelfth girl, resonated. She had to be the hero, the one who had stopped it all. Fanciful plots were set up: she had been rescued by a hiker and together they had plotted their revenge; she was an undercover agent; she was a 'Wonder Woman' with superpowers. Most agreed she was not from Georgia, as that state had had three victims, the other states only two each, so she was from one of those four as the murderer's rotation continued. So much for pattern analysis. Volumes of speculation, but it was a cold trail for now.

Maggie and Lauren followed these threads online, as did millions of Americans. There was no danger of their interest being noted by the mastermind. Maggie was an older single woman. They were known to be especially vulnerable to online conspiracy theories, the modern soap opera. The two ladies were constantly amused by most of what they read. A few posts were alarming, especially one about a person who wanted to set up a similar operation. They parsed the posts that showed solid critical thinking and consideration of the evidence, and how to do a true investigation. The ones who spoke of canvassing Grundy County to question locals about who had seen strangers gave Maggie and Lauren the most unease, but then Maggie had presented as older than she really was, whereas Lauren had presented as younger and a different sex. The motel manager Lucy had noticed the Florida plates on the rental, but that had been done under the Davenport name. For now, Lauren and Maggie looked to see how they could venture into this online media world, and begin to steer people to, as OJ used to say, the real killer.

CHAPTER 27

THE REAL INVESTIGATORS

"WELL DONE PRESS CONFERENCE," Sal said over the phone, Tom appreciated the compliment. "I imagine you are still in the middle of a media frenzy. By the way, thanks for being so circumspect about FBI involvement, we have had very few inquiries."

"If you want more credit, let me know, I'll hold a press conference and say the FBI knows everything, so call Sal," Tom joked back. "OK, what's up?"

"We have been informed by the big brass in D.C. that the Grundy County Massacre should be considered a top priority case for the FBI. Nine of the eleven women were transported across state lines, then murdered, the mastermind remains loose, Dossett's killers are out there, all sorts of stuff that needs to be acted on. It is me and Peter in charge."

"So how do you want to play this?" Tom asked. "I doubt my boss will give up any jurisdiction to the FBI, you guys being part of the Deep State and all."

"We will be the very best teammates, we will share everything except our beer," Sal replied, chuckling. "You could tell Roger Basten that we will be a cooperating agency and make all our resources available to you."

"Meaning you will pay for everything." Tom stated.

"Pretty much, especially lab costs, transportation expenses if we travel as a team, that sort of thing."

"That will work. Roger doesn't respond well to sticks but he loves carrots," Tom responded.

"Have you been paying attention to the online traffic?" Sal asked.

"No, I haven't. No time, and reading too much stuff written by crazy people can warp one's mind," Tom answered.

"Peter has been doing it; he calls it the UFO effect," Sal offered.

"UFO effect, as in 'unidentified flying objects,' that nut case stuff?" Tom was astounded.

"UFO reports are 99% complete bullshit. Another 0.9% are possible, but unlikely. It is the 0.1% that needs attention," Sal contended. "There are some very good thinkers out there, people who pay attention, are fact based, and think on both sides of the box. What they write about Grundy County warrants attention. Peter has been sifting those and he thinks he may have something we can act on. You have probably already thought of them, too, but we want to meet with you, in Monteagle, and do some real detective work. Bring Sally, we need her perspective."

"When are we going to do this?" Tom asked, thinking of his tasks for the week ahead. It was Monday.

"See you tomorrow for lunch at the Comfort Inn. I already cleared it with Director Basten," Sal replied, his enjoyment at having put one over on Tom Stass obvious.

■   ■   ■

"Here we are again," Tom said, as Sally drove the department minivan back down I-24, a stretch of highway Tom was getting to know far too well. He lounged in the front passenger seat, visor turned down to block the morning sun. She was doing over 80 mph; the state troopers had been alerted by Roger, so Sally turned on the emergency flashers and away they sped. Tom had checked the tires before he got in the car, just to be safe.

"So, how do we play this?" Sally inquired. "Are we in a competition, or do we give the FBI everything?"

"If it wasn't Sal and Peter, I might hedge my bets, but trust is a funny thing, hard to get, hard to keep," Tom mused. "I trust these guys, and I really want to solve this case. So we are open about everything."

"Suits me, Sal and Peter did not once give me the eye, or make a snide remark," Sally volunteered. "My gender was only referred to for perspective, as I see things as they can't see. To them I'm a pro, and I really like that."

"You're a pro to me!" Tom exclaimed sheepishly, wondering how many times he had given offense.

"I know Tom, and I appreciate how you keep Basten oriented in regard to me and my career," Sally replied. "I am torn between appreciating your help and being pissed that such help is needed at times. Anyway, where are we in our investigation?" Roger Basten had ordered Sally and Tom to stay home over the weekend, to let the situation settle, to clear their minds and get some rest. Roger understood how to keep his troops in top shape. He also had junior personnel who wanted a piece of the action. They spent the weekend going over financials for the five Grundy accomplices, as well as phone logs, police records, and anything else that might indicate who they had worked for. Boring, tedious stuff, but necessary work.

"The financial reports on our Grundy Five indicate that any payments may have begun over two years ago, a few weeks before the first abduction," Tom reported. "As might be expected, they were cash payments, large amounts, $5,000 each time according to Dossett's notes. More for him as the local organizing honcho."

"They put that much money in the bank each time?" Sally queried with astonishment.

"No, the bank deposits are for small amounts, in the hundreds of dollars," Tom explained. "It is an amount 'above background' as they say, but not enough to draw any real attention. It looks like they spent the rest and probably stuffed the residual in a mattress."

"If so, then Koslowsky should have found it. We will have to ask him," Sally surmised.

"The point is, we cannot trace the payments to anyone," Tom concluded.

"People must have noticed that these guys were spending money," Sally accused.

"Dossett paid his house off. The mortgage was held by a bank in Chattanooga. His local bank never saw anything," Tom said. "I bet we find it was that way with all the guys. Some took a vacation to the Florida Keys, some bought new guns for cash at a gun show, some hit the bars more often. Dossett bought a big expensive new truck. I bet it was with cash."

"So the Grundy Five are a dead end," Sally sighed. "Ketchum knew something, not about the master mind, but about the twelfth girl. But it seems he won't talk."

"He's a dead man walking, and he knows it. He has little incentive to talk," Tom responded.

"So what is our next avenue of investigation?" Sally inquired, blowing past an eighteen-wheeler.

"You tell me," Tom chided.

"How the perp got to and from the Dead Rock Holdings property," Sally offered. "If we assume he worked that part alone. If he lives within a few hundred miles, he probably drove. If not, he had to rent a car at an airport, unless he hitchhiked. He might have rented a car even if he was within a few hundred miles."

"Let's do the math," Tom stated. "Eleven murders, five accomplices, minimum $5,000 each, each time, although Dossett got more. That's $275,000, more than a quarter of a million dollars. That is big money. This isn't a successful small businessman, this is a successful big businessman."

"Inherited money?" Sally queried. "You haven't looked at his overhead, his other expenses. He used a variety of weapons. How did he acquire those? Where are they now? If he flew, how did he get them to Grundy County? Did someone stockpile them for him in Grundy County? Dossett makes no mention of any action like that. If someone else did, then it was more than five accomplices in Grundy County."

"He has a private jet," Tom exclaimed. "He flies in from a long way away, to give him separation from his crimes. He can carry what he wants on that plane — domestic flight, no customs inspection."

"He could keep a car permanently at the airport and just pay long-term parking. However, by renting, it is a different car, a different plate, every time he drives into Grundy County," Sally proposed. "He would probably have a cover story for the city he flies into, something business related."

"Did his business schedule drive his murders, or did his murders drive his business schedule?" Tom asked.

"I bet we can take Chattanooga off the airport list. He would go into and out of Atlanta, busiest airport in America, dozens and dozens of corporate jets fly in and out every day," Sally advised.

"Yes, but which ones flew out the day of the murder," Tom replied. "He would take care of business first, and then do his play."

"Looks like we have another job for Roger's young lackeys," Sally surmised.

"Oh no, this is a bone we can throw to Sal and Peter. Let the feds do the work, make it look like a drug smuggling investigation," Tom advised.

They drove on in silence for about ten miles, which was fewer minutes at the speed Sally was carrying. "Ketchum said he took the money, but he also said he was going to get a record expunged," Sally said suddenly, breaking the quiet. "Does that show up?"

"I bet that those young punks back in Nashville just made a list of the police record for each man, but didn't really look at it," Tom said, digging out his cell phone. "I am going to tell them to make a real close examination, check for any change in the initial state of things, look for cases expunged, look for dropped cases, for police reports that seem to have ended without resolution, all that stuff." He began to make a call.

"Could Koslowsky have been a part of that, not as a true accomplice, but maybe that is where some of the money went, as bribes?" Sally volunteered.

Tom didn't answer, his call had been picked up and he was giving instructions. After a few minutes of painstaking procedural discussion, the call ended with "If you don't like it, tell Roger." Tom pocketed his cell.

"Ketchum seemed to think the perp could help him with his police record. I don't think anyone was bribing the Sheriff after all," Sally said. "Someone was doing this online perhaps."

"The twelfth girl went to ground, dropped out of sight, from the very beginning," Tom observed. "Then she says in the letter that the perp likes observing the families and their miseries. She thinks this guy can find her online, track her down just as he tracked down all his victims."

"But he didn't know their identities. The girls weren't even searched," Sally protested. "Oh, wait, that was part of the game, take them, hunt them, kill them, bury them, and then try and figure out who had been killed. The hunt was game level one. Game level two, find out who you just killed. Game level three, watch online the missing person's reports, the family asking on TV for help finding their girl, the long drawn-out end game, the descent from hope to despair."

"That's the perspective you bring that Sal was talking about," Tom acknowledged. "It means this guy is a tech wizard, and probably very, very good. It will take the skill set of the FBI to see if he left any signature, any indication that he did these things."

"You think she figured this all out while running away?" Sally said, referring back to the twelfth girl.

"She sure had motivation. She saw at least four and maybe five men hunting her. She knew it was a big operation, and she maybe went with a worst-case interpretation to be certain she stayed alive," Tom offered.

"That big an operation, she had to worry if anyone in authority was involved," Sally replied. "We already know she is capable and smart. She got away. She tracked down Fred Dossett. She interrogated him with dramatic efficiency. She let us know so we would take on the case. This is one damn smart lady."

"Still a murderer," Tom responded, but his heart wasn't in it.

"If I were her, I'd come forward, and use the burning bed excuse," Sally contended.

Tom turned and gave her a look. "Say what?"

"A case from 1977. A woman set fire to her abusive ex-husband while he slept in his bed, killing him," Sally explained. "She was acquitted on temporary insanity protocols. He had abused her until she was crazy. The twelfth girl would modernize it, use PTSD to achieve the same result. I wouldn't convict."

"I might," Tom replied, a bit stunned.

"You ever been raped, abused, stalked? I thought not," Sally responded. "What you call a 'woman's perspective' is 'woman's survival' for the rest of us, and it is serious business." Sally took the off-ramp at Monteagle.

CHAPTER 28

RUN SILENT, RUN DEEP

SALLY PARKED AND THE TWO OF THEM WALKED into the Denny's that was attached to the Comfort Inn. As expected, Sal and Peter were already in a booth.

"I have to hit the ladies' room," Sally said and walked off in that direction. As she did, a woman followed. In the hallway to the restrooms, the woman tapped Sally on the shoulder. Sally swung around, prepared to halt an assault, then she stopped.

"Linda, what are you doing here?" Sally said in surprise.

"I am not here, I have something to give you then I am going back to Chattanooga," Linda said quietly as Sally stood with her right hand on the women's rest room door. Linda passed an envelope to Sally, who took it in her left hand. "Stay off-line about this. You can share it with Tom but assume every electron that crosses your desk has ears." She walked away and was gone. Sally went on into the restroom, sat in a stall, and looked at the text pages inside the envelope. She was there quite a few minutes, reading and re-reading. Then thinking. She returned to the booth.

Tom slid over so she could sit down, giving her an inquisitive look, but he knew better than to ask a woman how her bodily functions were doing. A waitress hurried over, seeing that the booth had finally gotten its fourth person, a bit surprised it was a female. They placed their orders, as Sally tried to catch up with the conversation, which seemed to be about how the perpetrator had gotten to and from Grundy County, so Sally wasn't out of the loop at all.

Sal looked at Sally. "So you think the assailant brought his weapons with him, and took them back with him?"

"Dossett never saw any weapons, just their effect on a human body," Sally replied tersely. "The detailed inspection, the cadaver dogs, the GPR, none of those located a place on the Dead Rock Holdings property where weapons might have been buried or stored."

"How many storage units are there between Grundy County and the Atlanta airport?" Peter queried, rolling his eyes.

"You are both missing the point," Sally interjected with some frustration. "It isn't just how he stored the weapons, or transported them, it is also how he acquired them. Did he get them all at once, or did he decide after each kill? If he decided to cut off his Tennessee operation, as Dossett stated, what did he do with a storage locker full of bloodied weapons?"

"I agree, he did each victim differently; he came with one weapon at a time, from his home site, and took the weapon back," Tom said. "That was his trophy, not who was killed, but how she was killed."

"So you two have settled on the private jet aspect," Sal proposed.

"For now, as it explains many things simply," Sally continued. "It also offers a quick way to get a lead on the perp. We know the dates of his travel, an examination of private jet flight plans around those dates will be instructive."

"Good first step, a lot better than trying to get commercial air flight manifests," Peter said. He reached into his pocket for his cell phone. "I'll call some guys at Quantico who do this sort of work for the DEA and get them on it."

Sally reached across the table and slapped Peter's hand with the cell phone to the tabletop. "No, we are changing procedures. We do nothing, and I mean nothing, electronic."

Peter quietly drew his hand back and tucked his phone into his pocket. "OK, what is this all about?"

"Think it through," Sally began. "Our killer has big bucks and spends it freely. He flies into and out of Atlanta by private jet. The letter writer thinks he watches his victim's families online and gets off that way. She goes into hiding and communicates only by snail mail."

Tom looked over at her, he nodded. "If this guy is an uber-wizard on the net, he may be able to watch what we do officially. Assume he has penetrated our data banks, is reading our e-mail, and perhaps watches our phones."

"That is a lot of watching," Sal snorted, "he can't do it all."

"We are talking about a Silicon Valley tech entrepreneur, who understands AI and knows how to scout the web with bots," Tom rebutted. "He only takes a look himself when he gets an alert."

"He has seen our press conference, he has seen the video, he has seen all the news coverage," Sally added. "He knows who is doing the investigation, he has all our names. I bet he has our cell phone numbers, the passwords, our computer electronic addresses, everything."

"We can't go dark. That will tip him off," Tom stated.

"We continue with routine stuff as normal, keep the electronic traffic flowing," Peter recommended.

"This watching of us will become part of his game," Sal observed.

"Level four," Sally agreed, then she explained what that meant.

"He is probably seeing, right now, that we are investigating to see if he fixed any of the Grundy Five's legal problems," Tom said.

"That's fine. He knows it is a dead end, but we can appear excited about it," Sally continued. "The twelfth girl, she figured this all out. But she isn't done."

"What is her next move?" Sal inquired, looking at Sally with an appreciation of where she was going with this line of thought.

"She will bait him, try and draw him out somehow," Sally replied. "He knows she is dangerous, that was obvious from the video, but he doesn't think she can find him, let alone hurt him. He will become more and more curious about who she is. It will consume him. He likes to sit back and react to what comes to him passively. She will force his hand, make him be proactive, reach out. Then she will have him."

"Do you think he will bug our rooms here?" Peter asked.

"Only if there is a device, like Alexa or Siri, in the room," Sally suggested. "In that respect, your original comment is useful. He can't watch everything, evaluate everything. He starts with his bots; those are his scouts. He will use AI to evaluate what those bots find, and then he looks at maybe half a percent of what the bots find that the AI flags."

"We need to be very careful. Use laptops that have had their wifi disabled," Tom suggested.

"Hard copy," Sally added.

The moment was tense, Sal broke it with "I hope everyone has good handwriting." As they all laughed, their meal came.

"What's next?" Sal asked, ketchup running down a few fingers from his double cheeseburger.

"We go visit Sheriff Koslowsky. I have a lot of questions for him," Tom answered. "He knows we are coming, I called ahead. It will fit our pattern of looking like we are focused on the Grundy Five."

Peter looked contemplative with his BLT. "How will she flush him out?"

"She will use the 0.1%," Tom said. "She will go online, release details only he will recognize, only she could know."

"She will recruit her own stable of conspiracy theorists," Sally proposed. "They will be her army and her cover."

"How does she do that?" Sal queried.

"The same way I would do it," Sally replied. "Pick one of the brighter minds in her conspiracy group and send that person snail mail material that then gets uploaded. Again and again."

Peter looked at Sally, he smiled. "She becomes Q," he said.

"Q, for the quick and the dead," Sally agreed.

CHAPTER 29

HE BECOMES REAL

THE LUNCH RAN LONG, as they had much to talk about. Being after 2 p.m., they could all check into their rooms, so they did. Sally soon knocked on Tom's door. He opened it cautiously, and saw it was her. "Come in," he said, with the eagerness of a co-conspirator. Then, "OK, what is this all about, the sudden communications blackout?"

"Something that now seems obvious in hindsight." Sally said, handing over the envelope to Tom. "Linda Usteuss cornered me outside the ladies room, and gave me that envelope, told me to stay away from electrons, and left. Read it, and we will talk." She got up and left the room; she needed some fresh air.

Tom read the letter. It was addressed to Sally and him. The fourth victim had been clubbed to death, a wooden club but not likely a baseball bat. Primitive killing, it had taken several blows. She had gotten her hands on him, there were skin cells under a couple of nails on her right hand, not *her* skin cells. Linda had done the standard DNA analyses, then she worked with public and private data bases to determine that the cells belonged to a male person of eastern European descent. Based on mitochondrial versus Y-chromosome data, both parents were from eastern Europe. The mother was a carrier of Tay-Sachs disease; being a recessive gene, the pathology of the condition would not be expressed in the child. The gene was especially common in Ashkenazi Jews, although it showed up at high levels in some other populations, such as French Canadians and Cajuns in Louisiana, indicating an early appearance in North America that followed population migrations. The overall genome affinities for eastern Europe indicated that the parents were probably Ashkenazi Jews, and they or the male child were recent immigrants to the United States.

Then there was a folded page, a photocopy of a news article about Ted Keller, a billionaire tech specialist who had dozens of patents and a business setup not in Silicon Valley, but in Los Angeles. He was quoted on how he came from the former Soviet Union as a child, fleeing with his parents to the United States which had succored him and allowed him to achieve the spectacular success he held today. His family name had been Theodore Kellinski; he had become Ted Keller to be more American. Asked if he had any regrets, he responded only that America seemed to have a lot of crime. His older sister, Karmia, 18, had gone missing in 1992 and had never been found. "That tragedy still hurts," he had said.

The final page was short. It merely said Linda thought Ted Keller was the killer, and that his research into artificial intelligence and web-based alternate reality games made him a danger to anyone who looked into his affairs. Her recommendation was to keep specifics, such as this letter, out of any electronic format. They were to assume Ted Keller could get anywhere an electron could go.

Tom sat stunned; he understood Sally's actions entirely. He was impressed how the four of them had analyzed the situation, with three of them not knowing how risky the communication situation actually was, but making appropriate adjustments anyway. He also realized that the investigation was over. It was Ted Keller. He had motive, a dead sister; means, he was a billionaire; and he created out of whole cloth his opportunities in Tennessee. Tom also needed to think about how to corner and arrest this man, who would see them coming from thousands of miles away. Tom was certain any actions he or the rest of the team made, like buying tickets to L.A., would be known to Keller. He knocked on Sally's door, but she didn't answer. He saw her at the end of the corridor, leaning against an open fire escape door and looking outside at the rugged plateau scenery. "Hide this again," he said as he approached her, handing her the envelope. She looked him in the eye, saw the understanding there, nodded, and went back towards his room as he went to rouse Sal and Peter. They still needed to talk with the Sheriff, if only to maintain their cover.

■　■　■

"You two are different this afternoon," Sal observed as they drove up to see the Grundy County Sheriff, the estimable Phil Koslowsky. "Family fight?"

Tom looked to Sally and nodded.

"I received information upon arrival in Monteagle that has identified the perpetrator," Sally began.

"So it wasn't a twenty minute crap," Sal rejoined. He was treating her as one of the guys, when she just wanted to be herself.

Peter had the appropriate look of surprise. "Why didn't you tell us at lunch?"

"Had to let my partner know first, the data were from within our operation," Sally explained.

"Who is it?" Sal now went professional.

Sally decided to read the letter, then the news article, then Linda's closing.

"So a person of interest. We don't know it is his DNA," Peter observed.

"I think we are beyond that to the suspect stage," Tom replied. "Our problem is how do we get more information, more proof, without alerting him?"

"We go back to my original move," Peter said. "We get our people to work on the flight manifests, but we disguise it as a drug investigation, and look initially only at private jet flights from a foreign country. We start with maybe the ten biggest southern airports, from L.A. to Charlotte, all within flight range of known drug exporting countries to the south. We let DEA do all the leg work."

"That approach will get Keller's jet flights into and out of Atlanta and L.A., we can do a cross correlation, fix his time windows, narrow the options," Sally responded.

"What about car rentals in Atlanta?" Sal asked. "Did he get them under his own name?"

"I bet he did," Tom said, turning in his seat. Sally was still doing the driving. "It is the best cover of all. He is just being his eccentric billionaire self, looking at hills that are Tennessee green instead of California brown. He might even have a hunting club 'membership' card for the Dead Rock Holdings property."

"He would just walk up to the car rental counter and get his car?" Peter gasped.

"Why not? He has nothing to hide. No one knows anything about what has gone on in Grundy County, no one who is going to talk, anyway," Sally noted. Other than Keller, sixteen people did, but eleven of them were dead, plus Dossett, four were in too deep. Oops, she thought, seventeen people; the twelfth girl knew enough to have blown up the whole operation.

"Outside of Grundy County, it is a one-man show?" Sal queried.

"It is all about control. He sees Grundy County as a personal fiefdom," Tom surmised. "He flies out, rents his car, and he is doing his thing for himself."

"The guns, the bow and arrow?" Peter inquired.

"Comes off his plane in his golf club bag," Sally guessed.

"So what's our plan?" Peter asked.

"We keep the focus on Grundy County, dig backwards into Dead Rock Holdings, do every possible piece of research on the Grundy Five," Sally stated. "He expects that, it is traditional, to work outwards from the scene of the crime, and it gives us a digital footprint for him to watch."

"While we do what in the background?" Sal asked.

"We watch the 0.1%," Tom suggested. "We send out our best cyber nerds to see if they can watch Ted Keller watching us. What do you think, Sally?"

"Fine by me. I have a trick up my sleeve," Sally replied with a hint of arrogance.

"And what trick is that?" Sal asked.

"It's a woman thing. You wouldn't understand," Sally said with a grin.

CHAPTER 30

SITE REVIEW

THE INTERVIEW WITH SHERIFF KOSLOWSKY had not been a waste of time. He had found stashes of cash, the smallest being in Dossett's house which, given the paid-off mortgage and the new truck, made sense even if he had been given more money than the rest. Maybe spending like that had eased his conscience. Josh Ketchum remained quiet; he had a public defender. Ketchum had only one statement, that he'd plead guilty if he got life without parole instead of the death sentence. The other three were trying to bargain but had nothing to really offer except the same arrangement Ketchum sought.

"What is your opinion?" Koslowsky had asked the team.

It was a Tennessee question, so Tom answered. "Two reasons to have the D.A. accept the deal. One, it is quicker and a lot cheaper than a trial and then all the subsequent death row appeals, which neither the prisoners nor the county can control, given all the anti-death penalty advocacy groups out there. Second, they may actually know something, and it may surface later. Josh Ketchum in particular seems to know more than he is telling about the girl who escaped. Alive, they might eventually tell us. Executed, most likely not."

"We haven't turned up anything regarding the actual killer of those girls," Koslowsky continued. "If it was a single male perpetrator, no one noticed his arrival or departure. The Dead Rock Holdings property leads right on to a desolate section of US 41. He could come and go and no one would see him. We haven't been able to get anywhere with the holding company. It seems to be a front in front of a front, if you know what I mean. The property was an estate transfer, handled entirely out of Nashville by lawyers nobody here knows."

"What about the girl who escaped?" Peter asked.

"No one saw her, not coming in nor going out," Koslowsky answered.

"We have been hitting dead ends too, Sheriff," Tom interjected. "We are as frustrated as you are." Koslowsky brightened at this comment, fearing they would think him incompetent. "Anything else?"

"Only that we have had family of two of the girls show up, and they asked to see the Dead Rock Holdings property," Koslowsky said with a deep sigh. "I couldn't deny them that, even though I thought it didn't do them any good."

"They had to know, Phil, even though it hurt. Good that you gave them that ease, painful as it was," Sally said, looking at him softly. "In fact, I want to see it too, from the north gate. I want to walk where those girls ran."

"Why, to feel their pain?" Peter asked sarcastically.

"No, I want to see what the twelfth girl saw. I want to get a feel for how she did it, how she got away," Sally rebutted.

*　　*　　*

Sal and Peter dropped Sally and Tom off at the north gate, said they would pick them up at the south gate after they checked a few things. Sally walked down the dirt road, imagining the twelfth girl, bound up in a tarp or blanket, bouncing around as the van maneuvered its way down the bumpy track. Hell, all twelve girls had done this trek. Then an open area, the valley going south, the cliff to the west, the floodplain to the left with a cliff distant to the east.

"Which way do you think she went?" Tom queried.

"She must have seen the hounds, Ketchum with his shotgun, the other men," Sally answered. "They were where we are, to keep her from going north or back up the access road. The forensic party sent up on the scarp said there was a trail across the top of the cliff. They found a cigarette butt. The DNA was from one of the van abductors."

"Their job was to keep her from climbing up and out," Tom suggested. "I don't know why. The cliff has an undercut shale band below the sandstone — a really difficult climb. Maybe it is easier farther south."

"East is too open, too obvious. The hounds would have had her easily," Sally observed. They were alone, the two of them. She could talk freely. "Ted Keller sat in his blind straight south, not far from the stream, where he could hear the girl coming, then kill her. Dossett said in his notes that he walked the west bank of the stream, to push the quarry back to the east bank." She looked around. "Let's go, we are a scared woman, men with guns behind us, hounds baying, slightly back and to our left, keeping us near the stream."

They walked slowly, no real trail, a lot of investigators had worked these woods; it was all messed up from a tracking viewpoint. They got to the two yellow markers.

"Keller was just ahead, ready to do his thing," Sally announced. "She got away before this point."

"Was she faster than they thought, did she break contact and then make a move?" Tom queried.

Sally had her cell phone out. "No reception, not a surprise." She turned and walked back north. "She got up the cliff somehow. Dossett and Ketchum were trackers, but the two van guys up on top weren't. She evaded them and went west."

"Why west?" Tom inquired.

"They had kidnapped her to the east, from Athens they said," Sally stated. "She is trying to escape; she goes away from where they took her. I just don't see how she got up there. Even if she was six feet tall, there is no way up that ten-foot undercut wall without equipment. Let's go take the top trail."

* * *

"If she got up here, it is easy going," Tom said as they shuffled along the top trail.

Sally was looking at a map. "The cigarette butt was found here," she said. "Right on the edge of the cliff. Maybe they leaned over to see something, or to talk with Dossett or Ketchum."

"Going due west from here hits the access road twice as it winds around," Tom observed. "Then you hit US 41."

"You are running, scared out of your mind but competent enough to find a way up and out. You stay off the access road, you cross it twice and then you hit the fence. Over that, and on to the main highway. Then what do you do?"

"Flag down a passing car?" Tom guessed.

"Are you crazy?" Sally almost shouted as they walked through the woods to the access road. "Women know not to hitchhike even when they are not pursued. She was being pursued in Deliverance territory. We will take the access road out to US 41. It will be quicker, and I don't feel like climbing up a six-foot chain-link fence."

▪ ▪ ▪

Once on US 41, they walked south on the west side of the road, not good for traffic safety, but to get a better view of the eastern side Sally thought the girl had come out from. Soon they were at the 'White City 5 miles' sign.

"This is very close to where she would have come out had she kept going straight west," Sally observed.

"With that sign, she knows help is only five miles north," Tom proposed. "She walks north."

"But within the tree line, she can't afford to be seen yet," Sally said.

Sal and Peter pulled up in their car. "I thought you said the south gate," Sal explained.

"Saw what we had to see in there, now I need to see more out here," Sally reported. Tom was without expression. Sally was on to something, so he let her roll. "What did you guys find?" Sally continued.

"As you go north, there is a convenience mart called 'Red's Safety Stop', a real mom and pop operation," Peter said.

"Surveillance cameras?" Sally queried.

"Yup, and the Sheriff already has copies from the time of the alleged twelfth girl," Peter added. "All the earlier abductions were overprinted, 30-day cycle time."

"It's a long way south before you hit anything, house, business, anything," Sal added. "Probably why this place was chosen."

"Cell reception up here," Sally noted. "Either here, or borrowed at the store, she called for help, and it came. We could look at the nearest cell tower activity for that Wednesday afternoon and evening."

"Then she set her plan in motion," Tom said.

"Fast too. They took her on a Wednesday morning, and Fred Dossett was dead by a week from that Saturday after midnight," Peter calculated.

"Why did you do this little walk in the country?" Sal asked.

"I needed a feel for this place, the layout, see what she saw, try and think like she thought," Sally replied. "So when I get in touch with her, she will know I am for real."

"Get in touch with her? You know who she is?" Peter was exasperated, as it seemed he often was with Sally.

"Online, through the 0.1%, then I'll tell her it was Ted Keller, and let her drive him to us," Sally smiled. "I'm going to unleash a she-hound and give Ted a taste of his own game."

CHAPTER 31

ONLINE TIME

LAUREN AND MAGGIE ISOLATED A FEW PLAYERS on the web that seemed to lead a sizeable cohort of serious thinkers about what was called 'The Great Hunt Conspiracy' or the GHC. It was an interesting set of thinkers. One participant, 'Neurometer,' spent time analyzing the mindset of the Grundy County Massacre mastermind, attempting to determine what his mental configuration was to plan and execute such a scheme. Neurometer also had posts about the 'Twelfth Girl' or TG who had gotten away, killed Frederick Dossett, and then gone quiet. What was her mental state? What her overall plan was became a secondary focus. The leader of the site used the handle 'For The Ladies', but posts referred to this individual as 'Lady' even though the actual gender or orientation was unknown (perhaps even to the person themselves, some speculated).

As it was known that TG had originally sent information out using snail mail, Lady posted a P.O. Box in New York City as a way for TG to communicate with them in secret. Lauren and Maggie understood that to contact them to get the ball rolling would require sending some information that only Lauren could know. While both women understood that data in the law enforcement files in the case might have been hacked into by the killer, they were fairly certain that members of the GHC did not know that police information. Because only law enforcement had seen and read Dossett's journal from the safe-deposit box, or what the Grundy Five (minus Dossett) had said during interrogation, Lauren and Maggie weren't certain how much the people at the FBI and the Tennessee State Police knew about how the hunt had worked.

So Lauren and Maggie crafted a letter to go snail mail:

Dear Lady, I have followed your posts on the GHC site with great interest. I am TG, and I am certain that you may have had many mails, both electronic and snail, from people who say they are me. So my first task is to convince you that I am the real TG. To do that task, I will give you information only TG could know. When I ran, and I ran very fast, I found a way to hide. The hounds and the two men running them lost the trail on the east side of the stream. Fred Dossett walked the west side of the valley, right under the cliff. He could not find the trail either. The two van drivers walked on the cliff top, and they saw nothing. They all had a conversation, which I heard, expressing their frustration. The men on top called me a 'little bitch,' and told Fred I was 'kicking his ass,' which made him angry. They went north to try and find my trail, and I came out of hiding and escaped to the west. They were to drive me to the south, to 'the markers' they said. They failed, and I made Fred Dossett pay. I will send you information online. I will sign my input 'crack-crawler,' and underneath I will use a code word. If a code word ever appears twice, it means that posting is a fake. I realize that what I have told you could have been created in part by law enforcement, but only I heard what the men said. More later. Confirm receipt of this message, and acceptance of its veracity, by putting a line in your next post including the date of May 23, 1977. My purpose in writing you is that everything you do is watched by the killer. I wish to goad him into a reaction, which will help reveal who he is so final justice can be meted out.

Sincerely yours, crack-crawler

code words: 438; blue; odd number; kumquat; Detroit; fast
car; Venus; left hand; peanut butter; sandal; subway; tram

If I send 'Excelsior' it means emergency, I am in big
trouble. More codes will follow in snail mail if we use up
all the above. Remember the dead; I fight for them.

They mailed the letter from Atlanta and continued their reading of
the web.

▪ ▪ ▪

Ted Keller had become very frustrated. His entire operation in Tennessee had been rolled up, and he worried that Fred Dossett or one of
the others knew something he didn't realize they knew, and now the
cops knew it. He could not find his Little Miss. He had full access to
the police reports on the progress of the investigation, and they had
no idea who Little Miss was either. They seemed strangely focused on
Grundy County, as if they could milk information about him from
that place. He knew they couldn't; they seemed to be building the case
against the Grundy Five, which didn't make sense as he had access to
the County D.A. emails, and he and staff were discussing a plea bargain for all four that remained alive. He had trouble getting into the
FBI stuff; they understood cyber security very well, but he had access
to them through the Tennessee State Police, who leaked like a sieve.
Sally Quinn and Tom Stass seemed to be typical state employees, good
enough to keep their jobs but not really top-flight minds. Their FBI
counterparts, Sal Munoz and Peter Comstock seemed better, but they
weren't getting anywhere. He had hoped they would track down Little
Miss, and he could sweep in and gather her up and finish her game
forever. He saw no threat to himself. He followed the online groups.
Most were nut shops, but GHC and a couple of others had done some
good thinking. Then they would get an idea and spend time running
down a false lead, like the one that had him as a Chinese oligarch with
a hatred for white women.

His bots watched other things too, such as a download of flight plans by the DEA of private jets going to ten cities. That was for a drug investigation, so he moved on. A Fred Dossett in Montana was flagged, but it was, of course, a completely different Fred Dossett. His bots were mindless, his AI smart but not an original thinker. In the end, he had to take time to vet these red flags. It was going nowhere, so he focused on work and occasionally thought about Little Miss. Then his AI alerted him to a new posting on GHC, which appeared to come from Little Miss. Ted read it, and realized it was a law enforcement fishing expedition. The made-up dialogue was a nice touch.

        ▪   ▪   ▪

Rainy Sundin, aka Lady, had read the letter with excitement. She hadn't gone to the P.O. Box herself, of course; she sent a courier who passed it on to another, all the while doing John le Carré spy craft stuff to shake any tails. Rainy had found the part online about her own gender amusing, as she had transitioned several years earlier and felt, more than most people, that she was fully aware of her orientation, a proactive fix of nature's action. The letter's tone, the overheard dialogue, the detail on which way she had escaped, all seemed correct. Rainy took the admonition about a law enforcement plant seriously, yet it was silly from the start unless law enforcement thought she actually knew who TG really was. Everything Rainy and her group knew was open on the web. Why skulk around about it?

In her next post, Rainy talked about astrology influencing how people thought about major events. Not that astrology was true, but that some people thought it might be, so if the perpetrator was into astrology, how might that influence his actions? She threw in three dates, asking her readers to figure out what the three dates were all about, astrologically. All were made up, but one was TG's date. It would be fun to see what crap people came up with.

The next day, she got a reply from crack-crawler, with '438' beneath the name. It said the Dossett video was not totally complete, or it would have shown how the injection that killed the man was done.

Inside of the left arm, crack-crawler said. Dossett was killed so that the mastermind would learn he was next. He could expect to be strung up as Fred had been, but it would be days before he was allowed to die.

Lauren's post, sent from a McDonald's parking lot off I-20 near the Alabama border, was a sensation as Lady had immediately verified the source was true. Feedback was all over the place. There was great support for her plans to torture the mastermind. A few said it wasn't appropriate, that he should be crushed like a bug, quick and simple. Others noted that she was admitting to a murder, while others said there was only her word that she had killed anyone. No one had seen the autopsy report; it hadn't been released. She sent another snail mail letter to Lady, with a P.O. Box address in Atlanta.

■　■　■

Ted had seen the autopsy report, he knew where the injection had been done. He also knew that anyone watching the video saw that all the torture was to Fred's left side. It wasn't much of a leap to guess the injection had been to the inside of Fred's left arm. Lady had talked about the discussion TG had allegedly overheard — that sounded real and matched up with what Fred had done that fateful day. Lady and her posts warranted steady attention. He therefore instructed his AI.

■　■　■

Peter was ecstatic; he believed it was the twelfth girl. He knew where the cigarette butt had been found. He called Sally on a burner phone, they all had one now. It was against regulation, but Tom had gotten written permission from Roger who kept if off the books to both fool the mastermind as well as any internal investigator. It sure fooled Ted Keller.

"It fits, Peter. The cigarette butt was right on the cliff edge, where the van guys would have stood to talk with the people below," Sally offered. "I am going to take another look at that cliff."

That afternoon, Tom drove, doing 85 mph with full clearance. He hadn't checked the tires — after all, he was driving. It was a quiet drive, Sally was making a sketch, and looking at the map Sal and Peter had made. They drove down the access road, feeling the bumps that all the girls had felt. Soon Sally was on the east side of the stream, looking west. She stopped where a large rock jutted into the stream.

"This is right across from the spot on the cliff where that cigarette butt was found," Sally said, her eyes fixed on the cliff. The foliage screened her from getting a good look at the upper half of the cliff. She had brought waders and stepped into them, walking out into the stream. Tom had not brought waders; he stayed at the rock. She walked out into the center of the channel and got a good look at the entire cliff. Then she saw it, the little opening about fifteen feet down from the cliff top. Maybe two feet high, less than a foot wide.

Tom saw her stop and stare. "What have you got?" Tom asked.

"The person online, who says she is TG, isn't her byline 'crack-crawler?' Sally inquired.

"So she portrays herself as a drug addict, what does that have to do with us here?" Tom complained.

"Because there is a crack in the cliff a small person could just fit into," Sally rebutted. "She crawled into it, and from there, she would have heard everything said by people down here, and by the two guys on top. They went north, out of sight, she wiggled out, and went up the joint there and over the top. Then west to US 41."

"OK, nice story, but how did a small girl get up that cliff?" Tom's inquiry was right on point.

Sally shook her head in frustration, then walked upstream in the water past the angled jut in the cliff face. She saw the ledge. She went back downstream and saw that the ledge petered out after the turn in the cliff face, but there were footholds and handholds. She had only deferred the problem; TG had still to get to the ledge. She went upstream, swatting a leafy branch from her view, holding it with her left hand so it wouldn't fly back into her eyes while she looked up. Then she looked at the branch, then the tree trunk on the west bank, then another tree farther up the slope.

"Holy shit!" she exclaimed. "That's it, that's how she did it! What a fucking smart person, to see it, to do it, all while chased by hounds and men with guns. Fucking great!"

Tom was stunned by Sally's outburst: the force, the language, her obvious joy. "Explain it to me."

Sally looked around. "She is running, her head is on a swivel, she knows she is being driven, knows she can't continue south. She gets up on the rock, and steps off into the stream, that will momentarily confuse the hounds. She wades upstream and pulls a branch down."

"And what, uses it as a catapult to fling herself up on a ledge?" Tom was totally unbelieving.

"No, she pulls the branch down and walks up it, like this," Sally argued, pulling on the branch, going hand-over-hand into thicker branches until she starts to rise out of the water, she continues on until her feet are free.

Tom watched, seeing that it would work. "Well, Goddamn, she flings a leg up and over, stands up, goes up a few branches, goes out to the west, gets into an upslope tree, then out a branch to the ledge, and around the corner. I see it." He paused. "She would be dripping water, just like you are, Fred would have seen it."

"Not if she took off her shoes and socks, draped them around her neck, rolled up her pants, and went barefoot, the water would have dripped and the feet dried before she got to the second tree," Sally explained. "Fred wouldn't have had the trace he needed."

"Well, that explains how she did it. It all fits with what we know and what we suspect," Tom said, shaking his head at the intelligence of both women who had hung from this tree.

Sally let herself back down the branch and walked to the east shore, taking off the waders at the rock. "Only she would know to call herself crack-crawler. The lady who said she is TG is really the twelfth girl."

"Well, that is good work; we know she is out and trying to communicate," Tom said. "Then she has confessed to committing the murder of Fred Dossett online."

"We also know a bit about her stature, she is small, almost tiny, to have fit in that crack," Sally added.

"Is she signaling us as well?" Tom inquired. "No one in her online community, the GHC, could have deciphered her web name."

"Yes, she wants us to know, she wants us to know she knows we know," Sally admitted. "She wants us to get Ted Keller in case she can't."

"And we want to use her, like a goat staked out to draw a tiger, to bring Ted Keller out into the open," Tom said, his voice rueful.

"It isn't for her, it's for the other eleven," Sally said in rebuttal.

CHAPTER 32

CONTACT

THEY WERE IN MCMINNVILLE, playing tourist at Cumberland Caverns and now sat in the coffee shop to have their meeting. Tom related the tale of how Sally had figured out TG's escape from Ted Keller. He told it with gusto and obvious affection, the fever of the newly converted.

"We have the data on private plane flights into and out of Atlanta for the last two years," Peter began. "That time window encompasses all the murders. Recognizing that correlation is not causation, Ted Keller was in Atlanta for every murder."

"With the DNA evidence, don't we have him dead to rights?" Sally asked, displaying an eagerness with Keller that Tom showed with TG.

"If your guess that he kept the weapons as trophies is correct, it would cinch the deal if we could find them in his house or business," Sal countered.

"Surely we have enough probable cause for a search warrant," Tom said with exasperation.

"To paraphrase F. Scott Fitzgerald, the rich are very different from you and me," Peter counseled. "Ted Keller has resources, friends in high places, important secret DoD contracts — we have to be able to walk on eggshells to bring him down."

"I can see the truth in that, but we can't just wait," Tom protested. "The man is an eleven times murderer, and a sicko to boot."

"Then we don't go after him," Sally said with grim determination. "We stake him out in L.A., and we sic our attack dog on him. He will panic, dump his trophies, and we don't need a warrant."

"Attack dog?" Peter queried.

"The twelfth girl, the one who has come out online, we feed her information, she posts it, and we watch," Sally said, this time with an emphatic grin.

Sal looked over to Peter, his moral compass. "What are the rules, and the ethics, of doing that?

"We are telling her. She isn't telling us, so she isn't an informant," Peter began. "Actually, we don't know who she is. We are just posting information. None of it is classified, most is public record, like the FAA flight plans. The stuff about the weapons as trophies is simple speculation. We have no data on them except what the coroner's report says, and the fact that they were not recovered at the scene or anywhere."

"How do we get her attention? How do we get the information to her?" Tom inquired.

"We do a post," Sally replied. "Something like: 'We need to talk, I have seen the crack below the butt,' and let her respond."

"Not even Ted Keller knows that. It is unique to her," Sal noted.

"We work through Lady at the GHC. They have a confidential link to her," Sally offered. "Send a letter to their P.O. Box in New York City and let them communicate the letter's concerns to TG."

■ ■ ■

At Lauren's request, Maggie came in from the kitchen and read the GHC post. "It's from law enforcement. They figured out your escape route," Maggie was tense. "What do we do?"

"We don't know what the cops know, but the killer probably does," Lauren replied. "These guys are clever. I bet it was the woman from the Tennessee State Police, that Sally Quinn, if she walked the route in Grundy County, and felt it, felt the pressure, heard the hounds in her head, she might have seen a possible route, the path I took."

"So what do we do?" Maggie was letting Lauren flow.

"They figured out what my web handle meant. They know I am physically small, they are gradually closing in," Lauren responded. "They may have a suspect, but they know it is a rich and powerful man. If he is as tech savvy as we think, he may have CIA or NSA contracts."

"They want to go through you, have you post stuff, blast him out in the open," Maggie suggested.

"That's right, we are going to tag-team that son of a bitch and blow him up," Lauren promised.

"Do we send a letter?" Maggie asked.

"They will go through Lady. We wait," Lauren replied.

■　■　■

The letter arrived in Rainy's P.O. Box and made its circuitous way to her. It was an official government envelope — no deception, very upfront. Such a step, out of the dark and into sunlight, was strangely exciting for Rainy, who spent so much time in the shadows. There was a short note folded over a longer letter:

> Please forward the enclosed letter to TG, we believe her to
> be the true successful escapee. We would ask you not read
> the letter, as much as to protect you as anyone, but under-
> stand you may feel the need to do so. You and your website
> are not under investigation, and you have broken no laws.
> We are taking this route because we understand TG needs
> protection; a powerful man is arrayed against her. We
> think she can help us end it once and for all.
>
> *For the Eleven, Sally Quinn*

With an actual signature. Rainy was impressed, she didn't believe in the Deep State, but she understood law enforcement was a bureaucracy, and had a life of its own. Like any living thing, it sought to feed, to grow, to reproduce, and to protect itself. But it also had a duty, a driving program that was made up of human components. She sent the entire letter onward and did not read the enclosure. Not to satisfy the writer's request, but to do what she suspected TG would do. She added her own note:

TG, I think this document is for real. I haven't read the
actual letter, though I really wanted to. This is your game.
We are mere spectators, but we so want you to win. *Lady*

The letter sat in Lauren's lap as Maggie drove, taking a few turns and
cutting through a Walmart parking lot in case there was any tail, which
was silly, Lauren thought, because a GPS tracker could have been
affixed to the vehicle. One can watch too many old spy movies, and
Maggie was 'Cold War' old.

Lauren looked at the letter as if it might explode, or a venomous
creature would wiggle out. Finally, she opened it. She read Lady's cover
note, and then Sally's cover note, out loud. She paused. "What do you
think, Maggie?"

"It could be a con, it could always be a con, but we have to move
forward," Maggie advised.

"Once I read it, the message will always be in me. It will give me duty,
obligation, and perhaps guilt," Lauren surmised. "So it will have done to
the writer. Sally and I are now intertwined." The two had been intertwined for some weeks now, Sally had known it better than Lauren.

"Your call," was all Maggie said.

Lauren opened the letter, and began to read it to Maggie, as if she
were an off-screen narrator in a movie.

Dear brave woman, I am Sally Quinn, and I am on the
team investigating the eleven murders in Grundy County.
I am also investigating the murder of Fred Dossett but
have understanding. I have seen the crack below the
butt and am impressed. We have identified the Grundy
County killer. He is Ted Keller, a billionaire tech entrepreneur from Los Angeles. We have DNA from skin cells
under the fingernails of victim number four. His private
jet flights put him in Atlanta for every murder. We think
he might have kept the weapons he used as trophies. As
you clearly understand, he is smart, powerful, ruthless,
and well-connected in high places. We are as constrained

as you are about placing anything we do in digital form. He watches us all.

We have a plan, which is to have you release all these specifics on the GHC site while we have him under secret surveillance. We hope to force him to make a move, dispose of the weapons, come east looking for you. There is a risk for us, we are bending rules, but your risk is absolute. Now that we have connected, below is a list of code words you can use to determine which posts are truly ours. This is a one-time book approach, old-fashioned, but protected from high-tech. My copy of this letter is on carbon paper; another copy was photographed on 35 mm film on a copy stand. We are taking serious precautions because we know what we are up against. The same as you. We will take Ted Keller down with your help, and you will be free of him.

You tortured and killed a man, and the law may feel it must judge you on that, but you have my admiration for your courage, skill, and intelligence.

Sincerely yours, Sally

It was a handwritten letter.

▪ ▪ ▪

Maggie drove on in silence, Lauren read the letter again, silently this time.

"I have to do this," Lauren said simply.

"I think so, this must all conclude," Maggie agreed. "We can stop for coffee and you can begin it all."

"The beginning is to tell Sally I agree. It is time to prepare. I'll await the go signal," Lauren responded.

"Won't that alert this guy Keller?" Maggie asked.

"My post will say "the crack is open and awaits,' that should be clear enough to Sally.

"Sounds like porn, but good enough," Maggie chuckled.

CHAPTER 33

POKING THE BEAST

"SHE IS IN — SHE IS ON BOARD," Sally noted as she sat on a bench outside the main entrance to headquarters on a breezy and pleasant day.

"Then we have to move. We put out information that will force Keller to act. We cannot wait," Tom replied, his excitement rising. "Call Sal?" This was Sally's play. Tom, though technically outranking her, deferred with a will.

"Looks like we are going undercover in Grundy County," Sally answered, referring to a plan worked out with Sal and Peter so they could move quickly and with assurance.

"Yup, by way of L.A.," Tom said with a grin.

Peter had gone to Washington to report on progress, or the lack thereof, in the Grundy County Massacre case. Once there, he had arranged to meet with the Director in a secure room and had verbally laid out what they were prepared to tell him, which wasn't much. All Peter wanted was the cover to get the team to L.A. to do a specific task. An FBI plane would go to Atlanta, pick them up, and take them to San Diego. From there, they would take a vehicle left by the FBI up to L.A. and do their work. The L.A. FBI office had been advised that agents would be in town on a sensitive counter-espionage case involving China, and to not interfere, but be ready to offer assistance if requested. Sal and Peter were sent a memo that also went to Sally and Tom, explaining that their undercover operation in Grundy County had been approved, and could begin immediately. The hope was that action would explain why all four were suddenly going dark to Keller's watching bots.

Tom and Sally did yet another drive down I-24, but she blew right past Monteagle and on to Chattanooga and I-75 on the way to Atlanta and Hartsfield International. They met Sal and Peter at the main terminal and were whisked down side corridors and to a car that took them to the plane, a Gulfstream jet. It was quiet and formal until the plane began to taxi.

"Are we all set?" Sally asked.

"We are making a big play based on a lot of assumptions," Peter said, almost as a complaint. "We don't know if TG will do as we ask. We don't know how Keller will respond. It could all be a bust."

"Look," Tom interjected. "We know it is Keller, I have no doubts. What more do we know about him?"

"I approached, in person, the reporter who did the most recent piece on Keller, a lady who has filed on some big tech guys for years, and has developed good standing with most of them," Sal answered. "These are not fluff pieces, but in-depth analyses that are fair, but have been hard-hitting."

"How did you ask about Keller? Weren't you afraid she would tell him the FBI was nosing about?" Sally queried.

"I was doing a top-secret security clearance background check, very heavy duty, and, of course, it had to remain totally confidential," Sal replied. "I noted that it could end up with Keller getting a big contract, and the USA getting better security against cyber-attacks."

"Played the old patriot card, I see," Tom laughed.

"Actually, if she liked him, and thought he should be told he was being checked on, the contract thing would give her pause. She wouldn't want to upset that lucrative applecart," Sal added. "Anyway, I got some good stuff, let me read from my notes."

Sal leaned back as everyone else leaned forward. "Any contradictions to what was in the article Linda gave us?" Sally inquired. "That piece is what formed my mental image of the guy."

"No, but lots of additions," Sal answered. "Because his parents had immigrated from the former Soviet Union, she asked a lot of questions about them. She started with a feel-good question, how would his late parents feel about him now? Her answer to me was a surprise. She said that he didn't care. That led to some careful probing, but it was clear that Ted and his father did not get along, I got the feeling that Ted's father had been highly abusive. His mother died when Ted was ten. The reporter told me that it was suicide, covered up to look like an accidental overdose. Then his sister Karmia was abducted. Ted has no family here in the U.S., never married, doesn't date. The reporter said his personal life was quite a mystery. She felt he was probably gay, which in the old days would have meant no security clearance, but today, nothing."

"Let me get this right, his father abused his family, all of them. His mother can't take it anymore and commits suicide, then his sister turns 18 and runs away?" Sally recited.

"No, she was abducted," Peter corrected.

"Peter, this explains the last missing piece," Sally stated. "His sister wasn't abducted — she ran away at 18 because her father could no longer legally deny her. Keller presents it as an abduction to hide his anger."

"Anger?" Peter shouted, at least his raised voice seemed like a shout in the close confines of the plane. Sal was watching closely, the gears spinning in his head.

"His father abused him," Sally explained. "His mother tried to protect him, but she gave it up. His sister was his only salvation, and she ran away, gave him up to his father. I bet an analysis of his father's death might show that it wasn't accidental or medical."

"He killed his father to stop the abuse," Sal said, it was not a question. "Or did it later to get even."

"The women in his life had abandoned him to his fate," Sally proposed. "This murder spree is all about getting even, getting even with women who are in the age bracket of his sister. Then, watching the family grief, rolling in it, making them feel as bad as he had growing up. His motive is simple, he just cannot get enough. He kills and keeps on killing because it gives him momentary joy, but it fades, like an addict's high."

"When TG goes public on this, it will be another betrayal by a young woman. He will go nuts," Tom projected.

"We will need to be certain he doesn't fly east," Sal said, glancing over at Peter, who nodded.

"Once TG publishes, all hell will break loose," Tom noted.

They landed, and after a night in an FBI safe house, drove north on I-5, Sal renting a second car with a set of standard-issue fake credentials. Ted Keller lived in a gorgeous mountain-side retreat in the Hollywood Hills. His business was only a mile away, a small and plush campus. Sally and Peter took the business, Sal and Tom, in the rental vehicle, covered the house. Hillside houses are nice, but you can get above them and see everything with binoculars. The campus was more problematic, security was tight there; one doesn't park in the oval and then whip out a pair of binoculars. Sally went in wearing a wig and sunglasses, walking with a slight limp assisted by a stylish cane. She approached the security desk, which blocked access to the main lobby. Peter got a short confirmation call from Sal and used his burner phone to send TG the 'go' signal.

"May I help you, ma'am?" the uniformed security official asked politely.

"Where should I have my driver park the car?" It was a Mercedes, seized in an FBI drug bust.

"He can stay there if he sits at the wheel," the guard said, glancing at her cane.

"My horse balked at the third jump, I lost my seat," Sally sniffed. "It will heal in time for the Nationals."

"Uh, yes, I see," the guard replied, embarrassed to have been caught looking, like a batter with two strikes. "How can I help you?"

"I understand this company is an expert in AI. I am looking to break new ground in horse training, can I talk to someone?" Sally queried.

"Uh, sales are conducted online only, ma'am," the guard stammered.

"Well, equestrian competitions are not. Now can you find me some-one?" Sally challenged. "I am supposed to walk two miles a day to get this leg back in shape. Any clown can sit at a computer. Why aren't you an AI?" The conversation went back and forth, with no resolution, as Sally had planned it.

"Well, here goes," Lauren said, and she hit the enter key on the laptop. TG had just posted her story of Ted Keller, killer of young women, tech entrepreneur with a black heart, or perhaps no heart at all. She left out the DNA but noted he had flown to Atlanta in the time window of all the murders. She also stated he was hunting her, and certainly would read this post. TG's message to Ted Keller was that his billions, his friends, his tech savvy wouldn't help him, that the soldering iron didn't care.

The response on the site was immediate and dramatic. Ted Keller was a known recluse, had no family, was a tech wizard, worth billions. The viral hue and cry was enormous.

CHAPTER 34

THE BEAST REACTS

TED WAS ON A CONFERENCE CALL. He didn't use Zoom, but something much more expensive and intricate; however, no more reliable. One still had to remember to turn off the mute button. In the upper left-hand corner, a little white box began to flash. Inside were three exclamation points. It was from his patrol AI, and it had never used three before, which meant something big had broken. Ted wrapped up the call as soon as it was politic to do so, and went down the hall to his secure room. He logged in and saw the alert text. His name had appeared in conjunction with the Grundy County murders. It has been posted by TG, the escaped girl imposter, but Ted realized he might have been wrong about that — she was the real thing. He knew the FBI was watching this page, they would be all over him. He could explain the plane flights as coincidence; he flew a lot of places all the time. How did she know he kept the weapons? How had she gotten his name? Painstaking analysis of flight plans? No one could have talked, no one knew it was him. Except TG. She never saw him. Or did she? Had she escaped south, out-tracked Dossett, gotten to a position where she could see him? Then, once she got his name from the flight plans, she could have confirmed by any one of a dozen magazine interviews. Hard copies, no online signature of an image search. That was what had taken the time. She couldn't go to the feds directly; she had murdered Fred Dossett, so she informed them this way. Gave a name and data. Enough for probable cause.

Ted prided himself on his cool, controlled approach to life. He had won many negotiations by appearing detached, as if there was somewhere else he wanted to be. He always did his homework, knew his competitor. He was always steady and assured in social gatherings, not aloof but not approachable either. If he approached you, it was a compliment. But not now. All he heard was his father's voice, loud, yelling at him: he wasn't good enough, he was lazy, he was a failure, and then the beating would begin. His father would yell, 'this is nothing like what the Russians do, nothing like what the Germans do.' His mother would cry but keep her distance. Only Karmia could make his father stop. 'If you need to beat someone, beat me,' she would say, and he would stop. But if she wasn't home, it went on and on. If she left the house, Ted would hide. He'd made a hidey-hole off the back of his bedroom closet, out under the eves. He put in a small TV with an earplug. He would go there, wait it out, knowing that his father was soon to be drinking himself into a stupor.

The past is prologue, as Faulkner said, and Ted's past overrode his present. He panicked and sought to hide. He had gamed this out many times. First, he had to destroy the evidence, the bloody ones from the cutting and piercing weapons, the ballistics on the guns. And the club, she had nearly got him, fought like a hellcat. Then he would take his alternate IDs and head for the Mexican border. His resources were all online, accessible from anywhere. He smiled, with no business to run, he could devote his time to Little Miss. What would she think when he called her 'Karmia?'

He left the secure office after engaging all the security protocols. They could get in, but the thermite charge would go off if the computer was handled in any way but the correct way. No explosion, just a big meltdown that couldn't be stopped with water. No need to secure his office; it would do so automatically if he didn't re-enter and do a log-out within ten minutes. Down the back stairs, elevators were a trap, even though he felt it was far too early for anyone to be coming here. Warrants took time. To his alternate car, an American-made

SUV. He would take the back entrance out, it was closer to the house anyway, and avoid that annoying traffic light on Gabriel. He had plans, and they were working. So far.

Sal had pulled out of the circle to where he could watch the back entrance. He saw the SUV, so nicely described by the reporter, silver with racing stripes. He pinged Sally, then told Peter their boy was on the run.

"I understand, officer, just doing your job," Sally lamented, turned, and walked briskly, still with a limp, out of the main door to where Sal had returned. She got in; the astute observer would have seen she got in the front but had gotten out of the rear door with the driver's help. Only cameras saw, and they weren't astute. Off Sal and Sally went to the back entrance. They knew the way to Keller's house; they parked at the corner of the only street that went to that house and waited, informing Peter and Tom they were in position.

■　■　■

Ted's saferoom was cleverly hidden, but readily accessible, otherwise why have it? The back of the fireplace swung out, and a narrow staircase led down. By now, Ted had enough used weapons to fill two golf bags. He struggled up the stairs with each bag, then went down to get a roller bag that had many necessary items, a 'to-go' bag more sophisticated than what he kept as standard equipment in each of his vehicles. He was a billionaire; he could afford redundancy.

"He pulled into his garage," Tom said with frustration. "What if he has a secret tunnel?"

"To where?" Peter asked. "Relax, he will be back in his SUV in a few minutes and will leave, and then we have him." Peter seemed cold and remote at times, a momma's boy, but he was a pro, very experienced, he knew his game.

"What do we use for probable cause to stop him?" Tom was antsy, maybe it was being in California instead of Tennessee, not on his own turf.

"He will make a traffic violation, everyone does," Peter commented. "Roll through a stop sign, change lanes without signaling, speeding. Not a problem. For us," he added. "Ask any Black driver, like you."

Then garage door opened, the SUV backed out.

"He's running," came from Peter into the phone as they walked briskly back to the rental car.

Ted came down the hill and, of course, rolled through the stop sign. Sal and Sally were a block down the road, they saw Peter and Tom come down the hill behind Keller. It was standard procedure. Sal placed the Mercedes across the road, Peter did the same to the rear, and all four agents came out with guns drawn. They ordered Ted Keller out of the car, and he complied. He had personal experience with what a gun could do to a human body. It was that simple.

CHAPTER 35

IT'S NOT OVER UNTIL IT'S OVER

"SO WE PULLED IT OFF," Tom said with a grin as they flew back to Atlanta the next morning. Sal looked a bit worn; it had been quite a party at the safe house.

"Seems so," Peter agreed. He had handled all the paperwork of a formal arrest, and the transfer of custody to the local FBI office as the charges at this point were entirely federal.

"All done until the trial, and we get called as witnesses," Sal winced the words out. "Pre-testimony review with a federal attorney, no fun."

"Now we go after TG," Tom interjected.

"No, we don't," Sally countered. "TG is a cooperating witness. We cut a deal with her. We admitted she was putting her life on the line. It is in a series of statements we made, either online or on paper."

"This reminds me of the end of the movie, *The Firm*, when the hero negotiates his way out of a pair of concrete boots by becoming the mob's lawyer," Peter complained.

"And your point is?" Sally queried. "We in law enforcement make deals all the time. We got Keller easy because this woman trusted us and went out on a limb for us." She'd done that before, Sally thought.

"Seriously? You want to give her a free pass?" Peter appeared affronted. "Did you see how she tortured that man?"

"She interrogated him, with minimal damage and no gratuitous excess, even though she was entirely warranted to do so," Sally said with a cold firmness. "As I told Tom, I was at Abu Ghraib. I know what true torture looks like."

"She killed him," Sal noted.

"He had hunted her. She had PTSD. Do you really think a jury will convict?" Sally remained calm, but she was forceful, defiant. "The fucking ex-president pardoned war criminals, and you want to put her on trial?"

"OK Sally, I am sold," Tom came to her assistance. "We don't get Fred Dossett's safe-deposit box without TG's help. TG gave it to us gift-wrapped. We don't get Ted Keller as a simple walk-up and arrest on the street without TG's help. Do either of you want to testify about how she helped at *her* trial?"

"What would you recommend, Sally?" Peter inquired.

"I'd recommend we walk away, and we tell her we are walking away," Sally answered. "If you want to waste time and money trying to identify her, and the effort of a trial that will likely be unsuccessful, then involuntary manslaughter, five years probation."

"It is not our decision," Peter countered.

"Yes it is," Tom observed. "It's our investigation. We can close it anytime."

"And leave a murderer out there?" Sal asked, but he was being rhetorical.

"Will she kill again?" Sally asked. "I think not."

"Are you withdrawing from the investigation?" Peter asked.

"Hell no, we are a team, a team I like," Sally countered. "Your problem is that Fred Dossett's murder was a state crime. I don't see the FBI putting in resources so you can have lunch with us in Monteagle." Her last comment broke the tension with laughter and chuckles.

"Actually, Sally, I agree with you. I just need to sell it up the line," Peter smiled. "You just gave me all the ammunition I need."

■　■　■

It was all over the late-night news, 'Grundy County Massacre mastermind caught in California' with all sorts of coverage. Tom had called

Roger Basten and alerted him ahead of time, so he could be sure some of the good publicity splashed over Nashville. Maggie and Lauren already knew, the GHC had had it right away, the code word said it was Sally Quinn who had leaked the news.

"I guess it's over?" Maggie queried.

"I don't know. We did torture and murder a man," Lauren replied.

"We eliminated a beast, and used his death to eliminate a bigger beast," Maggie countered. She glanced back at the monitor; a new post had come up. "Sally Quinn's code word. She says 'the hunt is over for everyone, and I mean everyone' so I guess we are in the clear."

"I am in the clear. I would never have implicated you," Lauren stated.

"So, I guess it is really all over," Maggie sighed.

"I can come back for the fall semester," Lauren said with anticipation.

"What will you use for a thesis project? We lost our field trip to the Bahamas," Maggie noted.

"Does it matter? Just being alive to do a thesis, what a gift," Lauren murmured.

■　■　■

Three days later, Lauren logged on to the GHC site to see what people were saying. There was a code word and note from Lady: 'Excelsior in your box.' What was that all about? Another drive to Atlanta, it looked like. Lauren was tired of road trips. She wanted her own place again. Maggie had been wonderful, but now, with the danger gone, it would get old really quick. Time for a bike ride. Would she ever feel comfortable again, out on her own? Would she always be looking over her shoulder? Maybe a call to Sally Quinn, get into law enforcement, maybe forensics. Surround herself with cops. Being small, everyone could dominate her, men and women. It was what life was for her. Then again, Maggie couldn't have fit into the crevice. Face it, she was alive because of who she was, not because of who she wasn't. It was over; she had not only escaped, she had solved the entire case, killer in jail, bodies recovered, and her life back. It was over. A randomly selected victim had found safety. What was it like to be targeted?

Part Two

IT IS NEVER OVER

CHAPTER 36

THE WAGES OF ADDICTION

KARL WISLOSSTOL WAS A DEAD MAN, and he knew it. He had quite a story to tell, and no one would hear it. Who could he trust, who in his life had not proven to be false? He would miss his role as Neurometer, the voice of behavior for the GHC. That had been short-lived but wonderful, figuring out what made people on the site tick. Especially the mystery lady, the escapee, the 'Twelfth Girl'. He imagined her in his mind, strong yet eerily fine, elfin but powerful. She had courage, had baited Ted Keller into blowing up. Had fooled the best the government could throw at her. He trusted her; he would send his story to her. Even if they found out, she could deal with them. They would fall beneath the power of her thought, the steel courage, the sense of finesse. He stopped, realizing he had slipped from reality into adolescent dreaming. Still, he had time to send a package. Lady would get it to TG; she had done that before. They were coming. They had made that clear. He had been warned he was being hunted from some of his clientele, and thought that destroying everything should mean the hunters would leave him alone. He was wrong, obvious now. He had downloaded it all, now he tapped in a short cover letter that he would send to Lady. He knew who she really was; he admired Rainy because she had personal purpose. He heard banging downstairs. They would find him on the roof. He sent the file, turned off the phone, and threw it as far as he could into the brush behind the house. Then they were there. He was going to try and talk his way out, but they shot him to stop him, then shot him again to be certain he was dead, then they left.

■ ■ ■

"Slowly Carlos, I must fully understand what happened," Nate Follette soothed.

"The man, Wislosstol, is dead," Carlos said doggedly, stumbling over the name in a strong Mexican accent.

"Where is the body?" Nate asked, trying to draw the man out. Carlos was clearly scared; he had completed only one of the two tasks assigned him.

"On the roof of his house," Carlos replied.

"Why did you take him up there?" Nate pursued.

"That is where he was, up on the roof. He must have seen us coming," Carlos explained. "So we shot him, as we were told. Twice."

"Did he have anything on him?" Nate was used to coaching students, but Carlos was really slow.

"Only his night clothes," Carlos answered.

"He was in his pjs?" Nate asked, then waved it off. "Where was his cell phone?"

"We didn't find it," Carlos stammered, now copping to the failed part of the assignment. "We looked everywhere. I know how to hide things. I have stashed drugs in every possible place in a building. We looked everywhere. We looked outside the house, in case he had it in his hand and it slid off the roof. We didn't find it."

There was nothing in the house, Nate knew that fact. He had entered the structure the day before, during working hours, and looked at all the electronics. They had been clean, at least clean of the files Nate had sought. While Carlos had been hunting and killing Karl Wislosstol, Nate had been in the man's office and adjacent lab a mile away. There were burned papers and plastic in a deep sink, and the two computers, one in the lab and one in the office, had been wiped. This outcome was bad; now he only had a rumor and no proof either way about its validity. He didn't understand Wislosstol's actions. He had destroyed mountains of effort where he worked, out of fear, yet he had gone to sleep in his own house, as if it was a fortress of some kind, or maybe he thought they didn't know where he lived. What Nate wanted was probably in the cloud, with absolutely no way to get to it, especially as it was accessed through the man's iPhone. And Apple was extremely good with data security. The phone probably had everything on it; Nate knew he could break into it. His boss had purchased a very expensive but effective program that could determine what a phone's password was. It involved tapping the ID entry circuit, and when the entry comparison was done, sneaking a peak at what was being compared. It required having the phone, of course, but also knowing how to open it up and where to stick the four probes. It was something Russia's GRU had picked up from their internal hacking group. The GRU sold that scheme for money, sold it where its application would most discomfort America. No phone, no hack, no data. Mr. Guterriz would not be pleased. It would be Nate's job to explain the failure. That scene might get awkward.

■　■　■

"You have nothing?" Mr. Guterriz said in his harsh and demanding voice.

"We have no proof of the rumor either way, however, the man at the root of the rumor is dead, so it dies with him," Nate offered.

"Unless a copy is lying around somewhere, or he sent it to a friend, or worse, the U.S. government," Mr. Guterriz could speak without an accent, but when he was angry, it would reappear. It had re-appeared, Nate knew he had to tread carefully.

"We saw no evidence he did that," Nate stated, trying to keep cool.

"You have no evidence he didn't. That is the problem," his boss accused.

"I am looking into what he was doing, trying to reconstruct his work," Nate explained.

"If it stays secret, then we are OK?" Guterriz growled.

"It depends on which type of secret it is," Nate began. Guterriz waved his hand, indicating to go on. "There are inevitable secrets, discoveries that are bound to happen when science has progressed far enough along a particular line of inquiry."

"Give me examples," Guterriz demanded.

"The discovery of radio, or of powered flight. If it hadn't been Marconi or the Wright brothers, it would have been someone else within a few years," Nate continued. "The key in that case is to know it is coming, to be the first to benefit. If you owned a buggy whip factory, you could sell it before Henry Ford was making cheap cars for everyone."

"The other type of secret?" Guterriz asked, now quite calm, accent gone. He liked exploring concepts.

"The random secret, that is discovered by chance," Nate offered. "A good example is a password. If you have been able to see it written down, then you can unlock a computer. Or the code name for a spy. It is possible that Wislosstol made a random discovery purely by accident. It would be very unlikely that anyone else would make that discovery."

"An example, please," Guterriz requested.

"The discovery of penicillin was an accident that happened to occur in a lab where the man who saw his contaminated Petri dish, Dr. Fleming, realized its significance. But no one was looking for penicillin at the time," Nate said.

"So the man is dead, and if he made a random discovery, and it went on to no one, then it has died," Guterriz seemed satisfied.

"True but the central problem remains, many people are looking for the cure, the treatment, which is why you pay me to watch and see how that work is going," Nate continued. "If someone finds a simple and effective way to treat or cure addiction, your drug cartel, and all the others in the world, will collapse."

CHAPTER 37

IT'S ALWAYS A THUMB DRIVE

MAGGIE DROVE AGAIN, Lauren dressed as a teenage boy again, and they were quickly in Atlanta, yet again. Lauren's disguise was partly because no one in their right mind truly trusted law enforcement, and because the word 'Excelsior' in Lady's post indicated that something dangerous might be happening. In the post office, Maggie got in line to buy stamps, and Lauren hung out like a bored teenager. The box was in the Davenport name, and as Maggie turned to leave after getting her stamps, Lauren opened the box and quickly took out the contents, consisting mostly of the junk mail every box got. She followed Maggie out and they walked the three blocks to where the car was parked, cutting through a Starbucks on the way.

"Was all that spy stuff necessary?" Lauren asked, sorting through the pile of advertising circulars on her lap until an envelope appeared with a New York City postmark.

"We can't let down. We don't know what fail-safes Keller had set up were he to be busted," Maggie advised. "This letter from Lady may be an indication of that situation."

"I want it to be over. I get heady from a sense of victory, then I remember all the casualties of this war," Lauren sighed. "I have a letter from New York. Let's see what we got." She opened the envelope with her fingernail, and took out a folded sheet of paper, and the ubiquitous thumb drive. She opened the letter; it was typed. She read it aloud.

TG, I received an e-mail with a large attachment, from a person you may remember, Neurometer. I had known him for a long time, before all the GHC stuff started, and I believe what he sent me to be authentic and true. It came in late at night, with a short cover statement saying he was being hunted and that they wanted his secret research. He had wiped it all except for the file he had attached. He said it was important but very dangerous, and for me to forward it on to you without examination, to help protect me. He said it was nothing to do with Ted Keller, but was something else, something bigger than Keller. I have followed up on the net, and Neurometer, actually Karl Wislosstol, was found shot to death at his home three days ago. I have followed his instructions and not opened the file, let alone read it. I put it on the enclosed drive and deleted it from my machine. I haven't even plugged the drive into a computer to check if the file is truly there. Why he didn't go to law enforcement, I don't know, but he had had a lot of bad experiences with the police in his work with the homeless in San Diego. You may want to avoid getting sucked into this. A man is dead, and the reason why is now in your hands. Below are some code words for future communication. Be safe. —*Lady*

"Jesus Christ!" Maggie exclaimed, loud in the confined space of the car.

"All I wanted to do was break in my hiking boots," Lauren whispered, a quiet counterpoint to Maggie's expostulation. "I get kidnapped, and make the mistake of getting free, saving my life, and ending the plot; and now this — strangers from across the continent sending me their dire problems. I am not the law! I am not some superhero! No one out there even knows my true name. Now what?"

"We have three courses of action open to us," Maggie considered. "First, we do nothing. Second, we send it on to Sally Quinn in Nashville, unopened. Third, we open it, see what is inside, and then decide on option one or two."

"We don't decide what to do ourselves?" Lauren queried. "I mean, what if there is something we could do. What if it is something that the public should know, but that law enforcement wouldn't want the public to know?"

"So, our decision-making process is superior to that of law enforcement?" Maggie inquired. "What if it is how to make a plague virus on your stove top, or a bomb from cold cereal?"

"What if it is the secret for cold fusion, or the cure for cancer?" Lauren countered.

"I know someone in Montgomery who had experience with this sort of thing. Maybe he can help," Maggie suggested.

"Montgomery?" Lauren said, looking confused, then it hit her. "The guy at Alabama Southeast University, the guy who broke open the North Korean plot? You thanked him for his help with your dissertation in your Acknowledgements. I heard that the graduate faculty were scared to ask hard questions at your defense. They didn't want this guy to come looking for them."

"Dr. David Langwonaire, Professor of Geology. He has done some great work on carbonate island caves and their geology," Maggie replied, as if rating a pro-sports draft prospect. "I've been in the field with him, visited him in Montgomery. He is smart, honest, and a person of exquisite character. He will know what to do with this problem."

"You and he are lovers!" Lauren exclaimed, somewhat scandalized.

"We are good friends. How we express that friendship is no one else's business," Maggie mused.

That led to quite a few miles of silence. Lauren was troubled by the ethics of being intimate with a colleague, then realized Langwonaire hadn't been on Maggie's PhD Committee and had no official status at Georgia. He just helped her out in the field. They were adults, professional geologists, it was all between them. Finally, she opened up. "Maybe someday I'll have a friend like that."

"I am very careful, Lauren," Maggie soothed. "I do not date in Athens. No one in the Department does the type of research I do. I go elsewhere for my professional and personal enjoyment."

"What about me?" Lauren asked expectantly.

"My very first graduate student, my chance to impart to someone as a mentor, after so many have mentored me," Maggie said softly, with an earnest tone. "I could have lost you right at the beginning and am so glad to have been there for you."

"I really jumped right into your life, and disrupted everything," Lauren was apologetic and ever so thankful.

"You made a series of difficult choices that day. Hard, life-determining choices, that went far out beyond yourself," Maggie contended. "Killers brought to justice, families given final peace, not a bad day's work."

"So I come back in the fall, and we continue on?" Lauren queried.

"I hope so. I want to show you my islands," Maggie replied.

"But first we need to deal with this situation," Lauren noted.

"We will get advice from a very good source, and see what our path forward is," Maggie concluded. "In the meantime, we don't touch the thumb drive. David told me stories of what can happen in that realm."

CHAPTER 38

DR. DAVID

DAVID LANGWONAIRE SMILED as he looked at his email inbox. An email from Maggie. He hadn't heard from her in a while, and assumed she was getting ready for a field season in the Bahamas. He really liked her — she was worldly-wise, suffered no delusions about people, and yet was funny, warm, and saw him as what he was. She gave him more peace than anyone else, in small doses, never overdoing it, never pressing. She was smart, attractive, personable, and had mapped out her later path in life on her terms. He admired her, a flower in a field of weeds.

She wanted to visit, talk about her upcoming field season, maybe talk about recruiting another graduate student. He wondered how her current student was doing — a learning experience for both of them, he surmised. He replied in the affirmative, as classes were over and he was catching up on research paperwork, manuscripts, as well as thinking about retirement. She said she was bringing dinner for three, that was a hint. She had a guest and wanted David to meet that person. The email ended with 'see you in Damascus,' which was an indicator of possible trouble. Now David sat upright. Ever since his North Korean involvement, he had been caught up in a variety of events that had dealt with potential disasters of a human nature. You get a reputation, he thought, like Leonard Nimoy, you will always be Spock. Then disasters sought you out.

■　■　■

"David, this is Lauren Tammers, my first and so far, only graduate student," Maggie said with delight as they met David on the porch of his house. "Can we go inside?"

"Of course," David replied, holding the screen door open. "Nice to meet you, Lauren. I am sure Maggie has had plenty to say about me." To go straight inside on such a glorious late afternoon meant there was serious business to be discussed.

"Not really. She said you were best understood in person," Lauren answered with sincerity. "I did look you up on your department's website, but just for background. I have read a lot of your work on carbonate island caves." Maggie wanted the interaction to go on, but David turned to her, holding out his hands for the large casserole dish she was holding.

"I expect there are secrets to be shared tonight, which means drinks first," David stated, taking the casserole back into the kitchen. He could tell it was Maggie's lasagna, which meant it would be important secrets: she made the food fit the situation. "Lauren, will it be beer, wine, or a cocktail?" He knew it would be wine for Maggie, beer for him.

"Rum and coke, if you have it," Lauren volunteered.

"Island drink, I like it," David replied, and set to his tasks as the two ladies, without invitation, sat at the kitchen table, creating an intimate, personal environment, suitable for the discussion to come. He had anticipated this situation; his dining room table was unset. He set the drinks representing the three alcohol food groups on the table and sat down. He held up his bottle of beer. "To the presence of ladies in my house. May I meet your expectations."

Well, that's a challenge, Lauren thought as she sipped dark rum in darker cola, strong enough to have an effect, weak enough to let the evening flow. "Dr. Langwonaire, I have a story to tell. It is long and involved, and it does not as yet address why we are here."

Normally, David would have quickly corrected the speaker, saying "call me David," but he recognized there was a protocol here, a need for some simple formality as the story was not for entertainment, but for judgment. He nodded to Lauren but caught Maggie's subtle head movement towards him; Maggie wanted him to just listen.

"It begins with an early morning walk to break in my new hiking boots," Lauren began, as if those boots had been the talisman that put everything in motion. She explained it all. She had it worked out in her head, needed no prodding or corrections from Maggie. It took a second round of drinks for everyone, with the lasagna in the oven on lowest heat, waiting its turn. Lauren got to the news that Ted Keller had been arrested, and she stopped. "I'm hungry," she said, closing out the prologue to this trip to Montgomery.

■ ■ ■

David served out the lasagna. He had a simple salad and some garlic bread on the kitchen table. Lauren switched to water, but Maggie and David kept to their recreational beverages. "You eat while I comment," David stated, not a command but more than a suggestion. Maggie had said few words the entire evening and did not interject now. She had been proximal to all the events; not the center, but in orbit at the very least. She wanted to step back, be an observer, and let a third party, not any part of the current affair, observe and interpret.

"I followed the news of the Grundy County Massacre with interest, as I have done some cave and karst fieldwork up there, so I have that distant perspective available to me," David said after his first bite of lasagna. "Classic Appalachia. Coal is dying out, cheaper minerals are mined overseas, logging is minimal, these people depend on tourists, typical ones as well as eco-tourists, to sustain their communities. It builds resentment, to be dependent on strangers who do not respect your way of life, to get the dribs and drabs of their riches. I can see how Ted Keller could successfully recruit men to do really horrible things."

Lauren wiped her chin as she ate with gusto. "I wondered why those men would do that stuff, the hunting and the killing."

"They partitioned it. They didn't do the killing. They knew, but didn't know the end result," David offered. "They liked the thrill, being in on a secret that no one knew was even a secret. Until you."

"I murdered a man," Lauren said simply.

"So did I, shot him in the side of the head, then violated his person," David replied just as simply.

"For the greater good?" Lauren asked.

"I did it because it was necessary. The good or evil of it is for someone else to decide," David rebutted. "Same for you. It took more courage for you than for me. I had stumbled on to a plot, you had been drawn in against your will."

"So you are OK with my actions?" Lauren queried, a hopeful look in her eyes.

"I am beyond OK, I am impressed. Do what I did," David recommended. "Think of the outcome had you not acted." He turned to fix Maggie with a serious look. "You have been strangely silent, the co-conspirator, drawn into the plot as much as Lauren was. Have you properly reconciled your experience?"

"My perspective is so different from Lauren's," Maggie began. "I have seen more of the world than she, lived through difficult times. Much of what I see that is wrong in the world was because people did not act, did not take the necessary steps, as you called it. I am fine with myself, fine with Lauren. All the criminals have been brought to justice, one way or another."

"You didn't come here for a therapy session. But, if my words help, that's good," David said softly. "So, why are you really here?"

CHAPTER 39

NEUROMETER'S DISCOVERY

DAVID'S QUESTION WENT UNANSWERED as the meal was finished. David cleansed everyone's palette with sherbet, and after a quick kitchen cleanup, they retired to his living room to sit in more comfortable chairs. He leaned forward, an expectant look on his face. It was the appropriate trigger. This time, it was Maggie's story to tell.

"Lauren, as TG, the 'twelfth girl' was a focus of interest on the GHC site, and other sites as well," Maggie slipped into her role. "One of the major participants called himself 'Neurometer,' and he did all this psychoanalyzing of the perpetrators and the victims. TG was, of course, a focus."

"You, yourself, never became a person of interest?" David interjected.

"I was the mythical 'second person' at the interrogation of Fred Dossett; my existence, while suspected, could not be proved," Maggie explained. "I was pretty much ignored, although Neurometer hypothesized I was a loyal follower, an acolyte blinded by TG's brilliance."

"Which is partly true," David supplied.

"Well, I am loyal, she is brilliant, but we consider ourselves a team," Maggie knew David was teasing her. "We have a name for Neurometer, a Karl Wislosstol from San Diego, California. Almost a week ago, he sent an email with a large attachment to Lady, the person who runs the GHC site in New York City. She sent it on to us." Maggie pulled out Lady's letter and handed it over to David, who read it quickly.

"You have the file?" David asked with some urgency.

"Yes, it is here. Lady sent it on a thumb drive," Maggie responded, holding out the drive, which David quickly scooped up.

"Have you inserted this drive into any computer?" David's tone had gone very serious.

"No, we were going to, then I thought about how careful we had been avoiding electronic snooping by Ted Keller, and thought we needed to talk over the situation with someone with greater experience than we had," Maggie responded, as Lauren just watched. "You had warned me about thumb drives."

"Excellent, you made the correct moves by not making any moves but coming here," David was all business, this was an action in the now, the present, not a good story of escapades completed.

"So what do we do?" Lauren became part of the discussion.

"Well, we see what is on this thing, but we do it very carefully, with special equipment," David answered. "A man is dead because of what is on here, if all the commentary is true. What made you come to me, instead of the authorities?"

"Well, there were three choices," Maggie began, and laid it all out, repeating the examples she and Lauren had presented to each other.

"I agree with your assessment, coming here was a good first step," David was calmer, knowing some potential troubles had been avoided by the two women.

"What is next?" Lauren inquired again.

"We go to my secret laboratory in the basement," David said with a false accent; he did an atrocious Bela Lugosi. David's house was in an older part of Montgomery, close to the University, and on high ground so it had a traditional basement that didn't get wet. He had a small lab where he could look at rocks with a 40-power microscope, cut rock samples with a power saw that had a blade for slicing ceramics, and an ultrasonic cleaner. He didn't do lapidary work, but he did photograph his specimens. He also had a closet that he had turned into a faraday cage, with an old laptop computer that ran on a battery. The machine could be completely isolated from any snooping. No electrons in or out, no electromagnetic radiation either. There was a printer/scanner in the tiny room along with a DVD burner. All running off 12-volt DC from truck batteries. At times David thought he had gone overboard, but he was still alive because he took precautions.

"OK, we can all fit in if we don't mind being close," David said, maneuvering to have Maggie between him and Lauren.

"It holds two people, three if you are friendly," Maggie chuckled to ease Lauren a little bit.

David shut the door, turned on the tiny light, and booted up the laptop, which in its day had been a powerful machine, but then so had Eniac. "Here goes," he said, plugging the drive into the USB port.

"What are we guarding against, exactly?" Lauren asked.

"A drive with important or secret information on it may have built-in protections that send a signal when it is opened or cause the file to self-delete if transferred. I am watching for that sort of stuff," David explained. "OK, Windows says there is a really big pdf file in here, just about 350 megabytes. Probably a lot of images, or it is a very long read."

"Are you going to open the pdf?" Maggie queried.

"First, I am going to copy it to the external hard drive," David replied. "I'd also like to print it out, so I have a copy that cannot be electronically eliminated."

"You have to open it to print it," Maggie cautioned. "You can copy it without opening it. What if it won't print, and then self-deletes?"

"We open it and read it as it prints," David decided. He clicked on the file, and it opened. The title said *Treating and Curing Addictive Responses*, and the document was 238 pages long, single spaced with many illustrations. "Hope I have enough printer ink," were David's first words.

"I see why the man was killed, if we assume the title to be factual," Maggie added.

"So we are still hiding?" Lauren inquired.

"If the file transfer to Lady in New York City becomes known, she is in danger," Maggie offered. "If they see she sent it on to us, we are in danger."

"We have two options to stop that from happening," Lauren proposed. "One, we send it to the authorities, or two, we publish it online."

"Or, we do what we did with the Dossett tape: we send it to the authorities saying they have a week to act before the media gets it," Maggie suggested.

"If publicly released, there will be chaos in a number of places," David replied. Next to him, the pages were printing off. No one was reading the screen, and the title page stayed as the only visible sheet. "The drug cartels will go crazy. Their market will dry up and be unrenewable. Alcoholism could diminish, lessening sales. Same for cigarettes, and to a certain extent, some aspects of electronic gaming and electronic media. Lots of upset people."

"My first response is 'too bad for them,' my second is 'how many lives saved and improved?' I think of benefits," Maggie proposed.

"Look at the potential social unrest," Lauren noted. "Everyone with an addiction problem or with a friend or family member with one, will want the treatment, right now, no delays. What are the possible side effects, how much to manufacture, what if it requires fetal tissue?"

"Very good questions, but we are working in the dark," David cautioned. "Let's read the document, see what it says, and determine first is it possible, and second, what do we do?" Next to him the printer cranked on. He pulled out the finished pages, and they read, a page at a time, passing from David to Lauren to Maggie. Three blind mice, but would they have to run?

CHAPTER 40

SPLIT SCREEN

MAGGIE READ THE MANUSCRIPT WITH INTEREST and comprehension. She had a biology degree from her undergraduate days, back when she aspired to become a medical doctor, before she made the misstep of marrying the unlamented Mr. Davenport. The Wislosstol document was an entertaining read in its own right, with a semi-autobiographical introduction that explained the path Karl Wislosstol had taken to get to the situation that led him to explore the biochemistry of addiction. Karl had a younger brother, Kit, born with ACC, or agenesis of the corpus callosum, where the massive nerve tract that connects both hemispheres of the brain is underdeveloped or even absent. The condition was manageable; Kit was able to lead a somewhat normal life although he suffered from seizures and was slow in achieving both motor and intellectual development. Karl had doted on his brother and provided the social insulation that allowed Kit to mature at his own delayed pace. Karl completed an award-winning high school science fair project on Kit's condition; close proximity for years allowed Karl to document the progression of Kit's development, and he had kept a diary. Kit's condition motivated Karl to go to medical school in neurology. He opted for medical school over a PhD in biochemistry as he wanted the legal power to prescribe medications for people with neurological disorders. He had become interested in hallucinogenic drugs for the treatment of depression, PTSD, and addiction, among other maladies.

After graduation and the necessary Residencies, Karl set up shop in San Diego, running a small research institute that explored the behavioral causes of homelessness, specifically if some portion of that population had brain conditions or disorders that predisposed them to the unattached, nomadic lifestyle typical of the homeless condition. San Diego had a large homeless population, the climate allowed outdoor living year-round with less discomfort than in northern cities. He obtained funding from several private foundations, which freed him from numerous government regulations and methods of accountability. His analysis of medical records for a selection of the human subjects he was studying was a tedious chore, as many had no such records, or existing records were old and scanty. He had to build them one by one. In that work, he discovered that eleven of his subjects, out of hundreds, had had a procedure called a *corpus callosotomy*, the surgical severing of the corpus callosum to treat severe cases of epilepsy, where *grand mal* seizure events beginning in one brain hemisphere spread to the other hemisphere with catastrophic results. The procedure was reasonably successful. Karl was, of course, extremely interested in these eleven subjects, as they displayed the developmental difficulties that Kit had shown, but it had been imposed on them, later in life. They had had to adjust to their new neurological situation all at once. For these eleven that Karl worked with, they had not adjusted well and had slipped into society's fringes, surgically predisposed to homelessness.

Karl worked with his homeless patients, most of whom had PTSD, not only from past traumatic events, but in their daily lives. The majority had become addicted to common recreational drugs like opioids and meth. He began to apply specific hallucinogenic drugs, including the standards like LSD and psilocybin, as well as more exotic ones like the simple nitrous oxide and the complex phencyclidine. In the end, his results were mixed and not consistent. He got the best results from LSD, the old standard, but it was the best performance of an overall poor performing outcome. What is the joy in being the best player on a winless team? His results matched what was in the literature, some people had a powerful, positive response, others less or none. Except for his eleven induced ACC patients. They had all showed a remarkable decrease in PTSD symptoms, a lessening of depression, and a complete removal of their addictions. Eleven for eleven sounds impressive, but it wasn't a classic statistically viable sample; he would have needed about thirty cases for that condition to be met. He could not go out and give another twenty homeless people a corpus callosotomy. Ethics aside, he was not about to do neurosurgery, too expensive, too complex, too 'mad scientist'. Then he got to thinking, could he induce an ACC state biochemically? Reversibly? He began to do some literature review.

He discovered a drug that was used to control the phantom pain associated with amputations, which inhibited certain long nerve-cell fibers, called axons, from sending their pain signals back up to the brain, given that the cells that were supposed to originate the pain signal were no longer there; they were in the discarded limb. The drug worked because it was only effective if it was in the axon for some time, so only the long axon pathways from the limb to the spinal cord were affected. Karl reasoned that the longest axons in the brain were those connecting the two sides of the brain, the corpus callosum. If the right dosage of the drug was delivered to the brain, could he induce ACC? If he could induce ACC, could he follow with a psychedelic drug and remove addiction, depression, and PTSD? The blood-brain barrier would be a problem, but he had hopes for using a nasal spray, or perhaps eye drops. In the end, it was an injection along the rim of the eye socket that worked. He could create true brain hemisphere isolation, a mimic for ACC, that would last for hours until the drug was metabolized away. Long enough for the psychedelic drug to perform its magic. Karl wasn't sure of the mechanism of action; he suspected that isolating the hemispheres prevented the neurons affected by addiction or PTSD from talking to each other across the hemisphere gap, and the psychedelic drugs would clean house on each side. He reasoned that the inconsistent results were that the psychedelics worked at different rates in different people on each side of the brain, such that the addictive response moved from one side to the other, taking advantage of the lack of phasing of the biochemical treatment. Isolating the hemispheres, either surgically or biochemically, prevented that action, and the PTSD, depression, and the addiction configuration in those neurons was removed. A treatment, and perhaps a cure.

The second half of the document was all the data, the spreadsheets, the graphs, the procedures. A classic scientific or medical journal write-up of methods and results. Maggie set the last page down; it was closing in on midnight. David had read first, handing each page off as he finished, and Lauren had gone second. Maggie, as the biologist in the group, had gone third so she could subject what she was reading to more analysis. Lauren and David both looked at her. They had been waiting some minutes, Lauren was back to rum and coke, and David had switched to water; he refilled Maggie's wine glass.

Lauren, with the impatience of youth, or rum, came right out with it. "Is it for real, or is this all bullshit?"

"If it is bullshit, it is fragrant and substantive," Maggie answered. "Of course, any good con would be believable on the surface. Let's say that I saw no obvious errors, mistakes, or leaps of faith."

"We should, therefore, act as if it is for real," David stated. "Someone else thought it was real, real enough to kill to stop it. They weren't trying to steal it; they saw this procedure as a threat to their business model."

"So we are next on the list?" Lauren asked, a flash of fear crossing her features.

"If they have a list, our job now is to stay off of that list," David replied.

CHAPTER 41

THE LOST DATA

NATE FOLLETTE HAD A PROBLEM, or rather, the problem was what he didn't have. No firm conclusion on what Dr. Wislosstol had done. He knew that the doctor had been working with homeless people and studying their behavior. All Wislosstol's paper records had been burned in the lab's deep sink; it must have taken some time, but then, these days, most everything was electronic. There were pieces of melted DVD in the sink, what looked like pill bottles, so his backup files and drugs had been torched as well. The two computers were wiped, nothing on his home computer or his laptop. Wislosstol had been well known in the homeless and shelter community, including the people who ran the soup kitchens, the flop houses, and the like. Mostly do-gooder charities with hard working and honest people. Nate had posed as a writer working up a story on the good doctor, so he got a feel for what Wislosstol was doing. The doctor's grant proposals were on record at the public health department, as he was dealing with a public health problem. While Wislosstol had stayed clear of government funding, he had to work with local government officials to get access to his clientele and to provide them with medical services. The Health Department thought he was doing useful work, the police, not so much. They felt he was supplying drugs that would make an on-going problem worse, even as their data showed that where he worked, crime levels by the homeless had gone down. Karl had been threatened with arrest many times, Nate learned. It was why the homeless, and those who provided social services to them, had admired Dr. Wislosstol, even if they thought he was a bit weird.

Nate had gotten word of Wislosstol from Mr. Guterriz, who had reports of decreased drug sales amongst the homeless from his pushers, and that a doctor guy was responsible. It was a fringe market, where they sold dregs and low-quality stuff to a customer base that could not choose to be selective or discerning. Low quality drugs sold by low quality pushers, so Nate had to weigh the quality of those doing the reporting. He had strolled around personally, doing his writer's act, and had determined that Wislosstol was executing something that affected a fair number of the homeless such that they were not buying anywhere near the amount of drugs they had before. The simplest fix was to have Wislosstol killed. But if he had come up with a treatment for addiction, it had huge consequences for Mr. Guterriz and his drug cartel, and by extension, all drug cartels. Nate reported his findings to Mr. Guterriz, and was told to get all the information in Wislosstol's possession, and kill him, preferably all at once. The doctor had a reputation, it could not be a long, drawn-out affair. No interrogation — what would anyone be looking for? No need to alert competitors or law enforcement that Wislosstol was doing anything interesting. So Nate had done a couple of break-ins with help from the ubiquitous Guterriz thugs, and then sent the hit squad to kill the doctor and get his cell phone. Slam bam and done. Except Wislosstol had left no records, they hadn't found his cell phone, and now he was dead.

Nate decided to tip off local law enforcement that Wislosstol was grooming the homeless for the drug business, and that they should see what he had been up to. He was hoping they would investigate Wislosstol's cell phone use, see if he had transmitted anything the night he was killed, look at cell tower records. Maybe spice it up that he was working for the Chinese to create the next COVID-19 virus. Nate decided against that step for now; he waited instead to see what the locals could do. Nate had to be careful, he didn't want law enforcement looking at what the Guterriz cartel was doing. It was like thawing a frozen pipe with a blowtorch, you didn't want to burn the whole house down. Target specificity was the game. He wrote up a note saying that Wislosstol had been planning on using homeless people to run a drug ring, that crimes were down where Wislosstol did his work because the doctor was supplying the people with drugs so they would do his tasks. He wrote that the cops should check it all out, that Wislosstol got the raw drugs from a Chinese source. He used snail mail, making sure the letter and envelope were clean.

■   ■   ■

Tanner Nelson was a new detective, hired from Arkansas because the San Diego police department wanted some different perspectives; promoting from within only increased the level of rot. What they got was a tried-and-true southern white boy, racist to the core, but intelligently so. Black and brown people were inferior he believed, so one had to expect inferior behavior. Women had useful roles, mostly to serve men. He was careful on how he promoted his inner feelings. He knew to play the role of modern law enforcement: sharing and caring cops, protect and serve, and bust asses when necessary, which was usually always. Tanner was a bully, policing to him was legalized bullying. He was also smart and knew use of firearms had to be careful because everything ended up on video these days. The captain gave him the letter Nate had sent, and the file on the Wislosstol case, which had gotten nowhere, and told him it was all his, find out what had been going on.

Tanner read over the file. Wislosstol's body found on the roof after neighbors reported hearing shots. In his pajamas. What the fuck? Nothing stolen from the house which showed signs of forced entry and had been ripped apart. No cell phone found, that was probably stolen, but an iPhone without the password was basically useless, and eminently traceable. His lab had been breached as well, his computers were clean, the hard drives had been reformatted. Some stuff, papers, pill bottles and DVDs, burned in a deep sink. His secretary and his two lab technicians did not have much to say; they kept no notebooks. It all went into the computer. One of the techs was a registered nurse. She helped with the treatments that Dr. Wislosstol employed with the homeless. She didn't know what the chemicals were, they were all locked in a safe-like storage cabinet which had been found opened when they came into work the morning after Wislosstol's death. It was empty; no drugs, no chemicals. Only the doctor had the combination. The secretary kept a log of when the doctor was in or out of the office, but he rarely gave a destination. "The homeless are where you find them" he said many times, the man reported. The secretary was gay, which riled Tanner, but it made no difference. There was nothing about the office that would prove or disprove the snitch letter. Wislosstol kept his work close to his vest. His employees, now all looking for another job, could not give a coherent expression of what the doctor had been working on. They all said that the people he treated got better.

The specificity of the information destruction in the office and lab pointed to an inside job. Whoever had broken into Wislosstol's house had been looking for something, the place had been torn up. Not so with the office and lab; a completely different hand had been at work there. Tanner moved up from a rough street cop in Little Rock to become a detective because he had become tired of beating up suspects as he got older, and he liked solving puzzles and mysteries. He had one now. He decided to give it a true effort. He had Wislosstol's cell phone number. He would start there.

CHAPTER 42

BREAKFAST

DAVID COOKED FRENCH TOAST AND BACON for breakfast. He and Maggie had slept apart the previous night; the topic at hand did not create a sensual mood, and Lauren seemed unsure about that relationship. David ate his French toast plain, only butter, which pooled like a lake atop each slice. Maggie opted for maple syrup; Lauren took fresh blueberries. Coffee assisted each of the women in meeting the day. David had his 'English Breakfast' tea. The kitchen table commentary was mostly about the food. They all were intent on enjoying the moment, waking up, deferring the serious stuff for later. After clean-up, they again moved on to the living room, and the day's work.

Lauren was impatient, she with the longest part of her life to live; David and Maggie, who could see the end in the distance, were more appreciative of savoring the present.

"So, what should we do?" Lauren began the process of reaching a decision.

"I'd like to hear what you think should be done. You have shown excellent decision-making skills," David rejoined.

"I have shown fast decision-making skills, in a situation where speed was the key," Lauren answered. "I keep thinking I am tired of danger, of powerful forces looking to find me, and then dispose of me. Then I think of my cousin Jack, addicted to opioids, and all that my aunt and uncle have done to try and rescue him. At least he hasn't OD'd yet. This Wislosstol discovery could cure him, and millions of others."

"So, we just send it to Lady and tell her to put it out on the web," Maggie replied. "Then we go home. Or send it to Sally Quinn, or *The Washington Post*, or whatever."

"You have a problem similar to your initial abduction conundrum," David began. "To have Maggie's plan work, you need to make the public, and the authorities, take this discovery seriously, realizing that vast forces are arrayed against this finding, and a major effort will be made to discredit the addiction treatment. I expect the depression and PTSD aspects will face little resistance."

"In other words, we need to capture, interrogate, and kill a major drug lord, taping it all, of course," Lauren interjected.

"Well, it worked the last time," Maggie added.

David decided to play along. He had another idea, but he would see how these ladies advanced their idea. Maybe they had developed a taste for vigilantism. "Tell me how you would do it, tactically?"

"Blackmail or extortion," Lauren was quick to answer. "Say we have the data, we want to sell it, and set up a meet, then bust the boss."

"Too obvious," Maggie countered. "Too hard to pull off. Any big-time boss would send an underling and provide muscle to take what we had and keep his money."

"I agree with Maggie's assessment," David advised,

"Yeah, on second thought, too direct, too much we can't control," Lauren responded. "How about we let little things leak out, make them send their best man or woman to track us down, let them think they are in control, and that we are oblivious, then we snap the trap shut and the soldering iron gets more work?"

"I like that approach much better, think we can get that cabin in Grundy County again?" Maggie was obviously not concerned. "What about you, David, you have been involved in all sorts of clandestine operations, what would you do?"

"I would do my homework and find out what agencies and companies were working on the addiction problem and set them up to believe the document we have is real," David answered.

"How does one 'set them up' so they act on the information?" Maggie queried.

"Pose online as a Chinese refugee who worked in a military lab in China where they wanted to control addiction, so they could induce it to create loyalty to the state," David replied, smiling.

"To control addiction, you need to know how to turn it off so you can turn it back on as you like," Lauren said with admiration.

"If you approach select entities, you can have them all working on it simultaneously; this process needs to get out to the medical community," Maggie argued. "If a person's leg had been chopped off, you don't stand around and debate which brand of tourniquet to use."

"How many drug overdoses will occur while this plan works itself out? How many PTSD or depression suicides occur?" Lauren asked. "We need to move on this."

David remembered his discussion with Molly back in Langley when the North Korean affair had wrapped up. He had told her about the Superman problem, how even Superman couldn't save everyone, all the time. A lot of people could be saved here, as many as would have died in North Korean-caused nuclear explosions, more than would have died in China by the planted virus. He saw with clarity that this was a cusp, a moment to act. "I agree, we need to act."

"Because?" Maggie gave David a thoughtful look.

"Because we can," David replied evenly. "If not us, who?"

■　■　■

Karl Wislosstol's financials were routine, Tanner determined. He paid himself well off his grants and contracts; it looked like he did his taxes honestly. Actually, he had an accountant service do them for him. Never married, no dependents. Parents and a couple of siblings, all clean. No problems with his employees. No evidence of an angry patient, a jilted lover, family disharmony, gambling debts, or the myriad of other reasons people get worked up and shoot someone. Not likely a random home invasion; the degree to which the house had been ripped up spoke of a determined search for something specific.

Tanner was working up a plausible scenario. Wislosstol had been working on something that was important to somebody. That person wanted what Wislosstol had, and that person didn't want anyone else to have it. Wislosstol knew he was in trouble, and he knew the reason why. So he destroyed all his work, maybe to convince those after him that it was done, over, to leave him alone. That attitude, stupid as it was, would explain why he didn't think they would come for him at his house. Well, he had certainly found out he was wrong. So why the roof? No way the intruders took him up there to kill him; it was obvious he was shot there, as the second shot had been a through and through into the roof while Wislosstol lay on the shingles. No blood trail leading to the site on the roof, so he wasn't fleeing active pursuit — he had gone up there for a reason. To buy time, to do something. Tanner had Wislosstol's cellphone number, but it was a dead line, the phone was turned off. Tanner might be a hick from Arkansas, but he understood cell phones. Wislosstol had done something with the phone, that was why he was on the roof. He needed time, not to call for help, it couldn't reach him soon enough. He had sent his secret project to someone. That item would be the key to why he was murdered.

CHAPTER 43

OPENING MOVES

"DO WE STAY OR HEAD BACK?" Lauren asked Maggie when David excused himself for a minute.

"In other words, do we hand this mess off to David and go on our merry way, or do we assist him to get the discovery out where it can do some good?" Maggie inquired.

"Either way, you are both still in danger," David said, walking back into the living room. "If someone in San Diego figures out Wislosstol sent his work to a trusted destination, then the pressure will be on, and they might come after you."

"Lady doesn't know who we are, other than we are within reasonable driving distance of Atlanta," Lauren contended.

"We haven't acknowledged to her that we received the letter," Maggie noted.

"So a file was sent to Lady, and she is identified," David proposed. "The hunter merely looks over the logs for the GHC site and finds her P.O. Box number, knows she is in New York City. That will simplify running down her IP address."

"She doesn't know where we are or who we are," Lauren protested.

David went on as if Lauren hadn't spoken. "Soon, you get a post with the Excelsior code word pleading with you for help, saying that they have Lady and demanding the file back on pain of her death."

"Won't work, they will kill her anyway," Lauren said with a flat tone. "She's dead as soon as they identify her."

"We can send her a warning, including that we are severing all communications with GHC so as to protect both sides," Maggie suggested.

"Then she dies, and you won't even know," David rebutted. "If she contacts you for help, it tells you how far the San Diego threat has advanced. Lady's best defense is to go to the authorities right now, explain what she knows, and file an official report as there is an active murder case on the west coast, and she knows something about it. Make her too toxic to be approached."

"That is what TG tells Lady to do," Lauren stated. "Why would anyone take Lady seriously?"

"I can help there, I know people who will convince the New York City Police Department to take Lady's story and her threatened state seriously," David said.

"Would it also help if she told this entire story on the GHC site?" Maggie queried. "It might immunize her against any action, especially as everything will be out in the open — public knowledge."

"It will also give a scent to all those conspiracy buffs who read the site," Lauren answered. "We might get some investigative help, backdoor stuff."

"Who do you think killed Wislosstol?" Lauren asked. "I mean, not the actual killer or killers, but who ordered it, who went after him?"

"I suspect a drug kingpin in San Diego," David replied. "My question is how did he, or she, find out what Wislosstol was doing?"

"You say you know people. Can they find out what the police investigation on that murder has turned up?" Maggie asked.

"If it's a drug cartel involved, they probably have a source inside that police department. The cartel would know before my sources could tell me," David admitted.

= = =

Nate Follette had gotten a message from the boss. He was notified by his source in the San Diego Police Department that the Wislosstol case had been assigned to one Tanner Nelson. Nate talked with some of Guterriz's street enforcers about Detective Nelson and got the picture of a self-assured tough guy who really didn't like Hispanics. A guy somewhat isolated because he was from Arkansas and some thought he had been brought in to spy on his fellows, sort of an Internal Affairs rat. That meant if he were knocked off, fewer people would care. It all depended on how good this guy was. If he was somewhat incompetent, he wouldn't find out anything worthwhile, so Nate would let him thrash around uselessly on the case. If he was very good, and turned up something valuable, Nate would first find out what it was, and then eliminate him. For now, Nate had lots of other things to do. Mr. Guterriz would enjoy letting the detective do Nate's work for him.

■　■　■

The cell tower nearest Wislosstol's house had handled a contact from Wislosstol's phone mere seconds before the timing of the shots the neighbors had subsequently reported, Tanner determined. It had been a text, not a voice call, and it had handled a huge, attached file. So there it was: Wislosstol hears the people break into his house, he flees up to the roof to buy time, and maybe to be certain of a good connection. He gets his message away, and then he gets shot. Just like in the movies, that Star Wars scene, send the file and die.

So what happened to the cellphone? It had taken the police fourteen minutes to reach the scene, 'shots fired' not being an unusual call, and commonly not correct. With time enough only for a quick search, the thugs took off when they heard the siren. The fact that they delayed their departure, as one neighbor reported a car rushing away after she had heard the siren herself, indicated they had been looking for something, likely the cell phone. The phone was dead, dead before Wislosstol was shot, if the timing was accurate. He had turned it off. Then he hid the phone, on a roof? No chimney to drop it down onto a closed damper. It hadn't slipped out of his dead hand and fallen off the roof — that would be an easy find. Had he thrown it? Tanner looked up Wislosstol's obituary, and it sprang at him. Wislosstol had been a starting pitcher on his high school baseball team. He could have thrown a phone quite some distance. His house backed up on a brush-covered hillside. Time for a road trip.

Tanner was working alone; the Chief had not yet assigned him a partner, and felt he didn't need one for this case, cold as it was. Tanner understood the Chief was probably having a hard time getting one of his suspicious co-workers to agree to buddy with him. Too bad for them, he had snorted. He had done a lot of solo work in Arkansas. It made beating up a suspect easier, as there was no one to gainsay his story of fierce resistance that had required the sternest of measures. He parked in the driveway of Wislosstol's house, ducked under the fading yellow police tape, and walked around the house. The crime scene investigators mentioned a lot of indistinct footprints around the home, especially the far end, which agreed with the idea that the assailant or assailants had looked for the phone.

Wislosstol had come up to the roof from a hatch in the attic crawl-space, which was at the driveway end of the house. His body had been found at the far end of the roof, so he had climbed up and out, and scuttled along the peak of the roof to the end, where he had sent his message and been shot. And perhaps had thrown the phone. Tanner followed Wislosstol's path, and he stood where a chalk outline displayed the configuration of the body. Tanner had seen such outlines on a roof before, on city buildings, but not on asphalt shingles on a sloping residential house roof. The front of the house had a lawn that ran to the street — a bad place to throw a phone. The phone wouldn't have been thrown back towards the driveway. Wislosstol had come to this far end by choice. Tanner scanned the grassy backyard, which was narrow and quickly turned into a fairly steep, brush-covered slope. The phone was thrown into that wild stuff, Tanner decided. It was maybe a hundred feet or more. It would be a long search, too, based only on a hunch.

CHAPTER 44

TENDRILS

RAINY, AKA LADY, LOOKED AT THE POSTING and was immediately concerned. It was TG, based on the code word she had put on her note. That confirmed successful transmission of the thumb drive, and whatever was on it. It was an interesting line of text.

> Some stories deserve to be told to the authorities. This is
> one of them, it may feel incomplete, but they will find it
> interesting. Manus.

Manus was the code word; it was TG, but she hadn't signed it herself. Rainy knew she didn't know much about Karl's information, but TG thought she could be in trouble anyway. This was an inoculation against whoever had killed Karl. If that person came here for her, and the police were ready, she would be safe and then it would be a step forward to not only solving Karl's murder, but dealing out retribution to his killer. Rainy respected TG totally; she also saw the common sense of it. She sat down to compose a letter explaining her role in Karl Wislosstol's murder. She knew law enforcement already had TG's P.O. Box number in Atlanta. Sally Quinn had done that. She wished Sally was in New York now to help her with this. Rainy felt a little fear creeping in. Karl was dead, sprawled on his own roof. The Neurometer gone. She had a job offer in Denver. Maybe she should go west, but only part way.

■   ■   ■

"David, how nice of you to call. Do you have more fucking geologists for me to deal with?" Sal said, laughing.

"Hello Sal, I cannot go into details," David responded. "I have some information concerning the murder of a medical doctor in San Diego a week ago, a Dr. Wislosstol. Take a look at the case, and then call me back."

"San Diego is a long commute from Montgomery, what are you up to?" Sal queried. "This is serious, no joke?"

"As serious as fingerprints rolled in blood," David answered, referring to the case where he and Sal had first met, and David had decked him with one punch. "It is serious, lives are at risk. Take a look and think about who you know on the New York City police who can be trusted with a confidential source."

"Are you then going to send me to Fargo, so that we have the whole country covered?" Sal asked, laughing again. "No, I got it, I'll do a check and get back to you."

"I very much appreciate it," David replied. "Say hello to Peter for me."

In less than a half hour, Sal called David back. "OK, I see; could be a drug hit, seems to be a cold line of inquiry, but there is a detective working the case, a southern guy, Tanner Nelson, just hired from Arkansas. What is this all about?"

"I have information that a woman in New York City, who has an internet handle called Lady, had received from Dr. Wislosstol a packet of information mere moments before his death. She sent the packet onwards, and did not open it, so she doesn't know what it is, except that it must be valuable. I feel she is in danger should that call from Wislosstol ever be traced to her. She has been sent a message to take her story to the New York City police. I need you to tell your contact to take her story seriously, and that she may need protection."

"You are an honest-to-God fucking geologist, David," Sal exclaimed. "There is only one reason you would know something about an internet personality named Lady in New York City."

David suddenly realized that Sal was informed about the Grundy County Massacre, which made sense. "That may be so, and we can talk about the why later, right now I need to be sure not only that this lady called Lady is protected, but that you realize any approach made to her by an assailant may give you the perpetrator of Dr. Wislosstol's murder."

"I think we have a lot to talk about. For now, let your source know we aren't looking for her," Sal replied.

"Sounds good, I am developing other information at my end, and will keep you informed," David responded. "This came to me; I didn't go looking for it."

"Bees and honey, or flies and shit, your choice," Sal said with a chuckle, and the call ended.

■　■　■

"I called a guy I know in the FBI, he seemed to know who Lady was, that she is associated with the Grundy County Massacre," David confessed to the two women. "Therefore, my warning to him about Lady's danger indicates I have contact with who he knows as TG."

"Well, that's just great," Lauren said, staring away to her left.

"I assume we need to leave right away," Maggie stated.

"He said I was to tell my source that they aren't looking for her," David backpeddled.

"You trust the FBI?" Maggie pounced. "The TG case is still active."

"I trust Sal Munoz with my life," David countered, realizing than he had said the name out loud, and this was not his intention. The ladies had him rattled, and for good reason.

"Sal Munoz?" Lauren shrieked. "He was one of two FBI agents on the investigation team into the Grundy County Massacre, he and Peter Comstock. I should have mentioned that in my tale last night."

"I know Peter extremely well, and trust him completely, also," David again backfilled. "If they are not looking for you, then the FBI is not looking."

"Fine, but what about Sally Quinn and Tom Stass, from the Tennessee State Police?" Lauren fumed. "They worked with Munoz and

Comstock, thick as thieves those four were. The FBI doesn't need to do anything but tip those two off."

"And you know this how?" David queried.

"From the GHC site, run by Lady," Maggie replied.

"The same site you were planning to use to help smoke out Wislosstol's killer?" David asked. "This isn't all a coincidence?"

"It is to some extent, David," Maggie proposed. "Wislosstol, as Neurometer, was a major player in the online analysis and conjecture about the Grundy County Massacre. He wrote extensively about the skills and character of TG. He was clearly enamored with her. He is in a crisis and wants to send his life's work to safety before that life ends. He warns Lady of the danger, and says send it on to TG, the wonder girl, who will not only make his data safe, but who will avenge him."

"It all makes sense. Wislosstol is linked to Lauren through the Grundy County Massacre," Maggie added. "It is not fate or coincidence, it was a planned event. What we didn't know," Maggie continued, looking over at Lauren, "was that your contact at the FBI would be involved in the Grundy County case. That is the coincidence."

"Well, here we are. What now?" Lauren inquired.

"First, I call Sal and tell him to keep the Tennessee State Police off this Wislosstol thing, to keep the Grundy County Massacre out of play," David suggested.

■　■　■

Sal looked over at Peter. "That was David, following up on what we were discussing, urging us to not tip off the Tennessee State Police about his contact with someone who must be TG."

"Sally Quinn would carve me with a soldering iron if we told anyone over there what we now know," Peter said, with some seriousness. "David was OK with your response?"

"I think so, I am interested in this Wislosstol case," Sal stated. "The connection to TG is obvious, the guy is in trouble, and as Neurometer, he calls on his superhero."

"Well, she didn't save him," Peter scoffed.

"She may have saved his life's work, and she may have set in motion the payment in full for the taking of that life," Sal rebutted.

"Fine, then what is it about the Wislosstol case that intrigues you?" Peter queried.

"There is a rumor out in the homeless population of San Diego that Dr. Wislosstol could fix your problems, make you a complete person again," Sal answered.

"Pass out drugs to druggies, and you are God," Peter mused.

"I have an old acquaintance who runs a shelter down near the docks, so I called him about this doctor, and got only good stuff," Sal continued. "He also said that another guy was nosing around, asking about the good doctor, said he was a writer doing a story on the man. My contact said he thought the guy worked for the local cartel."

"Was Wislosstol handing out drugs, costing the kingpin some business?" Peter was now more interested. He hated drug lords.

"I doubt it. Maybe he came up with a therapy or treatment for addiction, that would piss off a drug kingpin," Sal speculated.

"Then both Lady and TG could be in big trouble," Peter replied.

"That is why they went to Dr. David Langwonaire, the world's leading fucking geologist," Sal smiled.

CHAPTER 45

PHONE HOME

IT WAS HOT, but Tanner was used to hot. San Diego was a few degrees latitude farther south than Little Rock, but the heat was not oppressive or muggy. It didn't beat on you and suck your energy away; it just reminded you that you were going to sweat. And sweat he did, working his way through the brush in a grid pattern on the steep hillside, searching for the mythical cell phone of Dr. Karl Wislosstol. It took over an hour, he was patient, not in a hurry, and he had started early, but he found it, and bagged it with all the evidence protocols that were required. He couldn't access it, of course, and he had to check it for prints to confirm it really was Wislosstol's phone, but finding it confirmed the scenario he had worked up, of a man cornered and trying to keep his life's work out of the hands of a drug kingpin. Tanner retreated to the comfort of his air-conditioned vehicle after brushing off dust and debris and stared at the clear plastic of the evidence bag as the car engine idled. He jotted down all the information available, which wasn't much; like most people, Wislosstol had put a protective cover on the phone, so serial number and similar information was not directly available. He did measure its dimensions, and sketched its configuration, camera lens position, etc. He also took the phone carefully out of the bag and made a minute mark on the face of the phone, in the upper left-hand corner, a habit to make certain he would know this phone in the future. He had been caught in court once, on the stand, testifying as to the owner of a cell phone not knowing the defense attorney had made a switch. The judge had berated the attorney after Tanner had blithely said it was the correct phone and had then been exposed, but Tanner learned a lesson.

Tanner took the phone straight to forensics to get the fingerprints lifted. They proved to be a match for Wislosstol. He left the phone with forensics to let them remove the cover and log all the data on the back of the phone. He sent an e-mail to the Chief reporting his finding of the phone, and his scenario of what had happened to Wislosstol. He then decided he should go back to the dock area and talk to a few of Wislosstol's patients, to see exactly what had been done to them.

■　■　■

Nate got a text from Guterriz, it only said 'phone found', which sent both a chill and a thrill through Nate. Nate texted back 'where is it?' and assumed the police had somehow recovered it. He did not get an answer right away, which probably meant Mr. Guterriz was scheming to acquire the phone. If it hadn't been found by chance, but as the outcome of a purposed search by the police, then Detective Nelson was more capable than initially thought. That, too, was an important data point, as separating the phone from the police would need to be carefully done to keep that man from sniffing out the importance of the phone. Nate suddenly stiffened. If the detective had sought to find the phone, then he must have already felt it had unusual value. This Nelson guy saw what had been done at Wislosstol's lab, had examined the crime scene, and had realized there were secrets in the wind. Where had the phone been found? It should be on the evidence bag, part of the chain of custody procedures. A deliberately hidden phone was a signal of secrets hidden, an accidentally lost phone carried no such import. As Nate pondered all the implications and side trails, his phone pinged with a text. 'See me' from Mr. Guterriz.

■　■　■

Nate entered the private office from the side door, unseen by the clerical staff of Canyon Imports, the business front of Mr. Guterriz, after being escorted up the back stairs, and frisked, of course. Nate thought frisking stupid; he could think of a few ways to kill the man as he sat behind his immense desk — poison, for one. One look told Nate all he needed to know, a cell phone sat alone on the desk, looking small on the extensive flatness of that piece of furniture.

"Do the authorities know you have this?" Nate asked, trying to determine if the phone was here for good or merely visiting.

"My source was able to switch it out with an identical model, so we have time to play," Mr. Guterriz gloated.

"Is it enough that we have it, or do we try and get inside it?" Nate queried.

"It was found behind Wislosstol's house up on a bushy slope, or so said the evidence log," Guterriz responded. "What do you think?"

"I think he sent something from the phone, then turned it off and threw it into the bushes behind the house," Nate replied. "That is why he fled to the roof."

"The search for the phone indicates that Detective Nelson also figured that out," Guterriz proposed.

"He can't legally open the phone, and with the two phones now switched, it doesn't matter," Nate advised. "What is on the substitute phone?"

"Nothing, it was completely cleaned," Guterriz answered.

"Not good. Why turn off and throw a phone that is blank?" Nate asked rhetorically. "Nelson will see that as a problem if he can defeat the password."

"Perhaps, but still, he sees nothing. He doesn't know what Wislosstol was doing," Guterriz contended. "However, you need to break into the phone we have here and find out what Wislosstol was doing, yes? Is the secret random or determinative?"

"Of course. We can't plan if we don't know what is on the phone, and we need to know if he went on the roof to send a file somewhere," Nate agreed. "I can have Alexa assist?"

"Obviously, but keep your hands off her," Guterriz said, and both men laughed. Alexa was over fifty, obese, and now in a perpetual state of anger over the use of her name as an artificial intelligence moniker by Amazon. She was very, very good in all aspects of IT work; she would get into the phone, and then she would track what it had done.

CHAPTER 46

PARTS IN MOTION

RAINY HAD COMPOSED HER LETTER and sent it to NYC Detective Carla Conyors as Sal, through David to TG, had recommended, suggesting a meet at a coffee shop a few blocks from Rainy's apartment. The recognition symbol would be a copy of the book *Lean In* by Sheryl Sandberg. The meeting went well, especially as Sal Munoz alerted Carla to the excellent work that Rainy, as 'Lady', had done in the Grundy County Massacre issue. The result was that Rainy felt she was covered, and so informed TG.

■ ■ ■

"Well, that is a loose end potentially wrapped up," Lauren said after receiving Lady's post. "I understand, no guarantees but we have improved the situation."

"I hope so, because if we are going to taunt the beast, we need be ready," Maggie responded.

"Have you decided how you will do that?" David inquired. "More importantly, have you decided what you will do when the cartel comes after you?"

"Soldering irons, the ultimate tool for interrogation," Lauren replied. "We will induce the San Diego person to read up on the Grundy County Massacre."

"What she means, is we will have Lady publish a piece on Neurometer and his identity as Karl Wislosstol, and about how TG was the person

212

he most admired and trusted. That will put our guy on the scent. Once he is sniffing, we will do a *Cool Hand Luke* and pepper his nose." Maggie came across as triumphant.

"I expect he will subcontract," David rejoined. "These guys do each other favors all the time, especially when all are threatened at once. It will be hard to track, hard to pick up. It isn't one crazy guy with a lot of money, like Keller, but an international organization."

"We have to choose between releasing the addiction treatment, or avenging Karl Wislosstol?" Lauren asked.

"True revenge for Karl is getting his treatment out to the world," David admonished. He was trying to keep these two people under control while he worked with Sal and Peter to disseminate Wislosstol's procedure.

■ ■ ■

"So how do we play this?" Peter asked.

"We don't know if the procedure actually works. We only have what David said he read," Sal noted.

"Are we going to give him a contact list he will approach as this Chinese refugee?" Peter continued his query. "Why the multiple entity approach, both private and governmental?

"Yes, to the first part of your questions," Sal answered. "The only way to make certain this idea doesn't get squashed is to disseminate it widely to entities that compete in a variety of ways, politically, socially, and economically. I'll do the Chinese approach."

"The Chinese will hear about it. How will they respond?" Peter asked.

"They literally won't know what to do," Sal laughed. "First, they have to determine if they are actually doing what my straw man says. Then they have to decide if they want to claim intellectual property, which is fraught with problems, weaponizing addiction, holding back a critical medical cure. They can't prove it is theirs anyway. If they do, you know David will drop the truth on them like a bomb."

"You see this as more than avenging a man's death or curing addiction. You want to stick it to our international adversaries as well," Peter complained.

"You have a problem with that?" Sal inquired.

*　*　*

Alexa looked up from her laptop with a smile. To her side was Wislosstol's cell phone, cover and casing off, four tiny hair-like probes linked into the circuitry.

"How does it work?" Nate asked, he was good at programming but bad at electronics.

"You can't actually probe the chips, but when you punch in your four-digit password, or use a photo or a fingerprint image, you begin with a circuit that you can actually isolate. So, suppose you enter a four-digit number, the actual true password, let's say 4718. The circuit can either be set up to approve each number as it is entered, or all four at once. If you do it as each number at a time, and the first number is wrong, you can't have the phone say 'incorrect password' as it would make it easier to iterate your way in. So, you have the phone compare the entire four number signal at once. When you do that, you get what I call a 'circuit ghost,' a bleed-back of the actual comparison process, and if you are carefully sensing the input port, you can see what was compared. Bingo, you are in. And Bingo, I am in."

"What is the pass code?" Nate was eager.

"Why I told you, 4718, probably his high school gym locker combination."

"So we are in. Can you tell me what he did on the night he lost the phone?" Nate queried.

"The night you had him shot?" Alexa asked. Nate was naïve if he thought she didn't know everything.

"Yeah, well, OK, yes," Nate stumbled.

"It will take some time. I am in the phone, but I don't know how he organized his files, and if he put in any other safeguards," Alexa replied. "But you can tell my little brother I have it all under control and to be patient."

*   *   *

Tanner was stunned when his forensics IT team said the phone was locked. Tanner had gotten the phone's password from the gay secretary, who had been told to memorize it, never write it down. The man had not told Tanner initially because he thought it was private or protected under some sort of privilege. Tanner had only asked as he met with the man again to check up on who Wislosstol had worked with at the soup kitchens and flop houses. He had just asked, sort of offhand. Then when the secretary had shown resistance, he had gone and obtained a warrant. He gave the 4718 string to the IT team, and the phone had not opened. He then asked to see the phone, and there was no mark in the upper left-hand corner of the screen. He knew the phone had been switched out, but he gave no sign. Not a surprise that the cartels had an inside person. They probably knew all about Tanner's work. He would have to watch his back, but he also wanted to find the mole. It wasn't some custodian, it was someone with real access, a fellow cop.

CHAPTER 47

THE CIRCUS HAS THREE RINGS

SAL BEGAN THE LEAK PROGRAM. He set himself up as Bo Huang, a technician at the Academy of Military Science in Beijing, who had fled China by way of Hong Kong when his work with the COVID-19 coronavirus came under direct supervision. Huang had only been looking at the neurological consequences of the disease, he knew nothing of the origin or epidemiology of the virus, but he did notice the neurological effects were like a military-grade virus he had once been working on. When he noted that fact to his superiors, he could sense he had stepped into an area he should not have gone. His current main line of work was on addiction and how to use it to control human behavior, which meant controlling the process. Fearing the hyper-paranoid government would want to silence anyone who could deliver even a germ of truth about a Chinese-manufactured origin of the virus, he decided to take his addiction notes and flee. Huang's actions were so rapid and so complete that he was gone before his superiors had even reached a decision on his situation. Now he had a secret to peddle, and he would bargain for both his safety, such as asylum in the United States, and a bundle of cash so he could enjoy that asylum in splendid comfort.

"So, what do you think?" Sal asked Peter as he related his scheme with the fake Bo Huang.

"You should be writing *Tom Clancy* spy novels," Peter responded. "It's creative, I'll give you that. You had him flee to Hong Kong, then where did he go?"

"To Thailand, posing as a person who wants to do a gender transition, that will give him cover to look furtive and a bit scared, but not unusual" Sal answered.

"How will you host his emails?" Peter queried.

"Glenn helped me out. There is an operative in Thailand they use to mask email IP addresses. His new position gives him the authority to approve such an operation," Sal responded.

"I miss Molly. Do you know what she is doing after that Texas affair blew up her job?" Peter asked.

"Well, she is pregnant, so the term 'affair' seems appropriate," Sal replied, "and enjoying retirement in far western Kentucky."

"I don't understand that at all," Peter mused. He moved on. "So who will get the emails; Pfizer, Moderna, CDC?"

"Actually, I will approach drug companies not associated with the COVID-19 vaccine, companies hungry for both the good profits and good publicity those rivals have achieved," Sal explained. "On the government agency side, DEA of course, but not the CDC or Homeland Security, their plates are full. Veterans Administration, they are always looking for good news, as is Housing and Urban Development."

"Won't that look too targeted for a simple lab tech from Han China?" Peter inquired.

"These guys all compete, they silo and don't cross talk." Sal replied. "Does Macy tell Gimbles?"

"Who is Macy, some undersecretary?" Peter queried.

"An expression my grandmother used to use about two big department stores in New York City, big competitors once," Sal laughed.

"How much information will you release?" Pete inquired.

"That is the tricky part. I am putting a straw man in front of my straw man, an international patent attorney who does contract work for the CIA, Glenn suggested it," Sal stated. "If someone is truly interested and begins a little background work to check for a scam, they will see that the attorney communicates with this address in Thailand."

"And if they penetrate that cover and get to you?" Peter challenged.

"Then they have stumbled onto a federal counter-espionage case and will be asked to continue their negotiations as we feel the process is legitimate," Sal smiled. "In fact, that is what I would like to have happen, as it will indicate to us how serious any of these entities are about the process and allow us to provide a third-party validation."

"OK, I see it, maybe this approach will work," Peter was buoyant; addiction reversal, what a social and medical advance.

Alexa had a big smile on her big face. "I have a surprise for you," she beamed as Nate settled into the chair across from her desk.

"You know what Wislosstol sent?" Nate asked eagerly.

"Both times," Alexa dropped that statement like a hand grenade under Nate's butt.

"He sent the file to two different places?" Nate was initially surprised, then understood redundancy had value.

"No, he sent two different files to two different locations," Alexa responded, swelling up with pride. She so wanted to prove her value to her little brother, the big money man.

"All right, you have had some fun with me, tell me what you've got," Nate was curious.

"Let's dispose of the inconsequential file first," Alexa advised. "Dr. Wislosstol sent all his medical records to the Lightspeed Clinic down by the docks. He had been treating, and it appears, experimenting, on homeless people for quite some time, over three hundred different souls. For almost all those people, these are the only medical records they have, so he was ensuring their health and safety after he was gone. Pretty noble, actually."

"He was doing human experimentation on the side, that's noble?" Nate was confused.

"It is if you have cured their addiction," Alexa said. There it was, out in the open, Dr. Karl Wislosstol had created a successful cure for addiction, field tested it, and gotten superior results. So good for those people, so bad for Mr. Guterriz and his ilk.

"I see," Nate responded feebly. And he did. The second file that had been sent was the process report, the 'how to' aspect of Wislosstol's work. The ticking time bomb. "The second file, that is his medical report, the methodology and all that."

"Precisely, I can see why my brother keeps you around," Alexa was haughty and therefore happy.

"So where did the medical report go?" Nate tried to hide his anxiety and eagerness as they warred with each other in his head.

"To an IP address in New York City, a conspiracy website run by a person called 'Lady,' who had published a lot of material submitted by a person known as 'Neurometer,' who it turns out, is, or rather, was, Wislosstol. Looks like you are doing a road trip."

"Mr. Guterriz knows important people in New York, he will contract out the removal of this person," Nate argued.

"I doubt it. He cannot afford to have a competitor find out what that person has," Alexa countered. "This will have to be in-house, and we cannot send goons. It will be you."

Nate realized Alexa had already reported to her brother, and Nate was getting his marching orders in context. "I see, yes, and I agree. First, I will research this website and see what their game is."

= = =

"Lady confirms receipt of our story of Neurometer and his big discovery and subsequent assassination," Maggie said. "She will run it immediately."

"The GHC crew will go nuts, a mystery involving one of their own," Lauren chortled, then, "We have lit the fuse, and the bomb is under us."

"I would say so," David observed. "Sal tells me they have begun their marketing of the addiction cure process, that will be going on in parallel to our dealing with one specific drug group. He again asked if we wanted any protection, but I declined for the moment."

"We have already beat that horse deader than a doornail," Lauren complained. "We can't have the feds anywhere near us."

"The point is not to be that doornail," David reminded both women. "Your risk, and now, my risk too, varies depending on how good their IT people are. All they will be able to track down is the P.O. Box in Atlanta, and you are not going there again."

"We let them fizzle in frustration for a while, and then TG goads them again with an offer?" Maggie asked. "Will they take the bait?"

"These people are always transactional, they will readily believe you want to exploit the process for personal monetary gain," David replied. "They won't think you are after them because they are responsible for Wislosstol's death. That slant will give them a focus we can turn to our advantage, but the risks are huge, these folks don't play around. They didn't think it was worthwhile to interrogate Wislosstol, they just shot him."

"They wish now that they had taken him in for a few questions," Lauren noted.

"The false efficiency of the fearless," Maggie suggested. "They are fearful now."

CHAPTER 48

DISCOVERIES

NATE HAD BEEN SURFING THE LADY WEBSITE, seeing all the gory details of the Grundy County Massacre. He noted the mystery about the twelfth girl, or TG as they called her. Even the feds hadn't been able to dig her up. He stopped and realized they had dug up eleven others. Even for Nate, it was horrible stuff, all done by a sicko only ninety miles north. The Neurometer input was interesting, at times laughable but always with a professionalism that derived from Wislosstol's medical training. His posts regarding TG were powerful; he clearly had a strong interest in this mystery woman.

Nate stopped to get a bite to eat and when he came back, there was a new post, all about Neurometer and his death. How he had sent Lady a file and had requested it go to TG, that Lady hadn't opened it, but had gone to the New York City police about her personal safety. Nate saw through that move immediately, Lady's attempt to separate herself from a file that had gotten a man killed. Then he considered Wisloss-tol's fascination with TG, almost worship, all written well before his death. It was highly likely that Lady had followed Wislosstol's wishes and hadn't opened or copied the file.

The posts from the feds were obvious, but they yielded a post office box in Atlanta. That was consistent with an eastern Tennessee crime scene that TG had been involved with. Then Nate saw the video of Dossett's interrogation, and he paused, concerned. That was not ama-teur work, no hysterical woman there. Cold, precise, tracks totally covered. If he went after this person, he would have to be careful. Mr. Guterriz had briefed him coldly. The problem was Nate's, he had taken shortcuts, been sloppy. Nate was smart enough to keep quiet that he had done it the way the big man had wanted, no interrogation, just kill Wislosstol and get his files. He was a minion, and he would do as ordered. Despite the urgency and risk presented by the now-proven addiction cure,

Guterriz was leery of expending a lot of resources on the file recovery. It was out there. Who knew how many places it had gone. He was already making plans to transition more to human trafficking; the drug business with its huge infrastructure was soon going the way of the buggy whip. He initially failed to consider how much the state of addiction worked to make the human trafficking happen. Leverage would be lost. Marijuana legalization had been bad enough, but like cigarettes, the taxes and regulation placed on the product still made illegal sales profitable. Or booze for that matter.

Nate also understood the predicament. His job was in jeopardy, perhaps his life as he knew far too much. Like *The Shawshank Redemption*, Nate had kept meticulous records. All hand-written, then photographed with a digital camera, not a cell phone, and the pages burned. So much easier to hide a thumb drive, so small, so convenient. He hadn't done it for blackmail purposes, but to be a bargaining chip if he got busted by the feds. He had been thinking about going to the feds first, to get into witness protection and get out of this gangster life, which had become like any corporate white-collar job, so boring but with a lot more risk. Time to see Alexa and see what she could do with an Atlanta P.O. Box number.

■　■　■

It turned out to be a lot. A Russian iPhone hacking procedure wasn't the only thing one could get on the dark web, for enough money. A backdoor had literally been built into the US Postal System computers. For those who liked to ship drugs by mail, this was a useful tool, to see what postal inspectors were doing, their updating of equipment and techniques, all sorts of useful stuff. Alexa got a list of P.O. boxes in Atlanta that were opened after the date of the twelfth girl kidnapping, but before the date of the box's posting on the GHC site, a narrow time window. The first thing Alexa did was run those names against legal filings in several states, in fact, all of them as she had a computer of exceptional capabilities and she let it percolate overnight. She had seen the Dossett video after Nate had mentioned it and felt that the perpetrators might likely have criminal experience, so she had started there. She had known men for whom a soldering iron would have been appropriate. Again and again.

She looked at the list, only seven names long, still a healthy proportion of the twenty-nine boxes opened in that time window. She searched only legal cases, which meant she got three crime cases: a paternity case, a car accident case, and two divorces. None of those cases seemed to indicate anything until she realized one of the divorces had the box in the married name, but the divorce had been years in the past. Davenport. Her experience with divorce, and it had been many, was that you dropped the guy's name as fast as possible and went back to your maiden name. Why keep it to open a new box years later? Because you had your old ID and could open the box and not give away your current identity. It wasn't Nate who got the scent, it was Alexa.

▪ ▪ ▪

Sal was impressed by the response to his approaches to both private industry and government agencies. The most aggressive were from companies associated with fueling the opioid crisis, not to suppress the treatment, they were done with that market after billions in successful lawsuits, but to rehabilitate themselves and find a new cash cow. The government agency with the most interest was Housing and Urban Development; addiction played havoc with all their social planning, with their infrastructure, and with their public image. The Veterans Administration was a close second, as was a private foundation set up by families of opioid victims. Sal had his patent attorney negotiate with these and other entities, and it was progressing. There were enough hints in what Sal had put forth that within a few years some of the private companies could have duplicated the work, but Sal was offering a proven methodology up front, and a small clinical trial that proved efficacy. No one seemed to care that the idea came from China and the clinical trial from somewhere in California. A good investigative reporter would have found the San Diego anomaly and the link to an assassinated doctor, but then the trail would have gone cold. If Sal could close one or more deals with patent protection, then all would become public. That the patent application would eventually prove to be troublesome wouldn't stop the treatment from becoming accessible to the public.

    ■   ■   ■

Tanner watched and observed. He was still somewhat of a nobody in the department; he could poke around basically unnoticed. He looked for someone else who could do the same. The Chief had liked his report and was disappointed that the phone had proven a dead end. On the other hand, he agreed with the idea that the phone demonstrated that an important secret existed, and that tracking the secret down would be valuable, so he kept Tanner on the case. The phone now rested in a sealed evidence locker. He had a close-up image of the original phone and the mark he had placed, one that he had taken in his car, so he could prove the phone had been switched if need be.

So who was the mole? He was an excellent interrogator and could conduct a questioning where the target didn't realize they were being interrogated. He got information of value from the forensic team; he looked at watch schedules, he snooped and poked. He came up with a name. Nancy Privvat, on the force for more than a decade, female but without significant attractiveness for males, she was assigned to desk duty as she had trouble meeting the physical requirements for patrolling. She was basically invisible, always running papers around, going to every office in the building. Scooping up intelligence for the cartel. Nancy Privvat had to be busted, she was doing damage in real time, but she would have to be caught in the act.

* * *

"Shouldn't we go back to Athens?" Lauren asked. "I mean, I like it here, but we are using up your hospitality and also putting you in danger."

"Are you really trying to crush my male ego, feeling you have to leave for my safety, when my macho blood boils with the need to protect you?" David said, laughing. Then he sobered up. "Look, the danger is real, but the posting done with Lady has made it likely that those in San Diego think the secret is out, there is no longer anything to protect. Sal has things humming along."

"But they don't know that, those in San Diego as you call them," Maggie rebutted. "They could still think they have a chance to recover it all. We could end up dead."

"Well, dead but only after interrogation. They won't make the mistake they made with Wislosstol a second time," Lauren offered.

"Cool — tortured and then killed, so much more attractive," David said grimly. "You are one more remove from Athens, by being here. We know they might be coming. I could alert Sal that we might need some coverage down here."

"I have my Glock and two spare full clips. I assume you have weapons as well?" Maggie inquired.

"Matching butter knives. I can throw them with either hand with equal ability," David retorted.

"Equally bad with both hands, you mean," Lauren stated. "You shot a North Korean spy! You know what to do, and I must assume you know how to do it."

"I have a rifle and scope, and a .45 caliber automatic, US Navy issue, eight shots and two spare clips," David said, getting serious. "It is not a lot of fire power should they send a large team."

"So we prepare the house to withstand a shock attack. These guys certainly won't come to do a siege," Maggie advised. "How would you do it?"

"One sole attacker, at three in the morning, silencer on a .22 caliber pistol, double tap anyone I found," David said as if reporting a realtor's visit.

"That viewpoint isn't going to help me sleep at night," Lauren responded.

"That is why I have a dual security system, one obvious, one hidden, and why we are standing watches every night," David proposed.

CHAPTER 49

TWINING THE FIBERS

SO THERE IT WAS, MARGARET GERELLI DAVENPORT, now just Margaret Gerelli. Age 52, so she wasn't this mysterious TG girl the GHC site babbled about. Why rent a P.O. Box in Atlanta when you lived in Athens? It took no time at all to find her on the faculty at the University of Georgia. The Department of Geosciences website had some background information, and the name of her first graduate student, Lauren Tammers. Lauren could be TG, the twelfth girl. A rigorous search showed that Lauren had been absent from any electronic communication since the day of her abduction. That was significant. Alexa realized that if she had TG, then this is the person, perhaps with Dr. Gerelli's help, who had tortured Fred Dossett so efficiently and effectively. Had also gotten away from Ted Keller, and then brought him down. Sending Nate out alone to corral this person, or perhaps both ladies, could be a task far beyond his skills. Alexa saw how the GHC site had been manipulated to push Ted Keller into several mistakes that got him busted. Fred Dossett was dead, and these two had killed him. Yup, Nate could be in real trouble. The website had already been used to goad him. But then her little brother was considering whether to keep Nate on or to dispose of him. Nate was well known to many of Guterriz's team. It was a question of whether eliminating Nate would be bad for morale or good for discipline. Sending Nate to meet Lauren Tammers might be a way to answer that question: come back with the goods, and all is fine; get killed by a woman, problem solved. A real Pontius Pilate solution.

■ ■ ■

Tanner considered how to bait Officer Privvat. He took the easy way out: he 'found' a second cell phone, allegedly hidden behind the medical cabinet safe at Wislosstol's lab. He came into forensics with obvious glee at getting a second chance. This phone was different, it was fully operational and had its GPS tracker turned on. It had been programmed to stay on even if it appeared off, and to record everything around it, sight and sound, straight up to the cloud, where Tanner could access it in real time. Tanner had wiped it down, there would be no fingerprints reported. Then he waited. It was like fishing in an oxbow lake: you knew the fish were hungry, you just had to be patient. The hard part would be approaching the Chief; no one likes bad news, but then, if the boat is sinking, plugging the leak is a good thing. There was an outside chance that the Chief was in on it all, but Tanner considered that a remote possibility. If Privvat took the phone directly to her drug boss, then it was accepting stolen property. It could be bust and bust. Sweet.

■ ■ ■

Sal was exuberant, he had two companies, a private foundation, and two federal agencies seriously interested in committing resources to obtain the addiction cure methodology, and the clinical trial data. He waltzed in to see Peter with the good news and stopped when Peter gave him a concerned look. "What's up?" Sal asked.

"TG is busted by the cartel," Peter commented dryly. "We have to move quickly to secure her, as well as the second person and David Langwonaire."

"How did that happen? I mean, Ted Keller couldn't figure it out, we only have a vague idea," Sal lamented.

"The P.O. Box in Atlanta, it was a giveaway," Peter answered. "I was keeping an eye on that box, seeing if any queries came in about it. There was a search for which P.O. Boxes had been assigned between the dates of the TG abduction and the GHC information drop."

"We should have done that, it's so obvious now," Sal exclaimed. "Well, we had sort of agreed that we weren't hunting for them, that we had called off the wolves."

"And we had, I was doing a security check," Peter replied. "Interesting event, the search looked like it was an official U.S. Postal Service inquiry, but it wasn't."

"Have you told the Postal Service they have a backdoor and it is being used?" Sal asked.

"Not yet. I don't want to alert the perp," Peter replied. "Anyway, I worked backwards from that point, checking out the twenty-nine names that had come up. Most were easily discarded as being unlikely. I ran a check on the rest, and one name fell out, a divorced woman who currently uses her maiden name but registered the box under her old married name. Margaret Gerelli Davenport. Margaret Gerelli is an assistant professor at the University of Georgia, and has one graduate student, Lauren Tammers."

"Lauren Tammers is TG," Sal guessed, but it wasn't really a guess. "Tiny in stature?"

"Exactly," Peter responded.

"It makes sense: Lauren gets kidnapped, escapes, and borrows a phone to call Dr. Gerelli, who goes to Grundy County and picks her up," Sal was enthusiastic, the rush of seeing the pieces fall together was exhilarating. "They then set off on a quest to avenge the dead and bring the killer to justice. Wow."

"So they are being hunted, and don't know it yet, at least, they don't know they are being hunted by name," Peter warned.

"They will go to Dr. Gerelli's house first. We can nab them there," Sal proposed.

"They said they didn't want protection," Peter noted.

"One, they aren't in Athens, they are in Montgomery," Sal observed. "Two, we are obligated to protect society. We need to stop a murderer from killing — think of possible collateral damage."

▪ ▪ ▪

"Seriously, what do we do if we have an intruder?" Lauren asked.

"We remove the threat immediately and quickly," David answered with an abrupt tone. "We don't need any information from that person. They probably don't know much anyway beyond who the target is."

"In other words, shoot to kill," Maggie offered.

"Yes, take no chances, don't try and be a hero," David advised.

"You shot a man and became a hero," Lauren protested.

"I hid behind a rock and when he walked by, I shot him in the head from two feet away, he never saw me," David retorted. "Not hero stuff, just a pragmatic approach to a problem, which is how we will treat it here."

"Ted Keller couldn't find us, the FBI couldn't find us. Are you truly worried, David?" Maggie asked, a longing in her eyes.

"The FBI called off the dogs, they knew a conviction wouldn't work anyway," David replied. "Keller didn't see you as an actual threat until the very end, and by then he had lost the initiative. Who hunts you now hunts people for a living, with serious purpose as you are a threat, a threat to their entire edifice of operation. Take it seriously."

"Or what?" Lauren challenged.

"Or I kick you out," David said sharply. "I won't put my life in danger for people who lack enough common sense to see a real death risk."

"I understand, David," Maggie replied. "We will take it seriously and prepare appropriately. We have been under the gun for weeks and weeks. It wears on a person, numbs the emotions and the senses. I think in part we invite the danger so we can confront it and end it."

"That last attitude worked with Keller, but it won't work with a cartel," David stated.

"What does save us?" Lauren wailed, close to her breaking point.

"The work Sal and Peter are doing, to make the addiction cure a matter of public record, and a treatment actually in operation," David said. "Then it ends."

"So we watch and wait?" Lauren sobbed.

"The waiting is always the hard part," David soothed as Maggie embraced Lauren.

CHAPTER 50

THE CANDLE BURNS AT BOTH ENDS

NATE FLEW EAST TO ATLANTA. He had a car rental waiting at the airport, and the address of one Dr. Margaret Gerelli in Athens. He also had her car tag number. He assumed that the TG girl, Lauren Tammers, was there as well. He had an address in Atlanta where he could pick up the weapon, no names. He had looked at images of the faces of the two women, committed them to memory. The women who had defeated Ted Keller, and who had stayed out of the grasp of law enforcement. He was to end them; it was regretful. Being eliminated by Mr. Guterriz was more regretful. Perhaps he should go to the FBI, ask for a deal. Walk into a lawyer's office in Atlanta and say he needed to bargain. He had the necessary bait with him, a file on a card in his camera. He was posing as a journalist again. He hoped to get close.

■　■　■

Tanner had asked for a private appointment with the Chief, who hoped he would be told Tanner was going back east. The man was smart, but he didn't fit in.

"OK Tanner, why the secrecy, the private appointment, is this a personal issue?" the Chief asked.

"Yes sir, it is a personnel issue, but it is not me," Tanner slid into the opening the Chief had provided. "You have an officer working for the local drug cartel, Guterriz's operation."

The Chief was stunned, he had suspected information was leaking out, and he had hoped it wasn't an officer. Looked like it was. "You wouldn't be here if you didn't have proof, what have you got?"

Tanner opened his laptop, and displayed the live feed from the bogus phone, now in Privvat's possession. As the Chief watched, Tanner gave him the narration of the original phone switch, and the subsequent second phone manipulation that Tanner had set up. "If we move properly, Chief, we can not only bust Privvat, but we can catch Guterriz in possession of stolen goods, evidence in a murder case," Tanner finished. "We don't even need a search warrant. Guterriz will pick up the phone and look at it, and he is ours."

"I knew you were good, everyone in Arkansas said you were smart and knew how to work a case, but I didn't expect this," the Chief showed some admiration. He also knew that if Tanner had felt isolated before, he would feel it double now, no matter Privvat's crimes. "We will do this bust together, try and break that lone-wolf role you have been forced to play."

■ ■ ■

The phone had ended up on Alexa's desk. She hadn't considered it a priority; it was most likely a duplicate of what Wislosstol had thrown off his roof. But her brother didn't work in 'most likelys,' the suddenness of events in the cartel drug business didn't allow for such guessing. He had told her to get right on it, and she had started the process of getting the case off, the back off, and the circuits exposed. She went to turn it on and thought she must have done that already by accident; the cases were so hard to get off. She pulled out the probe kit with its delicate wires, and began to link in. That was when she found that the phone was not only on, but open. It was transmitting to the cloud as she sat there. She heard the commotion in the outer hallway, the shouts of "drop it," the clink of cuffs, the pounding of feet. She thought of fighting it out, she thought of putting the gun to her head, but in the end, all she did was say "good morning" as they came into the office.

＊　＊　＊

It was mid-afternoon. Nate's flight had been a red eye and now he was in Athens. He might catch the professor in her office, he would wander there first, get a feel for the place. He reached her door, it was locked.

A male student came by and asked "You looking for Dr. Gerelli? She hasn't been in but a couple of times the last few weeks, try her at home."

"She's not home, I was by twice this week. I need a signature to get into her Geomorph class, its full. She must be in the field," the student's female companion said.

"Uh, thanks, no problem, I'm just a book rep looking to make a sale," Nate said and wandered off. He was not surprised that, in the end, Dr. Gerelli and Lauren Tammers were not in Athens. They had displayed no stupidity in the Keller affair. He walked by the Department library and ducked in, just to sit and think. Where would they go? In front of him was a bookcase that held hard copies of various theses and dissertations, some so old that hard copy had been the only option. He saw *Terra Rossa Paleosol Development in The Bahamas* by Margaret Gerelli. He knew from the Department website she had gotten her PhD here. He pulled it off the shelf and turned a few pages. The Acknowledgment page was interesting, who she thanked and why. Then a name leaped out at him. She gave a hearty thanks to Dr. David Langwonaire of Alabama Southeast University. He knew that name — half of America did. The guy who had single-handedly foiled the North Korean plot to auction nuclear weapons to terrorist groups. She knew him, she knew him well. Would she run there for safety?

Nate went over to the main library and asked for the guest code for internet access. He looked up addresses next to Gerelli's house, cross-checked with some faculty names, and found a business professor lived two houses down. He would start there.

＊　＊　＊

"Dr. Fandling?" he asked as an older man came to the door.

"Its Fandlin, no g," the man answered. "What can I do for you?"

"I work for a new company, Tissue Publishing," Nate began, but before he could continue, he was interrupted.

"Never heard of them, what is this all about," the man demanded.

"Tissue implies transient, weakness, a lack of permanence," Nate began a spiel he had thought up on the drive over from campus. "We seek to digitize books in different fields that haven't been digitized before."

"I thought everything had been digitized. Amazon started that work a long time ago, and the Library of Congress, too," the man rebutted.

"True, sir, but no one is digitizing multiple editions, they just do the latest one," Nate made his pitch. "Tissue Publishing thinks that how editions change, and the timing of those changes, is an interesting data set on the evolution of ideas."

"That's true, I wrote a textbook that went through seven editions, and I updated it every time," the man seemed to have some enthusiasm now. "Do you want to look through my collection?"

"Next visit, my instructions are to do reconnaissance this time," Nate evaded. "Is there a Dr. Gerelli on this street?"

"Yes, two houses down, but she has been gone for almost a week," the man said. "She won't have what you need, anyway."

"Not productive? I mean my database says she is in her fifties, I thought she would have done a lot," Nate tried to do a convincing stammer.

"Only got her PhD a few years ago; she is starting out a new life," the man answered, and then closed the door.

Nate had what he wanted, confirmation Gerelli was out of town, and that her house was under a stakeout; the officers were good, but he knew the signs. That told him two things. One, they were aware he or someone like him was coming, and two, they thought it would be here, and not at her hideout with David Langwonaire. He was off to Montgomery, it seemed. Not a good chance, but better than slim. If it didn't work out, he could go state's evidence.

CHAPTER 51

THE LAST LOOSE END

IN THE END, IT WAS VERY SIMPLE. He had David Langwonaire's address, he drove around, he spotted Dr. Gerelli's car in the driveway, and he knew he had her. And Lauren Tammers as well. He probably had to take out Langwonaire too; that worried him, the man was a certified killer. He continued and parked some distance away and walked to a coffee shop right on the edge of campus. He needed some caffeine, and he needed it dark. He propped up his notebook computer and decided to calm his nerves with some card games. If he had gone to a newsfeed, he would have seen two things that might have changed his plans for the night. First, Guterriz had been arrested in San Diego, a major drug bust. Second, *The Washington Post* had broken a story about a new cure for addiction that would change the world. Tomorrow would be a different day for so many people.

■ ■ ■

In another end, it was also very simple. Nate had been spotted touring the neighborhood, David had checked out where he was parked, had seen him in the coffee shop. David had watched the news; he could have walked in and told Nate that it was all over, he had lost the reason to be here, and he had no place to return to. But David could not predict how Nate would respond, and if armed, it could get messy. He went back to the house to await the man's arrival. David assumed the man was working alone but remained aware he could be incorrect in that assumption. They literally lay in wait, behind sandbags David had placed in the kitchen and hallway to the bedrooms. The alarm was turned off. Nate appeared just before 11 p.m., impatient and unsure. He came in the east porch window, which had been left unlocked on purpose. Stepping into the living room, he noted the house was quiet and dark. The lights had gone off at 10 p.m. downstairs, 10:15 p.m. upstairs. He hoped the boards on the stairs didn't creak. He turned to the stairs, and a floodlight hit him full in the face with its powerful beam. One voice, male shouted out.

"Don't move, three guns are trained on you," It was David's husky male voice. "Place the gun on the floor, kneel, and then flop forward, hands and arms outstretched."

Nate did so, not surprised, almost relieved. They hadn't shot him. Yet. Behind him, he felt a gun muzzle at the base of his skull, he avoided trying to turn his head.

"As the man said, don't move," a husky female voice said. "Karl Wislosstol was a friend, and I would love to pull this trigger."

That statement froze Nate more than any command could ever achieve. He lay quiet, and was soon cuffed, ankles and wrists, then hogtied. He was hoisted up and into a simple wooden chair from the kitchen, and a few strands of rope kept him in place. There had been no other speech from his captors, but he did see the third girl, Lauren Tammers, so young and small. The floodlight was off, the window closed, the curtains drawn. Normal lighting was up. The older woman, Dr. Margaret Gerelli, sat to his left side, her small Glock in her hand. In front of him stood Dr. David Langwonaire, holding an ancient looking service .45 automatic. Lauren Tammers approached from the right, holding something in her hand that trailed an electric cord. An electric toothbrush? Then he saw it fully, and he moaned.

"I am very skilled with this instrument," Lauren said, holding the soldering iron carefully in her right hand. "I assume you saw the Fred Dossett tape, so you know that."

Nate was speechless with fear, he only moaned again.

"You will note there is no blue tarp, no video camera," Lauren continued. "What you face tonight is not for show. We seek results and have no inhibitions on how we achieve those results."

If Nate had not been fear blinded, he would have realized that there were no preparations to handle blood, urine, or feces, or that his screams would probably be heard all down the street. They planned to break him mentally.

David set up his phone as a recorder, then kept his .45 trained on Nate. Maggie holstered her weapon and came forward. Lauren stayed to the side but brought the soldering iron close now and then so Nate could feel the heat.

"Start at the beginning, and explain what happened to Dr. Karl Wislosstol, and why," Maggie demanded, her voice cold.

Nate swallowed hard, he was sweating profusely, he tried to control his bowels. "I didn't shoot him," he gasped.

"The pleading comes later; for now, tell your story," Maggie confronted the man. "Start with your full name and address, and a quick autobiography, stuff you know, stuff that does not reveal any secrets. Then you can move on. Lauren can motivate you if necessary."

Nate glanced at Lauren, saw only blankness in those eyes, distant from any emotion, machine-like. Nothing to react to, he thought. He began his tale, all the way to how he came to be in Montgomery. It took some time, but the four of them had all night. Whether all four would see the dawn was another matter, not yet decided. Finally, he was wrung out, his head lay back. David gave him a sip from a water bottle.

"Very good, now you can tell us why you should be allowed to live, or if we decide you must die, how long we make the process," Maggie said with an even tone.

"I have use as a witness to not only what Guterriz's cartel was doing, but other cartels nationally and even internationally," Nate began, his long rendition of what had brought him to this house had stabilized his thinking, although fear gnawed at the edges of his consciousness. "Guterriz dealt with them all, he was astride a choke point into Mexico. He had a lot of power."

"Guterriz was arrested today, as was his informant in the San Diego Police Department," Maggie continued. "We would need more than your words, anyway, we heard and recorded them all tonight."

"I have written records of everything, I wrote them up, photographed them with a digital camera, and burned the notes," Nate said slowly, with care and articulation. "I have account numbers, passwords, addresses, all sorts of stuff."

"You are willing to cooperate with the authorities? They like live witnesses," Lauren spoke for the first time in a while. "Me, not so much. We have your camera, and we have already checked the card, so we have it all. Why should we keep you alive?"

Nate finally had an inspiration. "You need to prove the validity of Wislosstol's work. I can be a hard point of evidence, that I was sent to kill two women to stop the concept from escaping to the public."

Maggie looked to Lauren, who nodded, as did David.

"I'm going to call Sal, it will feel great to wake him up," David said.

"Is it really over, for good this time?" Lauren asked Maggie, tears welling up.

"I came out of my divorce and made myself a new person," Maggie said, her voice soft with her victory. "You came through this horrific experience and gave peace to eleven families and saved the lives of millions more. You are now more whole than you have ever been."

EPILOGUE

LAUREN SAT ALONE ON THE BENCH to the side of the Quad, where the shade was dark and the breeze less fitful. She was lost in her thoughts, trying to focus on the future. But the past wasn't done with her.

"May I sit here?" a woman's voice said.

"Sure," Lauren said, not really looking at the stranger who had interrupted her reverie.

"Lauren, I love you," the woman said, and Lauren jerked upright and turned to stare. She recognized who sat with her.

"Sally Quinn, my God, Sally Quinn," Lauren breathed the words slowly, quietly. "Does this mean I am under arrest?"

"No, most certainly not," Sally responded. "I volunteered. Actually, I demanded to be allowed to bring you this message." Sally seemed to draw herself up, as if summoned to a royal duty. "The President of the United States, with the participation of the Governor of Tennessee, have granted you a confidential pardon; Margaret Gerelli as well."

"What sort of pardon is that?" Lauren asked, confused.

"It will not be public, but you can never be tried let alone convicted of any laws that were broken from the moment you were kidnapped until the moment you turned Nathan Follette over to the FBI. You are free, Lauren. Free with a nation's thanks."

"And the love part?" Lauren queried.

"A measure of my admiration for your courage, your skill, and your empathy," Sally explained. "You ended a monster and gave all those families some sort of closure. You gave me closure. Then you went on to help release to the world a true gift, escape from chemical control of people's lives."

"I did what I saw had to be done," Lauren said, tears flowing gently down her cheeks. "Even killing Dossett, that had to happen to bring the whole terrible scheme to light."

"I agree. I completely agree," Sally stated with conviction, her eyes leaking now, too.

"So, what is next for me?" Lauren asked with some trepidation.

"Whatever you want to be next. Just know that people out there in the real world admire you completely, even if they don't know you," Sally offered. "I just met you now, but I feel I have known you for a very long time."

END

ACKNOWLEDGMENTS

Much appreciation for all my friends who read early drafts of this work and provided commentary and insight, especially Jim Carew. Special thanks to Chuck McIntosh and to Michelle M. White for their patient editing and design skills. Most of all, my joy at having Joan as my colleague, friend, partner, and critic, who made it all possible.

ABOUT THE AUTHOR

John Mylroie is Professor Emeritus of Geology at Mississippi State University. After growing up in rural upstate New York, he attended Syracuse University, graduating in 1971 with a Zoology degree Summa Cum Laude and Phi Beta Kappa and also lettering on the soccer team. He met Joan Saxon, a fellow Zoology major and Phi Beta Kappa, in Chemistry lecture his freshman year, they were married in 1970. Draft number 69 in the first draft lottery sent John to the Navy for a year as a sonar technician. While subsequently working in the electronics laboratory of the Biology Department at SUNY Albany, John decided he wanted to turn his sporting interest in caves into a career. He entered the Geology PhD program at Rensselaer Polytechnic Institute in 1974, graduating in 1977 and taking a faculty position at Murray State University where Joan earned a MSc in microbiology and taught as an instructor.

John and Joan decided to start a family in 1981, and by November 1983 had three sons, the latter two appearing as undiagnosed identical twins (surprise!). Having now five mouths to feed, John took the Department Head position in the Geology and Geography Department (now Geosciences) at Mississippi State University in 1985. Joan later became a Geography instructor. He continued his island cave research program, often taking the entire family into the field. The National Speleological Society awarded John their Science Award for his work on island caves in 2000, and the Honorary Member award, the society's highest award, for lifetime contributions to cave science in 2008. Joan and John have done field work in 25 countries, and they have published hundreds of professional papers, reports, field guides and articles. Their work on islands across the Atlantic, Pacific and Indian Oceans, as well as the Caribbean and Mediterranean Seas, has given them insight into how peoples and cultures interact with the environment in remote settings.

After a career of writing tight factual material in the scientific literature, John decided it was time to make things up and write fiction. He has written books covering science fiction, fantasy, mysteries and spy thrillers. *The 12th Girl* is his first step into publication, the fifth book in his eight-book "David Langwonaire Thriller Series." The rest are in production, starting with Book One, *No Night As Dark*. Stay tuned.

He is used to feedback from students and journal editors, so if you wish to contact the author, he can be reached at cikmpub@gmail.com.